BLUE NOTES UNDER A GREEN FELT HAT

ALSO BY DAVID RITZ

NOVELS:
Search for Happiness
The Man Who Brought the Dodgers Back to Brooklyn
Dreams

BIOGRAPHIES:
Brother Ray *(with Ray Charles)*
Divided Soul: The Life of Marvin Gaye
Smokey: Inside My Life *(with Smokey Robinson)*

#3

BLUE NOTES UNDER A GREEN FELT HAT

GOLF
CC

REAGAN

by DAVID RITZ

DONALD I. FINE, INC.
NEW YORK

Copyright © 1989 by David Ritz
All rights reserved, including the right of reproduction in whole
or in part in any form. Published in the United States of America by
Donald I. Fine, Inc. and in Canada by General Publishing Company Limited.

Library of Congress Cataloging in Publication Data

Ritz, David.
Blue notes under a green felt hat.

I. Title.
PS3568.I828B55   1989   813′.54   88-45857
ISBN 1-55611-130-4

Manufactured in the United States of America

10   9   8   7   6   5   4   3   2   1

Designed by Irving Perkins Associates

This novel is a work of fiction. Names, characters, places and
incidents are either the product of the author's imagination or
are used fictitiously. Any resemblance to actual events, locales,
organizations or persons, living or dead, is entirely coincidental
and beyond the intent of either the author or publisher.

*Thanks to Don Fine, Aaron Priest, daughters Alison and Jessica,
and wife Roberta and sister Esther for suggestions.*

In memory of my beloved uncles:
LOUIS FOGLER AND LOUIS KAUFMAN

NIGHT OF THE
FIGHT

Madison Square Garden was packed. The Mayor and the Fire Chief and a gang of well-known Mafiosi were all in attendance. So were the stars—Myrna Loy, Jimmy Dorsey, Joe DiMaggio, Rita Hayworth, Hemingway with his bushy beard, and the ones who wrote for the rags—Walter Winchell, Elsa Maxwell, Leonard Lyons, Cholly Knickerbocker.

Me, my sister and our dates had ringside seats, smack in the middle of all the celebs.

December 5, 1947, my twenty-third birthday, the night Jersey Joe Wolcott challenged Joe Louis, the night I enjoyed a sensational piece of ass, and the night we discovered Clifford Summer, the most talented musician since Wolfgang fuckin' Mozart.

I remember walking into the Garden and thinking—*holy shit, this is for the championship of the world, and here we are, hobnobbing with the elite*—seeing the cloud of smoke above the ring, smelling the stinky cigars, the sweet perfume, the minks on the dames, blue sapphire pinky rings and dia-

7

mond earrings dripping like ice, guys flashing cash, nipping from flasks, wolfing down frankfurters, laughing and winking, flashbulbs popping, necks turning, colored fans decked out like crazy kings and queens, everyone worked up to fever pitch 'cause soon these two bears were going after each other and a shitload of money was riding on the outcome.

My man was Joe Louis, to the tune of three big ones.

See, when I was a teenager my pop, Myron Klein, the famous hatmaker, took me up to the Polo Grounds on a hot night in June to see Billy Conn challenge Louis. Now many experts (including my favorite, the late-great Damon Runyon) consider that the greatest fight in human history. Personally, I agree. For a while it looked like Joe was beat. Billy the Kid was a cute brute. He got to Louis in the third and fourth rounds, then it swung back to the Brown Bomber, then back and forth, blow for bloody blow until the thirteenth round when Joe finally landed a deadly right to the kid's noggin. They say if Conn had danced and dodged through the last three rounds, he'd win on points. But Louis knocked him out. Just the way Pop knocked me out by taking me to Lindy's afterwards where he introduced me to Joe Frisco, the stuttering comic. When Slapsie Maxie Rosenbloom, ex-light heavyweight champ, walked over to our table, Joe said, "Lay down, M-M-M-Maxie. M-m-m-more people will r-r-r-recognize you that way."

Funny thing about that night: After the pastramis and the cream sodas, Myron sent me home with a message for Mom. It was Uncle Nate who took me back to Brooklyn in his pirate cab.

"Where'd Pop go?" I asked Nate, who was about the sweetest numbers runner you'd every want to know, all two hundred fifty pounds of him.

"Don't ask."

"I'm sixteen, and I'm old enough to ask."

"Then you'se old enough to know."

Back in the huge apartment we had on Ocean Parkway in Flatbush, the door was shut to my parents' bedroom. Mama had gone to bed. My sister Peggy was sitting in the living room, reading a book. She was only thirteen, but she was halfway through some novel thick as Joe Louis' right arm. She was wearing this robe with her panties peeking through and I tried not to look 'cause, after all, she was my sister.

"Hi, Danny. How was the fight?" Peg asked.

"Beautiful. Joe Louis won."

"I heard. Where's Pop?"

"Some emergency at the factory."

Which is when I started making excuses for the old man.

By the time I was twenty-three, though, the old man didn't need any more excuses. Me and him, we didn't always get along, but I had to respect him 'cause he was the biggest hatmaker in the country—every well-dressed gent wanted a genuine Myron Klein on his head—and I was his heir apparent. In fact, he'd be at the fight tonight if he and Mom weren't down in Miami Beach soaking up the sun. Every December they'd go there for three weeks.

"Go, Joe!" cried some palooka at ringside with a fat red nose. "Beat Jersey to a fuckin' pulp!"

"Excuse the vulgarity," I apologized to my sister and my date, Monica Montgomery.

"Much obliged," said Monica, a redhead starlette with knockers you wouldn't believe and flashing green eyes the same shade as mine.

"I like the vulgarity," said Peg. "It's sexy."

I didn't like my sister talking that way, but a long time ago I stopped telling Peggy how to talk. Peggy was different. Even though she was petite, dark-haired and gorgeous with soft

brown eyes like Mama's, she was a brain, the smartest senior
Barnard had ever seen. Far as I could see, her date,
Winthrop Carrington, was a wimp. He'd just graduated from
Yale, but I wasn't impressed. You see guys like him all over
the city, blond and skinny and wearing tortoise-shell glasses to
make you think they read a lot.

I hid my true feelings about Winnie—I do that a
lot—'cause I believe in being nice. Besides, Peg said she
wanted to be with me on my birthday, my choice of place.
Well, my choice was a championship fight in the Garden
'cause there was no more action-packed place around except a
World Series at Ebbets Field or opening night of a smash hit
musical on Broadway.

Some guys like drinking; others play the ponies. Sure, I'll
take a belt now and then, and I'll lay a bet, but those aren't
my real kicks. Me, I get goose bumps sitting in the first row
when the curtain goes up; I gotta be in box seats right on top
of the dugout when the ump yells "Play ball!" That's when my
blood starts pumping and my heart starts singing and the
whole world is shining like a beautiful jewel, a beautiful
dream, with music and magic and all kinds of beautiful shit
running around my brain. I'm not saying I ain't a businessman
first. I am. Pop taught me business is survival, and you can be
goddamn sure Danny Klein is gonna survive. But underneath
it all, I got the heart of an artist. I swear.

"How'd you like these seats, Winnie?" I asked the college
kid. We were so ringside we could hear the fighters fart.

"Optimum," he answered, looking at me and Monica like
we was dirt.

"Isn't 'Optimum' the name of a cigar?" asked Monica, who,
leaning over to pick up her purse, gave me a bird's eye view
of her melons. Straining to see for themselves, the guys behind me nearly fell out of their seats.

"Very classy suit, Danny," said Peg, who admired me even though I quit school in the tenth grade. Sis knew I had style. She appreciated how I dressed; she saw the way I helped Pop's business. I was the one who made sure he was keeping up with the times by making snappier-looking hats.

Tonight, for instance, I was wearing a camel-colored cashmere coat, a white silk scarf, a double-breasted chalk-striped flannel suit and this green fedora with a wide brim—my own creation—tilted to one side. Like Mama always said, ever since I was a kid I could put together an outfit. Me and first-class clothes go together like coffee and cream, and green, especially dark green, is my color.

"You got such pretty green eyes, Danny," Monica mentioned earlier—which is when I knew that, by evening's end, birthday cake wouldn't be the only dessert I'd be eating.

Mom, Pop, Peg and me—none of us lack for sex appeal. Maybe that's the problem. Who knows.

Meanwhile, I'm sitting there watching my hero, Joe Louis, climb into the ring.

"Put him away, slugger!" I shout. "Put the bum away in the first round!"

He didn't. Fact is, the champ barely survived the first round when Jersey let loose with a vicious overhand, landing Louis on his knees.

Hey, this could ruin my birthday party. Could the champ be beat? Back and forth, the fifth was a roller coaster ride, a battle royal with both boys throwing out everything they had.

In round four, Jersey knocked down Louis again. Finally, at the count of seven, the champ heard me yell—"*Get up, ya' bum!*"—and obliged.

In round five, it looked like Jersey was toying with Joe, looked like the champ was about to crumble again, but somehow he hung on.

For the next two rounds, Walcott let Louis chase him around the ring, but it was Jersey who scored the points.

By round eight, the champ's left eye looked like a baked potato oozing with butter. Man, it hurt to look at him.

At the end of the ninth round, I would've sworn Louis swallowed Popeye's can of spinach. He nearly beat Jersey to a pulp. It looked like he had him, but damned if Walcott didn't come roaring back. At the sound of the bell, eighteen thousand fans stood on their chairs screaming bloody murder, crazy with admiration for both warriors. What a brawl!

"Keep running," the crowd yelled to Jersey who stayed on his bicycle, running from the champ during the last rounds, looking to avoid Billy Conn's mistake—getting knocked out at the last minute. If he held on, it looked like he'd get the decision, and I could kiss three thousand smackers good-by. He held on.

"Dear God, that was an uncivilized mess," said Winnie, who, at the final bell looked frightened.

"I'm thrilled," said Peg.

"I'm rootin' for you, baby," said Monica, her hot hand on my thigh.

I figured I'd lost, and so did the crowd.

The ring announcer got the votes and brought the mike to his mouth.

"Judge Frank Forbes scored the fight eight rounds for Louis, six for Walcott, one even."

You should've heard the boos. First time the champ was booed. Fight fans figured he'd lost and they were pissed by Forbes' poor judgment. I was ecstatic.

"Referee Ruby Goldstein had it seven rounds Walcott, six for Louis, two even."

A chorus of cheers. More hysteria. Shit, this was close. It all came down to the third vote.

"Judge Marty Monroe . . . nine round for Louis . . ."

Bedlam!

Peggy turned and saw Monica gently squeeze my dick. Surprised, I jumped out of my seat. Sis smiled.

"Who won?" asked Winnie, confused.

"*Me!*" I yelped.

"Happy Birthday, brother," said Peg, kissing me on the lips.

In the ring, Jersey fought back tears. Then the champ, a gentleman if there ever was one, went up to the challenger and said—I heard it with my own ears—"I'm sorry."

You gotta love Joe Louis.

Outside, waiting for Uncle Nate to pull around in the Packard limo Pop let him drive, we stood in the bitter cold, but I didn't care; I was living through the luckiest night of my life.

"Helluva fight," said Nate as we piled inside the plush limousine, the heater going full blast. "Where you kids wanna go now?"

"It's your birthday, Danny," Peg reminded me.

"Music. I gotta hear some music."

Ever since I heard Benny Goodman, I'd been hooked on swing. I was fourteen when my Aunt Bea, who runs the trimming room at Pop's place, took me up to Carnegie Hall—this was 1938—where the band blew my head off. In one night I heard Benny, I heard Lionel Hampton playing the vibes like they was on fire, I heard Gene Krupa beating the tom-toms like the world was coming to an end, I heard Harry James and Count Basie and Teddy Wilson, all the greats, the beat coming up under my ass—"Sing! Sing! Sing!" was the song—driving me out into the aisle where I started jitterbugging with two crazy broads with their tits flopping and them screaming "Go, man, go!" and me, a little dandy in a matching red suede cap and vest, causing a sensation 'cause I've always had dance moves that make folks up in Harlem wonder where I got my rhythm.

"Let's go to 52nd Street," suggested the Yalie.

"Yeah, Swing Street," I seconded the motion. "Great idea, Winnie."

I blew hot air in Monica's ear, whispering, "Is that okay with you, doll?"

"Anything," she whispered back, causing my manhood to harden.

"Uncle Nate, we're going to 52nd Street."

"Gotcha," he shouted over his shoulder.

Riding uptown, I thought how much I loved the city with the war over and families reunited and Times Square booming, the Camel Man smoking up a storm high above, the movie marquees screaming with stars, the Astor Hotel, the good news all lit up and rotating 'round the funny-shaped building owned by the New York *Times*.

"Fifty-second Street should be most intriguing tonight," said Winthrop Carrington lighting the kind of pipe Sherlock Holmes smokes.

"I'm surprised you like swing," I told him. "I saw you more as a symphony man."

"Win just got a job writing for Metronome, the jazz magazine," said Peggy. "He's a critic."

"Let's not stay too long," Monica whispered softly into my ear.

"A critic?" I said to Winnie. "Hey, that's something."

"You must understand," the critic explained in a tone designed to make everyone feel dumb, "that jazz is an art form undergoing critical changes. The style you refer to as 'swing' has been challenged—much as Walcott challenged Louis tonight—by an avant-garde form called 'be-bop.'"

"Then be-bop's gonna get bopped on the head," I jumped in, "'cause guys like Benny and Hamp are heavyweight swingers."

"Why don't you listen to Win," chided Peg, who can get a little snotty herself. "You might learn something."

"At Minsky's," said Monica, referring to the famous Newark burlesque house where she danced, "they play fabulous jazz."

"The be-boppers eschew the notion of jazz as an entertainment vehicle," Winnie went on. "They're true artists who refuse to create syncopated sounds merely for light amusement or ballroom dancing."

"Then they'll starve to death," I predicted.

"Remuneration is not the goal," Carrington continued, "self-expression is. The real innovators among them—Charlie Parker, Dizzy Gillespie and Thelonious Monk—have extended the music's harmonic range and pushed improvisation in a furious and fast-paced direction, brilliantly reflecting the anguish, the *angst* and, if you will, the frantic optimism of our post-war period."

"There's lots of dope on the Street now," Uncle Nate broke in from the front seat. "The vice squad's all over the place, so you kids be careful."

"History repeats itself," said Winthrop the historian. "In the early part of the century, Storyville in New Orleans, a breeding ground for jazz genius, suffered the same fate."

By then, though, Yalie had lost us. We'd arrived.

West 52nd Street, corner of 6th Avenue. Looking east towards 5th, this one city block of old five-story brownstones was wall-to-wall nightclubs. Getting out of the car, we could already hear sounds floating in the air—the blare of a trumpet, the moan of a trombone, clarinets crying like black cats. My blood started pumping.

Every club had an awning and a bright sign. On the south

side of the street were the Three Deuces, Club Carousel, Club Samoa, the Downbeat, the Famous Door; on the other side, the Onyx, Jimmy Ryan's, Leon and Eddie's, the Ha Ha, and the White Rose bar where the musicians hung out between sets.

"Which club are we going to ?" asked Peggy.

"We'll find the most serious musicians," said Winnie, "performing at—"

"We'll hit *all* the clubs," I interrupted. "This is gonna be a bar-hopping birthday like you've never seen."

"Can we do the bunny hop?" asked Monica.

"Later," I promised.

There were guys with berets and goatees and dark glasses and sailors and tourists and society folks slumming. The clubs were small and smokey, tables crammed together and no cover charge. The bandstands were tiny and the musicians were jammed together, jamming straight into our faces, blowing into our eyeballs while we downed highballs and listened to Winnie's lectures in between numbers.

"Art Tatum," he said, "is a transitional genius, a seminal figure who's designing a veritable architecture of lyrical possibilities for the modern jazzman . . ."

All I knew was that this chubby blind piano man was playing like God was licking his fingers, flying over the 88's faster than the speed of sound. I was eating it up.

I was happy at Jimmy Ryan's 'cause they was playing "Stompin' at the Savoy" while Winnie was calling it "dated and hackneyed" and I was telling him to fuck off 'cause Monica had her hand in my pocket and I liked all the jazz, who cared about the categories.

"Categorically, Coleman Hawkins, the first great master of the tenor saxophone, represents an older era," Yalie yapped on as we went into the Famous Door, "although he's been able to adjust to the younger artists."

Hawk blew his fat saxophone, saying things through "Body and Soul" I figured poets had been trying to say for centuries. "Blow!" I screamed while Carrington took notes.

It was hard to appreciate Charlie Parker and Dizzy Gillespie at the Three Deuces. Maybe 'cause I was a little tipsy, or maybe 'cause they were soaring over my head. Maybe that's why they called Parker "Bird." Buddha-faced Bird sucked his sax like a lollipop. I could see what Yalie meant. His music was new. I remember how Peg had showed me a painting where Picasso screwed up a woman's face; well, that's how the be-boppers screwed up melodies. I could appreciate their art, but they lost me until Dizzy started clowning around by rubbing his trumpet up against some lady's big backside and everyone howled and I said to Winnie, "I thought you said they wasn't entertainers," and he said, "Dizzy is prone to distinct lapses of taste."

Back on the street, the freezing chill sobered me up. Soft snowflakes started falling like sad little notes while the crowds thinned out and groups of guys gathered by cellar doors to buy dope. You could smell reefer in the cold night air. Monica took my arm while a couple of nasty-looking hoods looked her over like she was salami hanging in a deli. At the end of the block, I saw Uncle Nate surveying the scene—he never let me out of his sight for long—leaning against the Packard, a hack's cap on his head, tomorrow's *Racing Form* in his back pocket. He waved to me and I waved back. Nate was short with apple cheeks and a nose that looked like a cigar stub. His smile could make you happy for weeks and, as far as I was concerned, he had the disposition of an angel.

"One more club," I called to him.

"Knock yourself out, kid," he yelled back.

"Tired, Peg?" I asked.

"Exhilarated," said Sis.

"Fascinated," said Winnie as we went down to a basement club called Outside Inn.

Of all the joints on the Street, this was the dingiest. The sign said, "Opening Tonight! Clifford Summer."

"Never heard of him," said Winnie, which was music to my ears since it meant I wouldn't get an instant critique.

The narrow nightclub was half-empty. A couple sat at a side table necking, never once looking up to the bandstand where a strikingly handsome man with an oval-shaped face, high cheekbones, jet-black skin and sweet liquid eyes sat before an old upright piano. There were no other players. He had enormous hands, a tall thin frame, sloping shoulders and this graceful way of moving. He looked about my age.

I could barely hear his voice, soft and gentle, as he leaned into the mike to say, "I hope you like my blues."

My ears perked up. He hit a couple of dark chords and suddenly it felt like we were back in time and way down South in Alabama or Mississippi when they had slaves and everything was hard and cruel and hot. He didn't play many notes like Art Tatum, but all the notes were the right ones, the painful ones, and I felt I was seeing a movie about people suffering, bad suffering, the sun blazing and hearts longing. Peg had tears in her eyes. When he was through, Winthrop whispered, "Merely adequate," and I wanted to kill the critic 'cause he'd missed the man's soul.

His next number was a breakneck racehorse version of "Long Ago and Far Away" that didn't feel far away at all. The rhythm was right there, kicking my ass. He played a little like the be-boppers down the street, but I could follow where he was going 'cause he didn't jar. When Summer played the piano, he turned his torso toward us, his only listeners, and, seated at the bench, let his legs dangle and dance with the beat. He didn't even look at his fingers; it was like his hands belonged to someone else. He smiled this easy smile and I saw Peg smiling back, like there was something personal between them, like they already knew each other, and they even started laughing together as he teased and twisted the melody around so when Winnie started to say something Peg shut him up with a big "*shhhhh*" and I was glad.

Then the big surprise: Clifford Summer sang. You know what it's like rubbing against velvet or flannel or silk or satin? Well, imagine all those feelings and fabrics put into the voice of a man who pronounces each word like he's cutting diamonds with his teeth, and then underneath there's this quiet hurt—nothing's pushed, nothing's loud—and it's all so smooth that I swear to God, your heart's in your throat and you're convinced that even though he's just sung a song Sinatra used to sing up at the Paramount, "Speak Low," this guy's every bit as good.

When he was through, I turned to Peg to get her reaction. She was still smiling right into this guy's eyes when, just like that, she made this strange sound, tottered for a second and fell to the floor. Sis *fainted!*

Scared, I grabbed her, kneeling by her side. For a moment I thought maybe she was dead, but she was breathing and Clifford Summer came running over to our table. The guy was a gentleman 'cause he got a wet towel and put it across her forehead and she fluttered her eyes and opened them, staring at this man until all of us felt something very strange, the way they looked at each other, the way he helped her up, his arm around her, me still thinking about his talent and wondering what he was doing in a dump like this.

"I hope my songs didn't get you that upset," he said to Peg.

He spoke like a college-educated gentleman, not some saloon singer.

"It was nothing," said Peg. "I'm fine."

"You *sure*, Sis?" I asked, still worried.

A couple of hours later, me and Monica were back at my place, and the worry hadn't gone away.

I wondered what was going on with Peg. Why'd she faint? She recovered so quickly, like nothing had happened. When we dropped her back at her dorm, Winnie said he'd walk her in. But hell, they could have turned around and gone back to his place. I was sure she was a virgin, but I wasn't that sure, and I know men, and I know even critics get horny, but if she was laying this guy I'd be disappointed 'cause he'd probably still be talking about jazz theory while he was pumping her. Which is no way to talk about my sister, except she acted so strange, and this guy Summer made it even stranger, the way he stayed in my brain.

"He's some gorgeous man," said Monica when I asked her opinion of Clifford. "He's got some gorgeous voice. I'd say he's got sex appeal, even though I know it ain't right to talk that way about the colored."

She was cuddled up next to me on my silver brocade couch in my swanky penthouse that overlooked the East River.

"Your place looks like George Raft used to live here," she said, making me happy 'cause I loved his movies so much.

I just moved in last month despite Pop yelling it was too expensive and what did I need with a penthouse. I needed a penthouse for times just like this, for dishes just like Monica. Besides, Mom encouraged the move and even helped decorate. Without that wad of extra money she slipped me, I couldn't have done it. Mom was Pop's chief bookkeeper, and she'd always slip me cash behind the old man's back.

"I know it's your birthday, Danny," said Monica. "But you been ignoring me."

"Sorry, baby. I'm gonna make up for it."

I was thinking that maybe Monica really had a crush on me when I remembered her professional credentials. I'd met her through our ad agency. I'm in charge of advertising for Myron Klein Hats—I'm a great promoter—and sometimes we use models in the ads and this agency's got connections all over town. They connected me to Monica who I took to lunch last week. Right then and there I decided she'd be my birthday present. She was a real sweet kid who seemed to understand me.

Which isn't all that easy. See, I got an active mind. On the night of my twenty-third birthday, it was over-active, thinking of Jersey Joe and Joe Louis and Peg and the crazy music and that smooth singer. There was a terrific traffic jam in my head, thoughts colliding, bumper-to-bumper brainstorms, too many ideas going in too many different directions. That's why it's always handy to have a honey like Monica around to wipe out my confusion.

You don't have to tell a good stripper or a good hooker—and Monica, bless her heart, had been both—that men have simple tastes. Men like to look over the merchandise. So Monica came out of the bathroom looking like a wet dream. She was wearing my green felt fedora flopped over her face, and then this push-up bra with holes where her pink nips peeped through and scanty black lace panties against her pink skin and silky red pussy hair, milky thighs and curvy ass swinging from side to side, dancing to my victrola playing "Satin Doll," the sexiest song Duke Ellington ever wrote.

Monica, my Monica, undressing me like I was a little boy, making a fuss over my flat stomach and my stiff shlong, telling me just what I wanted to hear, that I'm the biggest and the best and how she couldn't wait to taste every last loving inch of me.

If I use the expression "sincere blow job," you'll know what I mean because some broads do it out of obligation and most don't do it at all. But Monica, she sucked like she meant it, cupping my balls in the palm of her hands and getting me so crazy I had to hold back until we switched and I tasted her sweet-smelling pussy, tongue-kissing her while my hands reached for her jugs, massive gorgeous smooth-skinned jugs, and if she didn't come while I was eating her then she deserved the Academy Award 'cause this one was wild, I mean screaming and making me worry about the neighbors, but fuck the neighbors, fuck Monica, "Fuck me, Danny, fuck me hard," she yelled, yanking me inside and squeezing tight, the lips and the muscles and the hips humping, my dick driving her down, jackhammering, bedsprings screaming, her creaming, "Keep coming, keep coming," my nuts slapping, tummies slamming, her fingernails in my ass, me, the birthday boy, riding her hard, riding her home, panting and pushing and pleading for more.

MYRON KLEIN
HAT*S* LIMITED

I love hats.

During the war we made caps for soldiers. Wearing a hat is the only way a well-dressed gent can truly top off an outfit. Hats mean class. They show style. Velours, suedes, shaggies, derbies, homburgs—hats make me happy the way, say, bees are happy buzzing around flowers, I'm happy buzzing around Myron Klein Hats Limited. When I was a kid, Pop's plant was my playpen. As a grown-up, my playpen became my work place. And, since all this would one day be mine, I took it seriously. It was like a whole country I'd get to rule.

Pop ruled with an iron hand, which is why he wasn't as popular with his employees as me. Me, everyone loved. Him, they feared. "If they're not afraid of you," Pop would tell me, "they'll steal from you." He had a point, but I like to try and see the other guy's point of view. Pop said I got my big heart from Mom. He always worried about me. But he didn't have to.

See, I wasn't about to be fucked-over by no one. Trusting

people, I used to tell Pop, is just a better way of getting more work out of them. Besides, the oldtimers at Pop's place remember me when I was a little kid, running around trying on caps and cowboy hats, and they was glad to see me grow up into the business. I didn't have to shout at them like Pop did. They liked listening to me.

And I liked Pop's plant down on Lower Broadway, four huge drafty lofts in an old dirty-brick building not far from where my folks grew up on Prince Street. You'd go up in a freight elevator and get to the fourth floor and start smelling the dye. Some people might say it stunk, but I liked the smell, I liked seeing the stacks of raw bodies—that's how the unshaped hats came in from Nutley, New Jersey—I liked thinking about how the furs sailed all the way over from Australia just to wind up at our place so we could turn 'em into something beautiful.

There's lots to making a hat, and I learned it from the experts. I learned to block 'em and press 'em, to flange 'em and finish 'em and blow a center-crease in the middle of 'em like Edward G. Robinson or John Garfield did in the movies. Oh man, I could handle hats. And my favorite part was the trimming, because of Aunt Bea, boss of the trimming room. I loved being in the trimming room.

Aunt Bea was the only one who'd stand up to Pop. She was Mom's younger sister by a few years, never married, a lover of music and sports, and strong as a man. That's why she got to play the radio when no one else did. She was short, with sturdy legs and a healthy chest. She didn't care about her teeth, which weren't good, or her eyes, which were a little crossed, but she dyed her hair a crazy orange color and dated a lot of different characters. Tough guys were nuts about her —Aunt Bea was a sparkplug—'cause they respected her. No man could scare her. And she loved to dance. The trimming room was always swinging with jazz.

See, a hat really becomes a hat in the trimming room. After it pops out of the hydraulic press, you got these gals—dozens of them—working for Aunt Bea, whipping in the leather sweats and cutting and curling the brims so they can fit on the flanges to be ironed and pressed, with the steam rising, the surplus hairs removed, the shiny rayon linings slipped inside, the outside bands attached with loving care, those smart little bows and ribbons put in place, then the hats slicked and buffed and shined by hand and finally packed into beautiful Myron Klein hat boxes with the distinctive green-and-yellow king's crown, sold at fine haberdashers and better department stores everywhere, just like our slogan says, "Myron Klein: Where Quality Is King."

"*Schmuck!*" the voice of the King reached across the floor, grabbing me by the back of my neck. "Get in here!"

I'd just gotten to work the week after my twenty-third birthday and the day Pop returned from Miami Beach with Mom. I was in the trimming room kissing Aunt Bea hello and greeting all the ladies who worked there—Goldie and Jean and Lillian and Reba, Mamie and Clara and Syd and Flo and Pearl—I knew all their names and asked about their kids, and some of them had grandkids, some of the ladies were portly and some pretty and some liked listening to the ballgames during the summer, the Dodgers and the Giants and the Yankees—I was crazy for the Dodgers—and some of them played the numbers and gave some action to the bookies who ran the shipping room. Sometimes I think we had more guys making book than hats, but that was the way of the world in 1947.

Pop's office was a glass-lined narrow room where he could look out and make sure everyone was working. (I didn't have an office, just a desk on the floor within shouting distance of Pop.) In Pop's office there was this long wall plastered with photos of him presenting hats to the Mayor, to the Junior Senator, to Leo Durocher and Jimmy Durante and a whole slew of stars. I loved these pictures very much, especially the two set up by me—Pops and John Perona, who ran El Morocco, and Pops and Sherman Billingsley, the bald guy who owned the Stork Club. There was also a blowup of Peggy, Mom and me smiling in front of our beach house at Sea Gate.

Now if I'm 5′ 10″, Pop's probably 5′ 6″, but you wouldn't know it when he's behind his big mahogany desk sitting in a raised leather swivel chair with an Havana cigar in his mouth and him talking on the phone. He's got this powerful voice that hits you over the head like a baseball bat. Pop's pudgy, but women like him 'cause he's rich and he's got all his hair—he's vain about his hair—a mass of black and gray curls he keeps real short and these intense brown eyes that drill you like bullets. His build is muscular and stocky and he doesn't walk, he struts like a cocky prizefighter. He played football in high school until he quit in the tenth grade—just like me. He likes to tell you how he made it to the top by himself and how I got it handed to me on a silver platter—which isn't true. But the thing about Pop is, don't argue. Just let him talk.

"Excuses I don't need," he was telling one of the salesmen on the phone. "You call from the Carolinas at my expense to tell me you haven't made your quota. What do you want from me? Sympathy? I'm telling ya' something, Harvey, there's not a fuckin' thing wrong with our spring line. It's one of our best ever. The merchandise would sell itself if you'd get off your ass and see more buyers, more stores, make more calls, there's no substitute for making the calls, making the rounds—am I right, Danny?—Danny's sitting right here, Harvey, and when Danny worked your territory he was a nineteen-year-old kid, a know-nothing, a fuckin' idiot, but because he was hungry he made the calls and he got the orders which is what I expect of you, a grown man, not this belly-achin' to me on the phone at my expense which eats at my gut because you just ain't doing your job."

Slam! Pop practically threw the phone into its cradle.

"Listen, Danny," he said, blowing smoke at me, "I'm putting you back on the road."

"What?"

"The South is falling apart on us."

"The South is the most miserable territory we got."

"It's the most important territory we got."

"I already paid my dues in the South."

"What dues? This isn't a club, this is a business. Dobbs, Knox, Adams, Stetson—they're killing us down South. Harvey can't handle it. He can't sell Southern buyers."

"They're crackers."

"Whatever the fuck they are, you sold them."

"I was proving something to you."

"Good. Go prove it again."

"Who's going to do the promotions? Who's going to see about the ads and the—"

"Me. How many hours a day does that shit take? One? Two? I've been watching you. You been acting like an executive, not a worker. Remember, a long time ago I told you, I said, a company's got one executive—one boss—and everyone else is a worker. Well, at this company the executive is Myron Klein until Myron Klein drops dead, which at this rate could be sooner than later."

"Why do you talk that way?" I asked, scared by the thought. "You're still a young man."

"When I go, I want to go quick. I pray to God, no suffering. I've suffered enough. This business is nothing but aggravation. I come back and we're ten days behind . . ."

"You come back," I interrupted, "and you don't even tell me if you had a good time."

"Three weeks with your mother in Miami Beach is no picnic. I played cards."

"You win?"

"If I'd won, I'd be smiling and handing you a raise. I had bad luck."

"How bad?" I asked, knowing that Pop's gambling was nothing to laugh about.

"How bad is my business? Your business is to start making this company money instead of spending it. You live like a fuckin' prince up there in your fancy-shmancy penthouse with your caviar and your women."

You're one to talk, I wanted to say, but what good would it do? "How's Mom?" I asked instead.

"You'll see at lunch. She's coming in the city to have lunch with you today. Then she's coming up to go over the books."

I was supposed to have Monica for lunch at my place. It was going to be our first afternoon delight. Now I'd have to cancel.

"When you talk to your mother," said my father, "I wish you'd tell her to be happy. I devote my life to making her happy. I give her everything there is to give, and still she's not a happy woman. Tell her, Danny."

"It's not that simple, Pop. You just can't tell people."

"You, she listens to. You're her sonny boy. She worships the ground you walk on. How else did you get so fuckin' spoiled?"

"Listen, Pop," I said, knowing I'd reached my limits, "I got some calls to make."

"Your broads will wait. You're talking to your father. And I'm telling you that after New Year's, you're back on the road."

I didn't answer; I just got up and left.

Monica didn't buy the line about me having lunch with Mom, but what else could I say? It was the truth.

"Then I want to meet her," Monica insisted, which is when I realized that Monica, for all her many charms, might be getting out of hand. Mom and Monica would go together like milk and vodka.

The cab raced uptown through the Christmas traffic and the slushy streets, filthy from last week's big snowfall, but pretty with twinkling lights and decorations and shoppers loaded down with bright packages, as merry as Manhattan ever gets. I got out at the Savoy Plaza, one of the classiest hotels in the city, at 59th and 5th, and hurried inside—I was a little late— looked around and saw Mom, the one and only Anita Klein, sitting in this regal armchair in the lobby, wearing an absolutely knock-out full-length Black Diamond mink and, under a wide-brimmed blue hat, her hair all done up and dyed with silver streaks, wavy and gorgeous like she was a movie star which many of the hotel guests presumed, I'm sure, because of how they was staring. Little did they know that behind the glamor was the sharpest bookkeeper in all five boroughs.

Years back Mom set Pop up in business with the money she made as an office manager at a big Brooklyn lumberyard. Even today, with all Pop's fancy CPA's, it was only Mom he trusted to scrutinize the firm's finances. Twice she'd caught key insiders trying to steal.

"Mom, you look sensational," I said, kissing her and helping her up. She took my hand and squeezed it.

"Handsome isn't the word for my son. The word is 'debonair.' To me, you're the Jewish Cary Grant."

We walked over to the dining room where Paulie had our reservation. I knew all the maitre d's at the swanky midtown joints and they all knew me 'cause of my big tips.

I slipped Paulie a fiver as he whisked us to a quiet banquette facing the door, a premier position. The atmosphere was low-key and high-class, chandeliers and tinkling glass, rich old ladies sipping tea and suave businessmen breaking bread over million dollar deals. You could smell the expensive sauces and Mom liked how we had a waiter and two busboys bowing over us as soon as we sat down.

My mother always smelled of expensive perfumes from Bonwit Teller and she had her huge emerald-cut diamond on one hand and her diamond dome ring, a beehive of shimmering pave stones, on the other. Mom was always decked out. When I was a kid she'd take me down to the Diamond Exchange on Canal Street and ask my opinion about necklaces and bracelets, buying herself only those items I approved.

"How was your vacation?" I asked after we ordered our food.

"Do I have to tell you, Danny? Your father's impossible. Him with his gin rummy, night and day. He lost a fortune. I felt generous, I wanted to be nice, so crazy me, I gave him five thousand dollars to play with, and he lost it all. The whole trip he didn't say two words to me. The sun was shining, the water was warm and your father's got his nose buried in the cards. They had shows, Sophie Tucker and Joe E. Brown, every big name was there, and my Myron, he couldn't care less. Luckily I met Ida from Eastern Parkway. Ida and Bernie Gruntstein. I went to the shows with them."

"That must have been nice."

"It was. But what about you, darling?"

"I've been working, Mom."

"You work too hard. Myron gives you too much dirty work. He treats his own son like a slave."

"He wants to send me back out on the road."

"Over my dead body."

I couldn't help but smile. I could always count on Mom to intervene on my behalf.

"It's dangerous on the road. Why should you go back on the road? You're a big shot now. He should make you president and retire—that's what he should do."

Lunch arrived. My lamb chops with mint jelly were delicious. But Mom barely touched her salad. I could tell something was on her mind.

"What is it, Mom?"

"It's Peggy."

"Peggy's fine. I talked to her last night."

"You're such a good brother, Danny. She's blessed to have such a brother. She looks up to you. That's why you have to talk to her."

"About what?"

"This man she's dating."

"Winthrop Carrington?"

"He's not Jewish, is he?"

"I wouldn't worry, Mom. I don't think it's serious."

"That's what you say. But every day in the papers you read about elopements. Peggy's young and impressionable and she's been seeing him since the spring. For me, that's too long."

"I've been with this guy, Mom . . ."

"That's why I'm talking to you. You know the situation."

"And I know Peggy . . ."

"No one knows Peggy. All we know is that she's a brilliant scholar. She says she wants to be a college professor. But I ask you, is that normal for a beautiful young woman like my Peggy? She reads and she reads. Reading's good for you, but enough's enough. This boy, Winthrop, I think he's also a college professor."

"A critic."

"Two peas in a pod. I'm worried."

"Mom . . ." I started to say, when all of a sudden I heard the strains of "Laura," one of my favorite songs, being played on a silky-smooth piano. There was something familiar about the musician's gentle touch, and when I looked across the room I saw Clifford Summer, dressed in a tux, seated at a Steinway grand, pushed in a corner. In the afternoon light, his skin looked darker than I remembered, and with his white shirt and black bow tie, he appeared very dashing.

I tried to concentrate on Mom's concern, but it was tough 'cause Clifford was playing like an angel. Funny how he was great in that jazz joint the other night, and just as good at the Savoy Plaza where his graceful runs were the perfect accompaniment to the tinkle of crystal stemware and the chit-chat floating around the room.

Mom didn't even hear him. "Will you talk to Peggy?" she asked me. "Will you just talk to her for me?"

"You could tell her yourself, Mom . . ."

"Coming from a mother, it does no good. But coming from a big brother she loves and respects . . ."

"What am I supposed to tell her?"

"To find herself a nice Jewish boy. Is that so horrible?"

Clifford finished a beautiful version of "Stardust" and I couldn't help myself. "Mom, excuse me for just a minute."

I walked over to the pianist, sipping water between numbers, and extended my hand. "Danny Klein. Remember me from the other night?"

"Certainly," he said, shaking my hand and enunciating like a voice coach. "How's your sister, Dan?"

"Great, just great. It's a little strange seeing you here after hearing you on 52nd Street."

"Trying to stay alive."

"Well, I just wanted to say hi and let you know I'm getting to be a fan. You're a terrific musician." Up close, I noticed that his tux was a little threadbare.

"Thanks. Try and stop back at the Outside Inn. I'm there through the end of the month."

"I'll try."

Back at the table, Mom was digging into her peach cobbler.

She hadn't noticed me talking to Clifford. "So you'll talk to Peggy," she said.

"I'll talk to Peggy."

"There's something else."

"What?"

"Your apartment, your beautiful penthouse apartment that you and I furnished together. Do you love it?"

"I love it, Mom."

"And the silver couch and the authentic Oriental rugs and the Chinese modern bedroom set and the satin quilt and the matching gold drapes. It's magnificent, isn't it, Danny?"

"Magnificent, Mom."

"No matter what your father says."

"I don't listen to him."

"Your mother has taste. You'll admit that, won't you, Danny?"

"Of course."

"And when it comes to you, your mother gives till it hurts. Isn't that true, darling?"

"It's true, Mom."

"Good. Now listen to me. Now that the apartment is set up and furnished and everything is just so, I need to use it."

I was confused. "What for?"

"You shouldn't ask such things."

Suddenly my heart started beating fast. "Mom," I said, "I don't think I want to hear about this."

"Look, Danny, it's time you knew. You've been hearing stories about your father for years. I wouldn't be surprised if he even asked you to procure for him. Far be it from me to ever ask anything like that. I'm just asking to use the apartment that you and I furnished together. I need it next Tuesday from noon to about three."

"Mom!" I was angry, I was disturbed. "That's wrong. That's very, very wrong."

"You're my only son, Danny, and you and me, we're close, we've always been close, so it's time to tell you a secret which you must take to the grave with you. Louis Shotkin—"

"Dr. Shotkin? Our family doctor? The guy who came to our house when I had the mumps, the guy we see up at the Cats-kills with his wife and his pimply kids and—"

"He's a wonderful man, and his children's complexions have improved a hundred percent. Of course he has a family, like I have a family. But between him and his wife Evelyn is like between me and your father. There's no affection. Two years ago he and I started up. He said he's had a crush on me for twenty-five years. Well, every couple of weeks we'd go to a hotel—not a cheap hotel, mind you, but the St. George."

"Mom, I don't want to *hear* this . . ."

"The St. George is Brooklyn's classiest—"

"I don't want to hear any of this . . ."

"But no matter how much the room costs—Louis would get a suite if I asked him—no matter how luxurious, I just don't feel comfortable in a hotel. At your place, though, with every-thing that I helped you pick out, I'll feel at home."

"Mom, this is terrible!"

"What's so terrible? Is it a crime to want a little love out of life? I don't have to tell you what your father's like. Sex is something he saves for his whores. It's been years."

"Then divorce him."

"Why? We love each other in our own fashion. He'd fall apart without me. And so would the business. Where else would he find an eagle eye like mine? He needs to yell at me, and I need to yell at him. Besides, a divorce would upset the children."

"Upset the children! What do you think you're doing to me now?"

"I'm talking about Peggy. You, I'm not worried about. You're a man of the world."

"I don't know if I can handle this. You mean, my father has no idea that you're . . ."

"Why should he? Would it be better for me to aggravate him? To drive him crazy with jealousy? The man has provided us with a good living, and I respect that. I leave him with his illusions."

"This is wrong."

"This is life, Danny. And this will be our little secret. Not a word to Peggy. Not a word to anyone."

"Dr. Shotkin," I said, thinking of how his hands looked so pink when he gave me a shot, how his breath smelled of medicine. "Dr. Shotkin!"

"He's a prince, a regular gentleman, kind and caring. And all I want from you is a key."

"Oh, Mom . . ."

"And by the way," she said, scrutinizing the check, "get the waiter. This is ninety-five cents too high."

After lunch, we walked out onto 5th Avenue, a cold winter sun shining, Mom's arm linked inside mine. She looked radiant as she continued unburdening her heart.

"It isn't one bit sordid," she said. "It isn't dirty. Louis is a clean man, an educated man, a wealthy man. We don't see each other that often because of his schedule. But when we do see each other, it's good enough to last for another two weeks."

"Every two weeks? Mom, that's *very* often."

"Look, darling, I'm not like my sister Bea. I can't have sex without romance."

Goddamnit, I didn't want to hear my mother talking this way, but what could I do?

She hailed a cab and we sailed down to Canal Street, all the while her describing how she was happy having two men in her life. "Myron is too talkative and Louis is too quiet," she said. "One helps me put up with the other. So I don't feel useless, I also go over Dr. Shotkin's books. You should have seen his billing. Until he met me, it was a mess."

At Pollock the jeweler she bought me a star sapphire pinky ring in a white-gold setting that I'd been eyeing for months.

"I'm paying with money I've put aside, money your father doesn't know a thing about."

"You don't have to do this, Mom."

"I do it, darling, because I love you."

"I love you too, Mom," I mumbled, heartsick.

"Now the key, Danny. We'll go make me a key. And you won't forget to talk to Peggy, will you?"

Back at the office I tried avoiding Pop but he caught my eye. Mom was in the file room going over the books.

"Did you tell her to try to be happy, for God's sake?" he asked me.

"Don't worry, Pop. She's happy, she's plenty happy."

On the afternoon that Mom was at my apartment with Dr. Shotkin, I was a mess. I'd broken off with Monica. Suddenly Monica seemed wrong for me. For the first time in my life, sex seemed wrong. I'd been enjoying the ladies ever since I was old enough to know what's what, but not now.

I'd grown up with Pop's affairs, and I didn't make much of them. They seemed normal. Or at least Pop made them sound normal. Sometimes when it'd bother me I'd talk to Uncle Nate who'd say, "Danny, human nature is such that everyone's got something wrong with him. The best thing to do is look the other way 'cause someday you'll see there's something wrong with you." So I took his advice.

And surely that same advice applied twice. But with Mom— with the woman who made my brown-bag lunches and hot dinners just the way I liked them every day of my life until I left home at age twenty-one—with her it was different. Or was it? I wanted to talk to Uncle Nate 'cause he'd sympathize. But I was under oath not to say anything. Besides, I didn't want Uncle Nate to know. I didn't want anyone to know. I was ashamed.

"Don't worry," Mom told me the night before her date. "I'll change the sheets before we leave."

That only made it worse—thinking about sheets, thinking about Dr. Shotkin and his puffy pink skin and the creepy way he talked, him drooling over my mom . . . I wanted to kill the bastard.

I thought about rushing home, throwing him out of my bed and breaking his skinny ass in two, just like that. But the idea of seeing Mom in my bed naked with this guy pumping her— the whole thing made me sick.

I didn't even want to go home that night. Which is why I decided to have dinner with Peggy. After all, I did promise Mom that I'd talk to my baby sister.

Peg asked me to pick her up at the Barnard library, and there she was, at a table in the back, buried under a pile of books. She was so lost in her studies that when I said "hi" she jumped.

"Sorry."

"Oh, Danny." She glanced up. "I was off on another

planet." Wearing a soft black wool turtleneck sweater, her small face half-covered by the collar, her dark hair cut short, she looked perky and pretty and happy to see me.

"What are you reading about, Peg?"

"Jazz."

"They write books about jazz?"

"They write books about everything. Jazz history is fascinating."

"I'm sure. Let's go."

Now I'm not much of a reader—mainly the sports section of the *News*, the *Post*, the *Journal American* and the *Herald Trib*. Those I read almost every morning and of course there were the columnists, like Grantland Rice and Red Smith, who wrote like people talk. I liked that. I liked looking over the movie page and finding out who Ed Sullivan was gossiping about and what shows were heading for Broadway. To be honest, though, I hadn't read too many entire books 'cause even in school I never finished *The House of the Seven Gables*, which I hated. Like Mom said, Peggy was a demon reader, and reading about jazz wasn't so great because of Winthrop Carrington. But I didn't want to discuss him right now because I was hungry and I was thinking about Dr. Shotkin and Mom.

We got into my white Studebaker, the little sports model, and drove over to a Greek joint on Tenth Avenue—I love stuffed grape leaves and spicy roast lamb—and all the time Sis couldn't stop talking about jazz.

"Do you realize that it's the only native American art form?" she asked me.

"What about horse racing?"

"That's ancient. They were racing in Arabia before the birth of Jesus."

"They have bookies back then?"

She laughed. I could always make Peggy laugh. "But jazz,"

she continued, her dark eyes reflecting the sparkling city lights, "jazz is original with America. African rhythmic origins, yes. And European harmonic influences, of course. But it's really the product of an extraordinary genius, developed by black people from the days of slavery till now."

"Do they teach you about jazz in college?"

"No, but they should. There should be courses. You should be able to major in jazz. Right now we're living through a major revolution in jazz—it's happening within a few miles of my college campus—and there isn't a professor at Barnard who knows the first thing about it. Look how we worship dead European composers like Bach and Beethoven and neglect people like Charlie Parker."

"I saw Benny Goodman at Carnegie Hall. That was something. Remember?"

"I remember when you came home with Aunt Bea. You were so excited. I used to play your Benny Goodman records all the time. You know, with Lionel Hampton and Teddy Wilson, his was the first big-name band to integrate."

"They weren't actually in the band," I added, not wanting to seem completely ignorant. "Benny put 'em in that little quartet with him and Gene Krupa."

"But that made it even more special," she argued.

In the cozy restaurant, warmed by a rattling radiator, we wolfed down our meal as Peg went on about jazz.

"I used to love ballet. Remember when I took lessons? Remember how Mom would take me to the ballet? She'd always tell me that she wanted me to be a ballerina."

"I wanted that too. Ballerinas are stars. They're so beautiful the way they twirl around in those little skirts."

She took my hand and forced me to look into her eyes. Like all us Kleins, Peggy was intense. "But do you know what was wrong, Danny? The rhythms. I never felt the rhythms. Ballet rhythms ran like running water. I missed the beat. With jazz —the kind of jazz Winthrop's been introducing me to—the beat seems to come from my heart. It's completely natural. It's wonderful..."

"The feeling's mutual," I said, "but I've been wondering about this Carrington character."

"He knows *everything* there is to know about jazz."

"I guess. But... well... is it serious?"

"Of course it's serious. Jazz is serious. It's the highest form of art. And art is the most serious, the most glorious, the most liberating emotional experience. It's nourishment for the soul—"

"I mean is it serious between you and him?"

"Why Danny!" She smiled. "You're being protective. How noble. But there's no need. We're just good friends. Hey, don't look so worried. Did Mom tell you to talk to me?"

"No."

"You're lying. I know she did. And that doesn't bother me. I just wish she'd treat me like an adult and speak to me directly."

"You know Mom. You'll always be her baby."

"Do you think she'll ever leave Pop?"

The question startled me. All evening I'd been wanting to tell Peg Mom's big secret—I felt like I had to tell someone—but I just couldn't. Peg was in love with life; she loved all these books and ideas and now she loved jazz the way she fell in love with lots of different guys in high school and college, but I didn't think she could take the news about our family doctor.

"Why should she leave Pop?" I asked her.

"Because she's unhappy. Neither of them know how to enjoy life."

"Well, I do. Uncle Nate's taught me a lot about enjoying life."

"Winthrop teaches me. He really does. Like the night of your birthday. Wasn't that marvelous? Didn't you love the piano player at the cellar club?"

"Hey, I ran into him."

"Where?"

I told her about my lunch with Mom at the Savoy Plaza.

"Is that when she told you to make sure I dated Jewish boys?"

"Peg, you can't exactly blame her."

"Who blames her? Just tell her I had an affair with my English professor last year. He's married, but he's Jewish."

"Are you kidding?" I asked, alarmed.

"That's for me to know and you to find out."

"I don't like these jokes."

"I don't like being watched like a baby, Danny."

"Mama's worried, that's all."

"Tell her not to be. Tell her I haven't fallen in love with Winthrop, but with jazz. Tell her I've fallen in love with jazz because *I'm* like jazz; I'm a free spirit."

"Nothing's free in this world."

"Oh, Danny, quit talking like Pop. Let's go over and hear that piano player. What do you say?"

"Swell," I said as we headed for the car. I was happy to put off going home to freshly changed sheets.

Driving to midtown, I wondered about Peg's sex life. I had to wonder because I'd known about Pop for years and now I knew about Mom and I certainly know myself—I've always been eager for beaver—but what about the baby of the family? What about that Jewish professor Sis mentioned earlier? Was she or wasn't she kidding? What about Sidney Kornfeld, the chess player she'd dated when she was a junior in high school? What about that time I caught them in her bedroom with her blouse off? I kicked the shit out of him, but he kept coming back when I wasn't there. And then there was this wiseguy med student her first year in Barnard, this stud from Columbia who asked her to his parents' place in Palm Beach and Mom didn't let her go even if the guy was going to be a doctor. What's to have stopped her from screwing him? Maybe she's been screwing all these guys, because Peggy, like she says, is a free spirit and that can get women in trouble and maybe she inherited it from Mom, maybe the whole fuckin' family is oversexed. Sure, I could ask Peg about her sex life, but the trouble was she just might tell me. I didn't want to know any more about it. I was thinking so hard I was making myself sick. Peg was going on about how some dead French guy really understood American music more than Americans and I was just glad when we got to 52nd Street. There was a parking place right outside the club.

We jumped out of the car and got hit smack in the face with all the different sounds. The jazz was jumping; business was brisk. Me and Sis were happy to can our conversation and just listen to the music. Downstairs in the basement I was surprised to see that the Outside Inn was packed. I was glad for Clifford. He was rocking through a chorus of "Fascinating Rhythm," peering at us through those pretty, peaceful eyes of his, nodding at me and Peg and us nodding back like we was old friends.

"*Peg!*"

Oh shit. It was Winthrop Carrington in a brown Harris tweed suit—a nice one, I had to admit—sitting at a ringside table alone, his notebook out, his pen poised, waving for us to come join him.

He kissed Peggy on the mouth. I didn't like that.

"I thought you weren't impressed with this guy," I whispered to Winnie as Clifford paused for the cause.

"I'm reevaluating. I may do an article on him, but I'm not quite certain he merits the attention. I've been asking the other musicians about him. Seems like he played piano with Ben Webster for a while and, after that, Fats Navarro—both the old school and the new. They say he didn't belong in either school. Musically, he may be somewhat confused."

"Because he quit those schools? Hell, that don't mean nothing," I said. "I quit school myself."

"He has technique," Winthrop went on, ignoring my remark. "But I suspect he's tainting his talent with this popular-styled singing."

"I think he's a fuckin' fabulous singer," I stated.

"Jazz singing is a strange and pure art," Peg added. "I've been reading about the blues vocalists like Lonnie Johnson and shouters like Joe Turner."

"Whom have you been reading?" Winnie wanted to know. "Was it Hugues Panassie or..."

And they were off in their spacey conversation while I surveyed the club. There were a few rough-looking customers, a few loose dames and some sailors. The usual mix. I ordered drinks for me and Sis and sat there thinking how here I was bringing Peg back to Winnie when I was supposed to be keeping them apart. I wasn't doing Mom much good, but on the other hand she wasn't helping my head by telling me shit I didn't need to hear. What I needed was this Scotch—man, it felt good going down—and a little music to lighten my mood and push all the thoughts out of my brain which was definitely overworked and overworried.

Clifford came back in and started the set with "Moonglow," a particular favorite of mine, which he played light as air, making it look as easy as a kid on a swing. When he sang, starting with the second chorus, he looked right at Peg, just like last time, only this time the look between them was hot, sexy, I swear it was, and even Winnie started squirming when, like a firecracker in our ears—*pop!*—a gun went off.

Remember, this was a tiny joint, and I turned and saw a big lug in the back, a white guy with a broken nose, standing and firing at this skinny colored guy two tables over.

Bam!

The black man takes the hit on his shoulder and he jumps over two tables and lands on ours and I throw Peg down on the floor and then Winnie turns around and says, "My word," and I throw his silly ass down too, and the guy in the back fires again, the bullet ripping off the dude's ear, skin tissue and dripping blood, and the lug in the back is heading towards us and the next thing I know his broken nose is up in my face and I catch him in the jaw with a clean right jab—my best punch—and Cliff is next to me, his eyes blazing, and just when I think I've got the guy's gun, it goes off, the blast blinding me and pain . . . oh man, terrible hot red pain passing over me and all I know is that I'm falling, falling . . . falling down a hole with Mom and Pop and Peg and so much pain, worrying whether my family's okay, whether I'll ever see them again, so much pain, so much worry, and I can't stop falling, falling, falling . . .

BETH IƧRAEL HOƧPITAL

The morning I came to, I got hit with two surprises. The first was the headline in the *Post*.

DRUG WARS ON SWING STREET!

Mobsters Shoot it Out
Famous Hatmaker Caught in Crossfire

In the article, they called me "Myron Klein." Careless reporters, those stupid fucks, mixed me up with Pop.

My second surprise came as I turned over and looked across the hospital room at my roommate, Clifford Summer.

His right hand was bandaged up and my left arm was in a cast.

"Where's my sister?" I asked.

"She's been here visiting. She's fine. No injuries. She's the one who insisted I be in here with you."

"Did anyone else get hurt besides us?"

"No. You coldcocked the guy with the gun. They say the cops came a minute later and hauled him off. The cat he shot survived."

"You gonna be able to play?" I asked, looking over his bandaged hand.

He turned his eyes away from me and paused before answering. His voice went down an octave. "I lost two fingers."

"Oh shit," I moaned, and turned my head away.

"The bullet went from your arm to my hand and through my pinky and the finger next to it. A freak hit. Your wound's deep—you've got a chipped bone—but they say you're going to be fine. It just took you a little longer to come out of that ether trance."

"Geez, I'm sorry about your fingers . . ."

"Hey, man, you don't have a thing to be sorry about. I would've lost my life if you hadn't pushed that revolver out of my face."

"I didn't know what I was doing."

"The hell you didn't. You were protecting everyone."

"Well, I didn't see *you* running out the back door."

"It happened so fast, I guess we were both acting crazy, thinking we could get the gun out of the guy's hand before he shot up the place."

"Can you make a living playing piano with eight fingers?"

"I couldn't make a living playing with ten. But it doesn't really matter. The music business makes prostitution look downright upright. I was through with music anyway."

"What are you talking about? With your kind of talent, how could you think of quitting music?"

"I see you're in the hat business," he said, coolly changing subjects.

"Myron's my old man. The paper got us mixed up."

"I know. He called before . . . screaming."

"That's normal for him."

"Intensity's not a bad characteristic."

"That's a nice way of putting it."

Knock-knock.

"Who's there?" I shouted.

"Your mother . . . and Dr. Shotkin."

"God help me," I moaned to Clifford.

"What's wrong?" he asked.

"You'll see."

Mom was in a silver fox jacket and smelled like the entire perfume department at Bonwit's. Tall skinny Dr. Shotkin was in a three-piece gray wool suit and smelled like he'd just bathed in Listerine. He carried his black leather doctor's case and didn't look me in the eye. Did he know I knew? While I was in the hospital, had they been in my bed? I wanted my key back.

"I've been worried to death," Mom moaned.

"I had a very good man work on his wound, Anita," Shotkin reassured her in his best bedtime manner. "I've told you a dozen times."

"This is Clifford Summer," I said. "Cliff, this is my mother and my doctor, Louis Shotkin."

"My pleasure," said Cliff, but Mom and Shotkin barely acknowledged him, looking through the guy like he was invisible. That embarrassed me.

"Make sure my Danny is all right," Mom told Shotkin.

"I've made sure, Anita. I was here when they put on the cast."

"Make sure again," Mama insisted, kissing me on both cheeks. "Feel his pulse, take his temperature, make like a doctor for God's sake. My Danny was almost killed."

Shotkin did as told. His fingers felt especially slimy against my skin. I thought of those times he stuck his finger up my ass or examined my balls when I was a kid. I never wanted this guy to touch me again.

"He's fine," he reassured Mom. "A couple of days rest and he'll be going home."

"What about Cliff here?" I asked.

"Peggy asked me to recommend a hand surgeon," explained the doctor like he didn't want to be bothered, "but the fingers couldn't be saved."

"Forget it, Danny," said Cliff, like he was angry.

"But he's a great piano player," I said. "Ain't there such things as artificial fingers?"

"You shouldn't be taking your sister to places like that," Mom scolded.

"He takes her because he's a fuckin' idiot," shouted Pop, rushing into the room like a locomotive.

"Myron," she said, "this isn't the time to chide the boy."

"He isn't a boy, he's a man with a dick for a brain," Pop proclaimed, not bothering to say hello to Shotkin or Clifford. "Only a dick-brain would take his sister to a nigger dive like that."

"Pop," I said, motioning towards Clifford.

"Not offense meant," said Pop, turning to the black man.

Clifford's jaw was tight, his eyes faraway. He didn't say a word but you could feel his rage.

"I'm upset," Pop repeated, "having a son without the guts to give his real name to the newspaper. Instead, he hides behind me and suddenly I'm in the middle of a nightclub with mobsters shooting over dope deals and the whole hat industry thinks I'm a basket case and my phone doesn't stop ringing for eight hours—eight hours it's ringing off the wall—with questions I can't answer and questions I don't understand."

"Pop," I said, "how could I say anything to the newspapers when I was out cold?"

"Myron," said Mom, "you're acting like an animal."

"*I'm* an animal!" said Pop. "*I'm* acting bad! I like that. I'm home listening to Jack Benny on the radio while my son takes my daughter to..." he paused, remembering Clifford, "to some dive and I'm the one she points a finger at. How do you like that, Louis?" he asked Dr. Shotkin. "How'd you like to have a nag like that at home?"

"Louis happens to have a very high regard for me," Mom answered.

I could see panic creeping over the doctor's face.

"Because you pay his bills on time," Pop retorted.

"Please," said the doctor. "The excitement isn't doing Danny any good."

"The only thing that's going to do Danny good is the road," said Pop. "I fired Harvey this morning. I'm telling you, Danny, I'm sending you down South to replace him as soon as you get out of here."

"Over my dead body," Mom maintained.

"Don't tempt me," said Pop.

"This isn't the time, Myron," the doctor pleaded. "It really isn't."

"You should be on your hands and knees, thanking God that your son's alive," Mom argued.

"He's alive, but Myron Klein Hats is dying," declared Myron Klein, "and now its reputation is shot to hell."

"The publicity can only help business," Mom shot back. "Besides, last quarter's profits were nearly as fat as you."

"This is how she respects her husband," Pop said to Shotkin. "You're a doctor, you're a civilized man, you tell me if this is how women respect husbands who dress them in furs and jewelry and whatever the hell else their hearts desire."

Shotkin smiled sheepishly.

When they left, I apologized to Cliff. "I feel terrible about that."

"Fuck it," he said, but I wasn't sure what he meant.

"They don't think before they talk."

"Even if they did, they'd probably say the same thing."

"Probably," I had to agree.

"Anyway, he's tougher on you than on me."

"Thanks for that."

"Besides, your sister arranged for me to be in here with you, so how pissed can I get?"

"That was nice of her," I told him, wondering what was going through her mind.

There was a long uncomfortable silence, and finally I said, "Look, I'm sure you'll be back to the piano in no time. That's a pretty good job you have at the Savoy Plaza, isn't it?"

"*Had.*"

"What happened? I thought you were doing great in there."

"I did too—until the owner said my music was a little too racy."

"That's crazy. What'd you say?"

"'Later for you, motherfucker.'"

I laughed. Laughing along with me, Cliff said, "No laughing matter. Especially when I got thrown out of my apartment the night of the shooting. The bum who owns the Outside Inn hadn't paid me in two weeks. That's why I'm not complaining about staying in this hospital room. Least it's guaranteed bed and board. And a chance to catch up on some reading. Your sister brought me some books."

"You got no savings?"

He laughed again and started singing softly. Even though he was my age, he could make his voice sound like a gentle old country farmer:

Ain't got no savings, no salary coming due
Ain't got no savings, I say nothing's coming due
Just sittin' here in ol' Beth Israel singin'
The eight-finger Danny Klein New York City Blues

"That's terrific!" I said. "That's a great song. You make it sound so easy. Look at you over there—you sing, you play, you write. You're bound to make a fortune."

"*You* make it sound so easy. I've been scuffling since I was twelve, and the only fortune I've known is the pure pleasure of creation. Which is no mean prize."

"You talk like Peg. But I'm talking business. Do you know how many clubs in New York City could use a talent like yours?"

"Look, Dan," said Cliff, cutting me off and suddenly flying off the handle, "my hand's throbbing and my head's hurting and I really don't want to hear any more shit. I'm sure you know everything there is to know about hats, but for Christ's sake don't tell me how easy it is making a living making music in this fucking city since you're looking at someone who's struggled at it—*seriously* struggled—for over a decade and is fed up, brother, too fed up to even discuss this shit any longer. So let me just nod out and hope when I wake up from this nightmare I'll have all ten fingers on my right hand."

I felt bad, but I understood what the guy was saying. I could hardly blame Cliff, he'd been through hell. So I just shut up and let him alone.

While he was sound asleep I had a nice little surprise. Monica came by to make me feel better. I gotta hand it to Monica: her hand job was a sweet get-well gesture. She simply closed the curtain between my bed and Cliff's and went to town.

She knew to be careful 'cause my arm was aching. But she

also knew I needed attention. It'd been a while since I had any relief. Monica understood me, and she understood pressure, the tight pressure of her fist, the smooth strokes of her fingers, long steady strokes, first hard, then soft, then slow, then fast, faster and faster, she worked me up, she had me wiggling and wanting it even more, licking my ear, kissing my neck, squeezing my boner, harder and faster, till I erupted. Monica used up half a box of tissues cleaning up. I appreciated her kindness and even thought of asking her to hang around and do Cliff—after all, he was a buddy—but I didn't 'cause something about that hit me as real wrong.

"Will you call me when you get out, Danny?" she whispered.

"Sure, baby."

"And will you dream about me, Danny?"

"Who else?"

She kissed me good-by and left the room. I dozed off, dreaming about Benny Goodman and Clifford Summer wearing wide-brimmed Myron Klein gray velours and charcoal pinstriped suits while playing jazz together in Carnegie Hall, which somehow became the Steeplechase at Coney Island, all of us riding the roller coaster, screaming and falling in space. When I woke up, I pushed back the curtains and saw Peg sitting real close to Cliff's bed.

I panicked. For a minute, I couldn't see her hands and figured she was doing to Cliff what Monica had done to me. I was about to say something when she got up to get him some water. I'd been imagining things.

"Hey, Peg," I said. "Aren't you going to see how I'm doing?"

"I already saw. You're doing fine."

A knock on the door.

"Come in."

Winthrop Carrington walked in wearing a thin smile.

"Just in time," said Peg. "I told Clifford you'd be here for the interview."

Cliff didn't seem thrilled with the idea, but I could see he didn't want to disappoint Peg.

To make matters worse, Winnie was wearing a Yalie letter sweater.

"Were you on the ping-pong team or something?" I asked him.

"Debate."

He pulled a chair over to Cliff's bed, sat down and started up. "I've been writing for Metronome. You might have seen my piece on Earl Hines."

"Missed that one," said Cliff.

"I'm interested in your background."

"Petroleum engineering."

Winnie looked confused. I loved it.

"Just kidding," Cliff admitted. "Actually, it's Italian Renaissance poetry."

"I appreciate your humor," said Yale. "I haven't met too many college-educated jazz musicians."

"Well, don't look at me. I went from my elementary school to jail."

"Why?"

"Got caught stealing hubcaps."

"Where'd you grow up?"

"I spent some time in Alabama, and some time in Dallas."

"Dallas is the home of Buster Smith," said Winnie, "Charlie Parker's teacher."

"I knew Buster. He taught me to fish."

"Was he the first jazz musician who influenced you?"

"He was the first fisherman to influence me."

"Were your parents musicians?"

"Philosophers."

"You're the child of academics?"

"I'm a musician—and a fisherman."

"How did you get to New York?"

"Broken-down bus."

"Really, Mr. Summer, I'm interested in your background and influences. I hear so many elements in your music—traces of Fats Waller, Basie, Erroll Garner, even Bud Powell. I wonder about the convergence of so many styles."

"I wonder too."

"Right now, though, I think you'd agree that jazz is at a crossroads. Be-bop seems to be reexamining the past—is it not?—in an attempt to forge a startling new future. Where do you see yourself in this new musical landscape?"

"Up a tree."

"I don't understand."

"My head in the sky, my roots in the soil."

"Could you explain that a little bit more?"

"No."

"Clifford," Peg pleaded, confused why someone so sweet had turned so sour. "You're not being helpful."

"I'm sorry, but Metronome's never been helpful to me."

"Well, maybe it will be now," Peg said.

"Now that I've quit playing."

"I'm sorry," said Winnie. "I didn't realize that the loss of your fingers meant you were giving up music."

"Thanks for arranging this, Peg," said Cliff, "but the timing's wrong. Look, Carrington, just tell your readers that music is all one thing and to stop reading and start listening."

"But what about your views on the compatibility or incompatibility of the swing schools and the modernists?" Winnie went on. "The conflicts are surely evident between the players, the arrangers, the fans, even the critics."

"Critics crave conflict. What else are they going to write about? If conflicts don't exist, critics invent them. Like I said, music is one thing."

"And what's that one thing?" Winnie asked.

"Music," Cliff answered.

With that, a frustrated Carrington gathered up his notes and put on his coat.

"I'm coming with you," said Peg, pissed at Clifford.

I was worried that Winnie, after being beat up by Cliff, might get some serious sympathy from Peggy. At the same time, I was glad Cliff had balls. He saw the Yalie the same way as me.

"I think you're arrogant," said Sis to Cliff.

"I think you're pretty," Cliff answered.

And with that, she and Winnie were gone with the wind.

Sometime that night, a nurse gave me a painkiller shot. The drug mellowed me out, but Cliff was still in a shitty mood 'cause when I asked him something about how he got started playing piano, he went off on me.

"Goddamnit, can't you people stop this interviewing shit!"

I didn't say nothing more. I just left him alone and fell back to sleep. A little later I opened my eyes to see that he had a visitor, a short black guy in a French beret, dark glasses, leopard skin jacket and red shoes that looked like spats. I'd never seen an outfit like this before. Across the room, their low voices sounded like dreamy jazz solos. Cliff's friend was saying, "Yeah, man, I just fell by this coffee shop and this weird waitress looked at me like I'd just stepped out of a flying saucer. All I did, man, was ask her for a couple of eggs with the eyes open."

"This is Fletch, Danny," Cliff said to me when he saw I was awake. I guess he felt bad that he'd yelled at me before. "Fletch plays trombone."

Fletch looked at me the way Mom and Shotkin had looked at Cliff.

He left a few minutes later and I dozed off again, dreaming about Mom, Pop and Doctor S. running up and down Miami Beach, throwing stones at each other. When I woke up, Cliff's mood had really mellowed. He was singing to himself. His voice was like honey dripping from a spoon.

I got up for a glass of water.

"Got a gift," he said, pointing to a fat reefer on his bed tray. "Ever smoke it?"

"Never."

"Interested?"

"What will it do?"

"Ease your troubled mind."

"Then light the shit up," I said.

"Crack the window."

Five minutes later I was back in bed floating free. "Hey, Cliff, I'm feeling pretty fuckin' relaxed over here."

"That's the point."

"Not bad. Not bad at all."

"This stuff can promote creativity."

"Shit, you're the creative one. You're an artist, a legitimate fuckin' artist. Me, I'm a hat salesman."

"You really dig hats, don't you?"

"The way you dig jazz. Hats talk to me. They got different personalities, like singers. When we get outta here, I'm taking you down to Pops' so you can pick out something snappy. What do you say?"

"I don't see myself as one of your family's favorites."

"My family's great, really. They just take getting used to. Peggy's in love with jazz, Pop's in love with money and Mom's in love with . . ." I almost said "Dr. Shotkin" but stopped myself. How could I tell my deepest secret to a guy I barely knew?

"Who's Mom in love with?" Cliff asked.

"Me. She drives me nuts."

"At least your family's close-knit. You're involved with each other. That's something."

"How about your family?"

"Scattered." For a guy who could be open, he could clam up just like that.

"Any other geniuses in the family besides you?"

"You've got a strange notion of genius, Dan."

"I got taste in music—that's what I got—and I know you're selling yourself short."

"It's that shit we smoked."

"No shit," I said. "I hate to see people throw away fortunes, which is what you're about to do. See, the only thing you lack is the right promoter."

"And that's you—is that it?"

"I wasn't thinking along those lines, but come to think of it, a lot of people think I'm an ace promoter. If I can promote Myron Klein hats, I sure as shit can promote your talented ass."

Cliff laughed. "You talk like an agent."

"You don't think I can do it, do you?"

He shrugged.

"Look, Cliff, you learn to play with eight fingers and I'll find you some work in 1948. And that's a fuckin' guarantee."

He laughed again and then, joking and smoking, started making up another one of his smooth blues:

Eight-finger jazzman and bright-eyed Jewish boy
Scufflin' jazzman and Mama's bouncing boy
 They gettin' into trouble
 Just looking for a little joy

BLIZZARD
OF BLUE*S*

All night long, the wind was howling. The storm was blowing something fierce, and I kept tossing and turning. When
morning came, I peeked out the window and could see
nothing but swirls of blinding white snow. Looked like the
world had disappeared. My left arm, still in a cast, was
throbbing and my head was aching and on the radio John
Cameron Swayze called it the Blizzard of '47, the worst
blizzard in the history of New York. The city was buried
under 25.8 inches of snow. Nothing was moving out there,
and I couldn't have cared less.

It was my first day home from the hospital and the perfect
atmosphere for recuperating. The phone wasn't working and
the cabs weren't running. No honking buses, no screaming
from the streets below. Lots of peace and quiet. I took an
aspirin and made myself a pot of coffee. I turned up the radio
'cause Lena Horne was singing "Ill Wind" in her sweet haunting way, when the doorbell rang.

Hurriedly, I slipped a maroon flannel robe over my red silk

pajamas. The colors were clashing, but who had time to coor-
dinate colors at ten in the morning? And who the hell could
have gotten through the blizzard to visit me?

"Mom."

"I was worried."

"About what?"

"You. I'm always worried about you."

"You look like an Eskimo."

An Eskimo covered in mink. She was wearing a long white
mink coat, a huge mink hood and big black golashes. She was
carrying two shopping bags filled with food.

"How'd you get over here from Brooklyn? The whole city's
shut down."

"Where there's a will, there's a way."

"But how'd you find a way today?"

"Ever hear of snowplows?"

"You came over on a snowplow? I don't believe it."

"The driver didn't believe me either when I told him I'd give
him fifty dollars to take me from Ocean Parkway. But I gave and
he took. Look, I had to come. For you, I'd cut off both arms. I
knew that this wouldn't be a good day for you to be alone."

"What's happening out here?" asked a groggy-eyed Clifford
Summer, emerging from my guest bedroom wearing a pair of
my long johns.

Mom looked at the lanky black man and said to me, "So
you're not alone."

"Cliff's staying here a little while. Just till he gets back on
his feet."

"Well," she paused, considering the situation, "there's food
enough for Cliff, if Cliff likes *kreplach* soup."

"Love it," Cliff assured her.

* * *

"Okay, so you don't love the South," said Mom an hour later, "but it'd only be for a few months."

We'd eaten the soup, Cliff had gone back for a nap, and Anita Klein had finally gotten to the point of her visit.

"Look, Mom, my arm's in a cast. I can't go anywhere."

"In five, six weeks you'll be fine."

"I can't believe you're changing your mind like this."

"I went over the books. You know me and the books. Numbers talk to me. I don't argue with numbers, Danny. Business down South is off sixty percent."

"And you want my apartment."

"Your apartment isn't the issue. The issue is Georgia, Florida, Alabama, Mississippi, the Carolinas—all that used to be Myron Klein territory. It was a gold mine for us. Half our profits came out of the South."

"'Cause I developed it."

"Don't I know? And so does your father. He's so proud. The knack you have with the people down there."

"Black people. They're the hat customers down there."

"The way all people love you, Danny. The way you can sell them. The way they listen to you. Peggy's listening to you. She told me she's through with that writer."

"Good."

"And the way you like to help people." Mom turned her eyes towards the guest bedroom. "Sometimes I think you go overboard."

"Cliff's a talented guy, Mom. Just down on his luck. I'm going to help him find some work."

"God helps those who help themselves, Danny. And right now it's your father who needs help. Would I come through a blizzard if this wasn't important?"

"I hate this thing between you and Shotkin."

"Then don't think about it. Meanwhile, he's a fine doctor
and a true gentleman. Look at the care he's given you." Mom
got up and kissed me. "There's nothing I wouldn't do for my
sonny boy. Nothing."

"How are you getting home? Is the snow plow driver waiting downstairs?"

"Don't be a wiseguy. It doesn't suit you. An ambulance is
coming for me."

"An ambulance?"

"Ambulances run in every kind of weather. Mine's coming
from Beth Israel Hospital, courtesy of Dr. Shotkin. I told you
he was a gentleman."

On New Year's Eve, the snow was still sticking and the city
barely back in motion. I was barely back in motion, still too
pooped to party.

Cliff had been moping. He wasn't real thrilled to be staying
with me. This guy was proud. On the other hand, my penthouse was big and comfortable and I had plenty of jazz
records around. I knew to leave him alone. Besides, I had a
baby grand piano which he kept eyeing but never touching—
at least not yet.

I could have gotten depressed. The start of 1948 and here I
was, being sent back on the road as a traveling salesman. I had
half a mind to quit. Why not tell Pop to cram it? Why not get the
hell out of the hat business and become a music manager?

"'Cause you don't know what you're doing, that's why," said
Cliff, as we sat around the living room getting bombed on a
bottle of French bubbly.

"Selling is selling," I said. "If I believe in a product, I can
sell it."

"Music is a filthy-dirty dishonest business run by a bunch of two-bit gangsters."

"The hat business ain't exactly run by saints."

"Besides," Cliff added, looking over his three-fingered hand, "I'm no longer playing with a full deck."

"You're good as new. It'll make you more inventive."

"I'll invent a scenario for you. Let's say you find me work at a club, downtown, uptown, crosstown, you name it. How much are they going to pay me? A hundred a week? A hundred and fifty would be a miracle. You take ten percent, or fifteen, or twenty-five. All that means is that we starve together."

"You don't understand, Cliff, I intend to get you a record contract."

"*You* don't understand, Dan. There's not going to be any recording in 1948."

"What are you talking about?"

"Just listen."

With that, Cliff got up and put on a freshly shellacked 78 RPM single that his friend Fletch had brought by yesterday: Dinah Washington singing "Record Ban Blues" with Cootie Williams noodling his nasty trumpet behind her.

"What's the point?" I asked while the record was still playing.

"Ever hear of a guy named Petrillo?"

"No."

"He's the boss of the musicians' union. What he says goes, and right now he's saying there's not going to be any recording for any major label for a long, long time. That's what Dinah's singing about."

"Strikes don't last forever."

"The last one back in '42 paralyzed the industry for a whole year."

"There's always a way."

"Look, Dan, you're a nice guy, and I wouldn't steer you wrong. But if you know what's good for you, stay out of the music business. Stick to hats . . ."

"This guy's trying to stick it to me," said Monica a few minutes later.

"Where you calling from?" I asked her.

"Work."

"Where's work?"

"Newark. Minsky's."

"I thought you were through stripping."

"Since you threw me off, I needed the money."

"I didn't throw you off, baby. I've just been laid up here, sick."

"I think it's sickening to force a girl to take off her clothes for strange men—that's what I've had to do—and this guy here says he's got a gun and if I won't go to his place he'll use it."

"It's just a threat."

"I'm scared."

"Call a cop."

"I'm calling *you*."

"What do you want from me, Monica?"

"I don't want you to be lonely on New Year's Eve."

"I ain't alone. Cliff's here."

"Cliff the piano player?"

"The same."

"Well, I can bring him a date too, if he wants one."

"Cliff," I asked, "you want a date?"

Cliff smiled. "*Si, señor.*"

* * *

Our little party started at two and ended at dawn. For the first time since the shooting, Cliff played the piano while Monica and her pal, a cocoa-colored dame named Smeralda, did a dance that'd make Salome blush.

Watching Cliff, I could see him doing with eight fingers what most folks couldn't do with forty. By instinct, he found graceful little tricks of flying around his handicap. He played fewer notes, his style was slimmer, but he sure as hell had the old bounce back, goosing the girls with the right rhythms, getting 'em bumping and grinding at all the right spots.

We loved the show and I presumed Cliff loved Smeralda 'cause when the phone rang at two the following afternoon he and his honey were still shut up tight in my guest bedroom. It was my sister on the wire.

"I still think he's arrogant," said Peg, talking about my roommate. "Winthrop could have helped him."

"Mom said you and Winnie are old news."

"I just said that to get her off my back. I think you should talk to Clifford, Danny. Make him see that an article in Metronome could be invaluable. Winthrop's angry, but I know I could persuade him to reschedule an interview."

"Look, Peg, I don't understand why you're so interested in this guy."

"Which guy?"

"Both guys."

"Winthrop's a brilliant critic and Clifford's a brilliant pianist. They need one another."

"You sound like you're setting up a love affair."

"Has Clifford played since his accident?"

"Last night he played his ass off."

"At a club?"

"A private party."

"Would it help if I talked to him about this interview?"

"Not now." Monica licked my ear, urging me off the phone. "Now I got my own business to tend to."

"It's business," said Aunt Bea, "or I wouldn't bother you."

"I'll come out there."

"You don't have to. I'll come to you."

"That's all right," I said. "I could use the fresh air."

It was the second Sunday of 1948, and I'd been making a big stink about not going down South. When Pop called I refused to discuss it. When he wanted to know when I was coming back to work I'd say maybe never. When Mom called I took the same position—leave me alone. Now with Uncle Nate it was different. Nate was Pop's older brother, but Pop considered him a flunkie. Him and Pop didn't get along, and Pop was always bailing him out of trouble. Like when Nate's pirate cab company got nailed by the cops or when Nate was caught running numbers. See, Uncle Nate wasn't a business-man, he was a philosopher, he looked at life like a street poet, and I counted on him when it came to matters of the heart.

"Someday you're gonna have to call your own shots, kid," he told me. "Might as well be sooner than later."

"So you're telling me to quit?"

"I couldn't tell you nothing. Except that my brother's never changing—that much I know."

"I'm a little nervous about going out on my own."

"Why? You can hustle with the best of 'em."

"But what's my hustle? What am I selling?"

"Yourself. We're always selling ourselves."

Uncle Nate's great at talking blue-sky bullshit until it's time to leave which is when he usually hits me up for a hundred bucks which he swears he'll pay back in a week. I know, though, I can kiss the dough good-by 'cause it's headed straight for the ponies.

Now Aunt Bea, she's Mom's younger sister and nothing like Nate. Nate's been married four times. All his wives were hardworking women, and all of them left him cold. They got tired of watching him gamble their money away. On the other hand, Aunt Bea's never been married and never will 'cause she says she don't believe in love.

"Most men are only good for one thing," she told me, "and if that one thing lasts for more than ten minutes, I'm a happy dame."

The one thing Nate and Bea got in common is neither of them has kids. They kinda see me as a substitute kid, which is fine since I never minded extra attention.

I admire Aunt Bea. She's self-sufficient. As foreman of the trimming department, she won't take shit from anyone. She also lives alone in Coney Island year round, which is strange.

Coney's way on the other side of Brooklyn and you usually go there during the summer. We got a place at Sea Gate, a private beach that's part of Coney, but Bea, a proud lady, refuses to use it even though it stays empty during the winter. Instead she lives on Surf Avenue at 32nd Street in a small apartment above an Italian grocery store, which is convenient for shopping, but oh man, the neighborhood looks awfully goddamn lonely in January with the wind whipping off the ocean and the sky a bitter-cold pearl gray.

I felt better, though, soon as I knocked on Bea's door and heard the victrola playing Artie Shaw.

"What's that song?" I asked my aunt after kissing her on the cheek.

"'Get Out of Town,'" she said, smiling. She was wearing a pea-green jacket and her crazy orange-colored hair pulled up in a tight bun, which made her crossed eyes look even more crossed.

"When they taking off your cast?" my aunt asked.

"Shouldn't be too long," I said, not wanting to mention Dr. Shotkin's name.

"Good. You hungry, hon?"

"Starved."

"You know me, I'm not much of a cook, so I figured we'd go to Nathan's."

"Great."

I drove us down Mermaid Avenue in the snappy Studebaker, heading for downtown Coney where there's usually more people than flies. Today it was deserted. The Thunderbolt, the Mile-High Chaser, Shoot-the-Chutes, the Rough Riders—all the rides looked so lonely, just standing there, like dinosaurs stuck in the sand. The Parachute Jump wasn't moving. Steeplechase Park looked haunted. Usually you heard bloodcurdling screams from the girls on the roller coasters and ferris wheels, but when we walked over to Nathan's, all we hard was the sound of the surf beating against the empty beach.

"I love Coney in the winter," said Bea. "I feel like I own the whole island. You mind eating at the counter?"

"Nope. Food tastes better at the counter."

"What are you having, hon?"

"Couple of franks, an orange and fries."

It was my favorite meal, especially those wedgy fries, served up in a paper cone, golden-brown and crispy. I particularly loved the extra-crispy pieces at the bottom of the cone.

"I remember you loved this joint when you were a little boy, Danny," said Bea. "I once brought you in here and you had this little red bow tie and matching red shorts. You were quite the fashion plate."

"I'm still trying," I said, smoothing the front of my camel-colored cashmere overcoat and snapping the wide brim of the brown felt number I'd named the Continental.

"You're always trying. That's why you're a good kid, Dan. And that's why I wanted to talk to you."

"If I can help with something, you know you can count on me, Aunt Bea."

The food arrived and I downed the first frank in a flash while Bea bit into a hot potato knish. Steam floated over her face.

"Me," she said, "me, I mind my own business. I don't have to tell you that, Danny, do I?"

"No."

"My private life is my own. If I got a problem, I keep it to myself. Why aggravate others with my own aggravation? Does that make sense to you, Danny?"

"Of course."

"My dear sister, your dear mother, is different than me. Anita, bless her heart, needs to unburden herself. So who does she turn to? Naturally, she turns to me."

Oh God, I thought to myself, *here comes more tales of Dr. Shotkin*.

"Recently," Bea continued, "Anita's been bending my ear, and, Danny, I gotta tell you, she's plenty worried."

"About what?"

"Your father. You know how she's devoted to that man."

"What's wrong with Pop?"

"He's got an ulcer."

"He's always had ulcers."

"This one's bad. He's worried about business. Worried to death."

I was relieved to learn that at least she didn't know about Shotkin playing doctor with Mom.

"Business goes in cycles," I said. "Pop's the one who told me that."

"But Anita says it's different this time. And I don't have to tell you, Anita knows. She says business down South is so miserable that—"

"Look, Aunt Bea," I broke in after wolfing down the second frank, "I got this feeling that Mom's put you up to this."

"No one put me up to nothing. I'm just worried about layoffs, that's all. My girls in the trimming department, I'd rather cut my own throat than lay them off. They got rent to pay, kids to feed."

"And I'm supposed to guarantee them work?"

"You're supposed to do what's right. Do you know what I'm saying? Ever since you were a little boy, you've been a regular little doll. So why does your mother say that now all of a sudden you're starting up?"

"Then she *has* talked to you."

"Sisters have a right to talk. And you should hear what she says about you. 'God gave my Danny talent,' she says, 'like He gave honey to the bees.'"

"What talent?"

"What talent! Why there's no better salesman in the whole hat industry, and that includes the great Benny X. Pushman from Stetson, no better than my nephew Daniel Jacob Klein."

"I gotta be honest, Aunt Bea, I'm thinking of changing directions."

"That's why I'm buying you another hot dog," she said, putting her money on the counter. "I want you to think about your responsibilities. I want you to think about your mother and father and what you owe Myron Klein Hats Limited. I don't want to beat a dead horse, Danny, I don't want to repeat myself, I just want you to do what's right."

She gave me a hug and turned around to leave, just like that. Aunt Bea always had a flair for the dramatic.

"Where you going?" I asked.

"I got a date."

Outside, she got into a truck where some guy had been waiting for her. The truck was marked "Gersky's Rye, Always Fresh." Kissing Bea hard on the mouth, the driver looked like a lug. She saw me watching and waved, shouting, "You're a good kid, Danny, we're all counting on you!"

The truck drove away, and disgusted, I decided to take a stroll down the boardwalk.

I tried putting the bad thoughts out of my mind. I tried enjoying the way the boardwalk felt under my feet, the way the long beams of wood were neatly angled, the way it was built so wide.

When I was a kid, I remembered, I'd walk here and make funny faces for my relatives. I'd sing songs and do little dances. They'd count on me to make 'em happy.

But going back down South wouldn't make me happy. The trips I used to make there were lonely and long. I figured I was beyond that. I was an executive. Why should I have to go back and suffer for everyone else?

I was tired of taking Pop's crap, and I was pissed at Aunt Bea for guilt-squeezing me. Besides, why did she have her truck driver date pick her up right in front of my face? Why did she have to flaunt that stuff? Wasn't that just like Mom telling me about doing the family physician? Hell, I was tired of being used.

But meanwhile, the winter wind felt good on my face. I could smell the salt in the air, the fried oysters and oregano from a pizza stand where a couple of chubby ladies were stuffing their mouths, watching the waves crashing on the beach and giggling at some nut running along the water's edge in his BVDs.

Thoughts kept running along the edge of my mind: Why did I think so much about Mom and Pop and sister Peg? Why did I care so much? Why was I the one to worry? How about my own worries and my own life? Why should I give such a shit about Myron Klein Hats Limited?

"Because one day you'll be taking over the place," said Cliff.

We were up at a crowded Harlem jazz joint on Lenox Avenue, talking between sets. The place was dark and smokey and smelled of barbecued baby-back ribs.

"You don't know Pop," I told my pal. "No one's going to be taking over. He'll run the place from the grave."

"You have to know yourself, Danny, and from where I'm sitting, you look like a natural-born hat man."

I had to admit that my center-creased crown homburg, in smooth baby blue, was a knockout. It featured this brim, flat in the front and pencil-curled in the back, that had guys turning their heads even in this part of town where fashion's always two steps ahead.

"Look, Cliff," I said, eyeing the ebony-skinned gals poured into red satin sheaths and long white gloves, "I'm tired of talking about my family. I said I'd find you work and that's what we're doing here."

"I've been hearing about this place."

"Owned by a guy named Pepper Katz, a friend of Uncle Nate's. See, I got music connections I never even knew about."

On the bandstand a Billy Eckstine-styled singer sang a couple of baritone ballads.

"You can sing circles around this schmuck," I assured Cliff. "Plus he don't even play the piano."

The singer was joined by a gruff-toned alto player who recognized Cliff and acknowledged him from the stand.

"He wants you up there," I said. "It's a good idea 'cause that must be Katz at the bar." I nodded to a tall bald guy with a bushy moustache and schnoz shaped like a tenor sax.

"I'm not sure I'm ready..."

"If you don't sing something I will, which means they'll start shooting at us again."

Cliff laughed and ambled up to the bandstand. He shook his friend's hand and sat down to play piano while the other singer sang some bland blues. He played well, like he'd been managing with eight fingers his whole life, but I wasn't happy since I wanted him singing.

"*Sing*, Summer," I finally shouted, and when he did, right there from the piano bench, the joint stopped still. You could hear a fuckin' pin drop.

He sang "That's My Desire," which was a big cornball hit by Frankie Laine, but Cliff turned it around, turned it salty, slow and sensual, bent it into a bluesy jazzy gentle thing.

The place exploded, and afterwards chicks came flocking 'round our table, all flashy smiles and squeaky nylons, making a fuss over Cliff and a couple of them rubbing up next to me. But business is business and I was there to score work, not pussy, no matter how sweet.

"Mr. Katz!" I waved him over from the bar. "You know my Uncle Nate."

"Nate Klein?"

"I'm his nephew Danny."

"Myron's kid?" he asked in his salami-sized accent.

"Myron's kid is right. This is my pal Cliff Summer. Hell of a singer. Hell of a piano player. You saw the reaction."

"You sound like an agent," said Pepper, who looked like he needed someone to pick out his clothes 'cause his plaid sport coat and striped tie definitely weren't getting along. There was also more white in his eyes than eyeballs and his neck was too long. His shiny head was too big for his body and his moustache thick enough to cut with a lawnmower.

"Cliff's been bringing in business all over town," I said. "Been working 52nd Street, been playing the Savoy Plaza. He can play anything and the people go crazy."

"Oh yeah?" said Pepper Katz, looking at Cliff's three-fingered right hand. "Well, maybe I'll try him out on Tuesdays. That's a slow night for me. We'll see what he can do."

"That's great. What are you going to start him at?"

"Tips. He'll keep his tips."

"I'm talking salary."

Throwing back two aspirins and taking a big gulp from a glass of club soda, Pepper looked at me like I'd just escaped from the funny farm.

"Salary is something bankers get. Here you work for tips. You sing good, people tip you. That's it."

"That's crazy," I said.

"Then let him go work somewhere else. You find him another club who'll pay him. Me, I'm a nice guy, I'm willing to give him a chance."

"You sound like he's a newcomer. He's already established."

"Then show me his records. Tell me about his hit songs."

"They're on their way."

"Look, kid," said Pepper Katz, "is your uncle still making book?"

"I ain't sure."

"With him, I can do business. With you, I can already see there's trouble."

"Why should there be trouble?"

"Because," he said, walking away, "you don't know your ear from your asshole."

Humiliated, I looked over at Cliff and saw he was fighting back a knowing smile.

*　*　*

The 92nd Street Y is a well-known hang-out for eggheads. Don't ask me why, but they stick around that joint like moths stuck on a lightbulb. They got poets over there, they got philosophers, they got every breed of highbrow you can imagine.

I only went 'cause of Peg. She insisted. See, Peg was pushing me to quit Pop's place and devote my life to jazz.

"You *are* a great salesman," she said, agreeing with Aunt Bea, "but why not use your talent to sell something meaningful? Like jazz. Jazz is the music of the future. You could be an angel of jazz."

"JAZZ: ITS ESSENCE, EVOLUTION AND FUTURE" was the name of the seminar. Who knew what it meant? Who cared? Peg did.

"Bring Clifford along," she'd urged.

"He moved out last week."

"Where'd he go?"

"I don't know. Found some place up in Harlem. He's a proud guy, this Cliff. He don't want to live off no one."

"You never found him work?"

"It's tougher than you think."

"That's why this seminar will be valuable to you, Danny. You'll meet some important people—writers, scholars, record producers."

Meanwhile, what else did I have to do? I hadn't been back to Myron Klein Hats Limited 'cause I hadn't made up my mind what to do. Monica had been after me something fierce, calling every hour on the hour. I'd put her off 'cause I still had the cast and couldn't enjoy the freedom of full movement. Full movement was always the best thing about Monica.

Peg was wearing a little pink beret and a black velvet cape when I picked her up at Barnard and drove over to the Y. She was really excited, ready with a stack of books and notes.

"This seminar will open your eyes," promised Peg. "You'll see the significance of this movement. I'm certain that somewhere in the world of modern jazz there's a place for you."

The meeting was in a small auditorium. There was an audience of fifty and a panel of six, one speaker tweedier than the next. The tweediest panelist, naturally, was Winthrop Carrington. This was his element. Like him, the place smelled of pipe tobacco and leather elbow-patches. Everyone looked thoughtful and smart and a little mean. Funny, they were talking about jazz but there were no black people around. And when the eggheads started talking, you could see they were out to nail each other.

I could see there were a couple of Commies on the panel. Peg called them "Marxists," but me, I knew they were Commies 'cause they were against anyone making money. Not that I'm against Commies or anyone else. I don't give two fucks about politics. But I do believe in making a good living and I could see that these guys were living off some university or fellowship scam, the way their heads were in the clouds.

"Societal restrictions," one of them was saying, "create tensions which the true jazz artist finds repugnant. Consequently, he's stymied in traditional emotional expression and, quite untraditionally, his music manifests an altogether different dimension."

"I quite concur," said Peg's Yalie. "It isn't only America's virulent racism which denies its only native art form, but this obsessive preoccupation with art as entertainment, art as pure profit."

"Wouldn't it be more useful," asked some bearded joker in a black turtleneck, "to view the question in purely existential terms? I'd suggest that if, for a moment, we use Jean-Paul Sartre's aesthetics, strictly as metaphor, we'll understand..."

I wasn't understanding shit, but Peg was scribbling down everything while Winthrop was trying to show everyone he knew the most. In fact, soon all the panelists were swiping at each other, dropping names like bomber pilots—Shakespeare! Schopenhauer! Strindberg! Stravinsky! Stanislavsky!—pushing their pet theories about why good jazz was being pissed on by a pigheaded public.

I had to raise my hand.

"Hey," I asked the boys, "ain't Louis Armstrong making a good living?"

I shouldn't have asked, 'cause I got bombarded with a dozen different answers. Louis' best work was behind him; Louis had sold out; Louis was a reactionary, an Uncle Tom. But I knew goddamn well that Louis was still the best goddamn trumpet player who ever blew the fuckin' horn.

"This seminar's basically concerned with be-bop," Peg whispered, embarrassed by my question.

"*Sorry*," I said.

From then on, I spaced while the panel rambled on, rubbing their eyes, wrinkling their brows, spewing their smarts, stinking up the room with pipe tobacco and bullshit.

In fact, I was about to nod out when, all of a sudden, who should walk in the side door in perfect view of the speakers and audience but Miss Monica herself, fresh from Minsky's.

For the first time all night, everyone shut up and just stared. You could see those eggheads' eyes popping out of their tortoiseshells; you could hear them gulp.

"Danny!" She waved. "There you are!"

She sashayed straight for me, red hair streaming down her back, big boobs popping through low-cut blue blouse, skirt cut up to here, black garters showing and thighs swishing. Monica stopped the show.

"What were we talking about?" Winnie asked the other panelists.

No one could remember.

Dr. Shotkin's waiting room smelled of rotten eggs and ether, that awful mediciney doctor-death odor you learn to hate when you're a kid. I thought about going to someone else to take off my cast, but what the hell, Shotkin had been taking care of me my whole life. Besides, who had time to start shopping for doctors?

At the same time I still hadn't adjusted to the idea of him and Mom. If the subject came up, I thought, I'd give him a piece of my mind. The problem was, I didn't know if he knew I knew.

So I sat there in his waiting room, thumbing through the paper: Gandhi had been shot by a crazy Hindu; Milton Berle was starting up a new television show; and some guy had invented a new record made of unbreakable plastic, something called a "long play."

Last night Monica was looking for the long play. And that, I swore to myself, was going to be the last night for Monica. The dame was driving me nuts. She had this way of tracking me down. Not that I wasn't glad that she'd showed up at the Y, it was just that her mind was set on marriage, and marriage wasn't any item I wanted on my menu. Plus, the combination of me, her, Winnie and Peg—I remembered this from my birthday—wasn't exactly your ideal double-date. After the seminar at a deli around the corner from the Y Winnie had been all worked up, still holding court, claiming the other critics were narrow-minded and uninformed.

"They fail to understand," he argued, "that jazz has a linguistics all its own."

"Eat your tongue sandwich," I said, "before it gets cold."

Monica took her tongue to my ear lobe. "This kind of talk is stimulatin', ain't it?"

Ignoring Monica, Peg kept pushing Winthrop. "You should write a book. Why should the French be the only jazz theoreticians with insight and breadth?"

"I once knew a Frenchman with lousy breath," Monica remembered. "But he sure could—"

"Why don't we get out of here," I suggested, "and let Winnie and Peg plan their book."

Back at my place, careful with my cast, Monica had gently fucked my brains out for a good half-hour. Professionalism pays. And her professional training had developed probably the best pussy muscles in the business. She could squeeze a quart of orange juice down there if she had to.

I was the one, though, who had made the orange juice in the morning 'cause I don't like to hurt anyone's feeling, and, even though the sex was sensational, I had to tell her the truth.

"It could be like this every morning, Danny," she said, smiling in her see-through nightie.

"No, it couldn't."

"I don't see why not."

"I like living alone, baby."

"You'll like it better when you're living alone with me."

"You're crowding me, Monica."

"You didn't mind it last night."

"I gotta go to the doctor."

"I'll go with you."

"I told you I like being alone."

"You're being cruel."

"I'm being honest, baby."

"But I honestly love you."

Silence on my part.

"I don't hear you saying you love me," she said.

More silence before I finally said, "The doctor's waiting." . . .

"The doctor's waiting," the nurse was saying in the waiting room.

I got up and went into his office.

Shotkin was standing there, a thin smile across his slender face. His puffy hands always drove me nuts, and now I couldn't help but think about those hands on Mom. I just wanted to get this over with. Fast.

Thankfully, he was a man of few words, and while he was cutting off the cast he only asked, "How's Father?"

"Fine."

"And Mother?"

"Fine."

"You've healed quite nicely."

"Fine."

A few minutes later I was gone, happy to be rid of the cast.

Riding down the elevator, though, I started bending my arm. It was still sore and I remembered I'd forgotten to ask whether I had to keep taking those pills.

I turned around, went back up and walked through the empty waiting room straight into his office.

The only problem was that another patient, her back turned to me, was already in there, and she had her dress up, and he had his pants down, and her name was Ida Gruntstein, Mama's bosom buddy from Eastern Parkway.

The book was entitled *Sexual Behavior in the Human Male*, the author was some doctor named Kinsey, and my father was reading it. I was at my folks' apartment in Brooklyn and Mom had gone shopping. Pop was wearing a brown cableknit cardigan and chewing on a cigar.

"It just came out," he said.

"Doesn't look like your kind of book, Pop."

"Your mother's making me read it."

"How come?"

"They're discussing it at her Current Books class at the synagogue. The rabbi says it's important."

"What does it say?" I asked.

"Who knows? It's got more charts and figures than the *Racing Form*. And all I think the guy's saying is that most men get laid before getting married."

"It takes all those pages to say that?"

"Here," he said, handing me the book, "you're a genius, you read it and tell me what it says."

"Aunt Bea says your ulcer's been acting up."

"That's 'cause your mother doesn't believe in blow jobs."

I hated when he talked this way.

"Blow jobs," he went on, "is the only thing that makes a man relax. That's why if a man's wife won't do it, he'll find someone who will. Am I right, Danny, or am I right?"

"Has Mom read this Kinsey book?"

"Who knows what your mother reads and what your mother thinks? Your mother's a mystery to me, your sister's a mystery to me, and now you, the one member of my family I can count on, my only son, now you've gone off the deep end."

"I haven't gone anywhere."

"You sure as hell haven't gone to work."

"I've been thinking."

"I hear you been living with your nigger friend."

"He's a talented guy, Pop, and that ain't a nice word."

"They use it to describe themselves. I've heard them. Don't I have them working for me in shipping? These are people you can't trust."

"That's what they say about us."

"And you know something, wiseguy, they're right. Except for family, you can't trust a goddamn soul."

"And you can't even be sure about family."

"Don't ever talk that way in front of me 'cause I'll smack you across that face of yours like you were a little kid."

"I'm not a little kid, Pop. That's the whole point."

"Look, Danny, I know I ain't the easiest guy in the world to get along with. Sure, I'm temperamental, I do my share of yelling, but if I yell it's for your own good and the good of Myron Klein Hats Limited. See, the guys I grew up with, the guys from Prince Street, they all turned into bums. Bernie Rothman, a contract killer, Charlie Barnes, another hit man, Weasel Cohen, serving time, my own brother Nate, nothing but a numbers runner..."

"I love Uncle Nate."

"Love him all you want, but he never made an honest dime in his life. If it wasn't for me, he'd be sharing a cell with Weasel Cohen. And meanwhile everyone thinks I got it made, everyone thinks I'm a king because I got my beautiful apartment in Brooklyn and my company in New York. But no one thinks about the responsibilities. I don't gotta tell you about the responsibilities I carry on these shoulders, Danny—serious responsibilities, family responsibilities. And it's about time you realized what real responsibility is all about. If that means going back on the road, is that so bad? Am I sending you to Siberia?"

"Yoo hoo, anyone home?" Mom shouted from the doorway. She was loaded down with packages from New York's finest department stores. "We're back."

"Sonny boy," she said, twisting my cheek with a long love-pinch, "look who I've been shopping with."

Walking behind her, wearing a feather red hat and the same

dress from yesterday, Ida Gruntstein saw that on my lap I was holding *Sexual Behavior in the Human Male*.

She looked at me nervously, but that didn't mean much 'cause Ida was a nervous woman. She'd been that way ever since her daughter Beverly, who I once finger-fucked after a Passover seder, ran off with a merchant marine.

I didn't know whether Ida had seen me in the doctor's office; I didn't know what Ida knew about Mom or Mom knew about Ida or what Mrs. Shotkin—a third-grade schoolteacher for God's sake—knew about her pussy-crazed husband.

All I knew is that things were moving too fast for me, and I wanted out.

The Outside Inn was open. I looked in the window and was surprised to see a sign that said Clifford Summer was playing. It was ten o'clock on a Friday night and I had nothing to do except avoid Monica who'd been bugging me to take her away for the weekend. Plus, Pop had been bugging me to leave and Peg had been bugging me to stay and I really needed a couple of stiff Scotches chased down by some smooth jazz.

I'd been wondering about Cliff anyway. I hadn't heard from him since he'd moved out a couple of weeks earlier.

I walked down the steps into the club and damned if that piano sound of his didn't get my heart to racing and my face to smiling. His music fueled me, he got me going. Cliff had this spirit, sometimes happy, sometimes sad, but always real, running over the keys, even with only eight fingers, like a slick skater over ice. Fact is, he sounded better than before, maybe 'cause the song he was playing, "Lush Life," was so rich that when he started to sing you could see the women in the joint starting to melt. You knew he was getting 'em where it counts most.

It was tough to categorize Cliff's music. Maybe that's why he drove Winnie Carrington nuts. It was ballads, it was blues, it was definitely jazz, it was modern, but it wasn't hard to understand if you had half a heart and listened with your soul. Besides, in his loose linen sport coat he looked especially cool. This guy was pretty, and you had to be pretty crazy not to see he could be a star.

"Hey, Dan," he said afterward, coming over to my table, "glad to see that the cast is gone."

"You know something, Cliff," I said, "you're an asshole. You lose two fingers and wind up sounding better, just to make every other piano player around here feel like shit."

"You always do my spirit good, Danny."

"And what are you doing playing here again? I thought this guy owed you."

"He finally paid. Besides, there's nothing else happening."

"You sound down."

"Been staying with Fletch. You remember Fletch."

"Sure. The little guy with the crazy red shoes."

"He's in bad shape."

"Sick?"

"Strung out on horse."

"Heroin?"

"Half the cats on 52nd Street are fucked up. It's an epidemic, the black plague of the jazz nation."

"Why don't you move back in? I got the room. And I still know some clubs where they—"

"Thanks, Danny, but no thanks. I've had it with New York. This cesspool city can run without me. I'm only playing this gig another two weeks to save enough bread for bus fare back home."

"Where's that?"

"Alabama."

"You mean you're going down South?"

"That's the general direction."

"Want a ride?"

"You heading that way?"

"I'm trying to decide."

*S*OUTHERN DI*S*COMFORT

Mom decided for me.

After Cliff's gig on Friday night, he and I stayed up half the night talking things over. Cliff was a great listener. He could see I was squeezed. The family was getting to me, and I wanted to escape, but escaping down South, selling Pop's hats, meant even more family business. At the same time, I loved Pop's hats, and I missed them. After all, some of the ideas for the snappiest styles were mine. But I knew that Pop would be calling me on the road every night to see how sales were going, and then he'd start yelling that I wasn't selling enough, and Peg would have no respect for what I was doing, and Uncle Nate was against it, but Aunt Bea would be proud, and the ladies in the trimming room would love me even more, and Mom would be caring for my apartment and her horny doctor would be caring for her and I cared about Monica except not in the way that she wanted. I just wanted to be left alone.

"Impossible," said Cliff. "The wheels keep turning."

It was the wheels that did the trick, wire wheels to be precise.

That Sunday morning, after a night of disturbing dreams, the phone rang early and Mom said, "Go downstairs."

"Why?"

"Listen to your mother. Just get dressed and go downstairs."

There, parked smack in front of the building, was a brand-new banana-yellow 1948 Cadillac convertible with green felt upholstered seats. The green and yellow was the same color combination as the green and yellow king's crown on Myron Klein hat boxes, and I'd never seen anything more gorgeous in my life. People stopped to stare. It had these wire wheels, this toothy grille and these big fins in the back. It was the first car ever made with fins. It looked like a boat that could fly. And it could. On the windshield was a note from Mom.

"Nothing's too good for my sonny boy."

That's all I needed—no more indecision, no more soul-searching. Mom knew how to get me going. Out of gratitude, I thought about warning her about Ida and Shotkin, but I decided not to. Mom was right; I just needed to get away.

The next week I was back at Pop's plant, planning the summer line, packing samples and getting ready. I was feeling good, I was heading out and leaving all the little love affairs behind, including my own. Monica would have to wait.

"I'm coming with you," she said.

"Like hell."

"I could be useful."

"How?"

"As a model."

"Modeling men's hats?"

"Men might like that."

"I'm sure they would, but I ain't sure it would sell hats."

"You'll be lonely."

I didn't tell her that Cliff was coming 'cause I knew she'd be jealous. In fact, I didn't tell anyone except my sister—and that was a mistake.

"Why is he leaving New York?" asked Peg.

"He misses his mother."

"Are you kidding?"

"No. Not all mothers are as nuts as ours."

"He's leaving New York at the height of the bop revolution. That's a mistake, Danny. He could be making musical history."

"He'd rather be making money."

"Down South?"

"He says you can always find work down there."

"Danny, there's something I must tell you. Winnie wants to marry me."

"Don't. He's a wimp. Plus, Mom'll disinherit you. You can't afford to do it."

"I told him he's rushing me. I feel like I'm too young."

"Good. You can do a lot better."

"I'll miss you, Danny."

"I'll miss you, too, Sis. But I'll only be gone a couple of months."

"You're the white knight on the yellow horse, off to slay the dragon of slumping Southern sales."

"I wouldn't go that far."

"You're the family favorite, the family hero."

"What are you talking about? You're an Ivy League college graduate, the first in Klein history."

"I think you're making a mistake, caving in to Mom and Pop like this."

"Look, I just want to get out of town for a while. I need to get away."

"Take me with you."

"Are you kidding?"

"Maybe I am, maybe I'm not."

"Well, I'm not. So forget it."

March 1, 1948. Blue skies over Manhattan island, bright sunshine, unseasonably warm, mild ocean breeze and me in the yellow Caddie with the top down, cruising over to Harlem to pick up Cliff. The car was loaded down with straw-hat samples, a hot summer line I'd personally put together during the past two weeks.

I would have been in a better mood if Uncle Nate hadn't come over the night before to ask if I could drop him off in Miami. It was tough telling him no.

"There ain't room, Uncle Nate. See, I already got a passenger."

"Who?"

"Cliff."

"The colored piano player?"

"Yeah."

"You can't take him down there with you."

"Why not?"

"They'll kill you."

"For what?"

"Colored and white don't mix down there."

"What are you talking? The colored are our biggest customers. Didn't I used to sell in the South?"

"You sold, but not by driving around with a nigger sitting next to you."

"I hate that word."

"You'll hate it worse when they start shooting at you."

"Didn't they already shoot at us right here in New York City?"

"It's different down there. Look, Danny, at least make him ride in the back seat. That, they'll understand."

"You don't understand, Uncle Nate. He's my buddy."

"Oh, buddy," said Nate. "You're really in for it."

I still wound up loaning my uncle the money for a plane ticket to Miami.

Thinking about Nate's warning, I pulled up to the place where Cliff was staying on 148th Street and there was my Studebaker, which I'd given to Peg, with Peg sitting inside. Next to her was Cliff.

I didn't like this. They were engaged in deep conversation and didn't even notice me when I pulled up.

Peggy was wearing this tight white blouse with the buttons practically popping and Cliff was staring at her with this earnest look in his eyes and they were sitting real close together so I leaned on the horn and nearly scared 'em to death.

"What the hell you doing up here, Sis?"

Sis rolled her window down. "I came to say good-by."

"How'd you know where he lived?"

"I told her," said Cliff. "You mind?"

"Goddamn right I mind, 'cause if we want to avoid the traffic, we gotta get going."

"Then let's go. Let me just go upstairs and grab my suitcase."

While Cliff went off for his luggage, Peg waited with me in the Caddie.

"I thought you were mad at this guy," I said. "I thought you said he was arrogant."

"He's such a close friend of yours, Danny, I knew that deep down he had to be nice."

"How'd you get his number?"

"Through musicians."

"What time did you get here?"

"What is this, 'Twenty Questions'? Clifford is an extraordinarily talented jazz artist."

"You're telling *me*?"

"And I think it's a shame that he can't make a living in, of all places, New York City, the international capital of jazz."

"So you've been trying to talk him into staying here."

"Winthrop knows a clubowner looking for a piano player."

"I thought Winnie was looking for a new girlfriend. I thought you told him to take a powder."

"It no longer matters. Clifford's convinced that he needs a break from New York."

"I thought we were talking about Winnie."

"I'm interested in Clifford."

"Look, why don't you give me a break and quit palling around with my pals."

"Why does everyone in this family spend so much time bossing me around?"

"'Cause you're the little sister, that's why."

"Shouldn't you two be kissing each other good-by instead of fighting?" asked Cliff who showed up with an old beat-up black suitcase.

Gently, Peg pecked me on the cheek and got out of the car.

"Yes," she said to Clifford, "we should kiss each other good-by," and she kissed him hard on the lips, surprising him, surprising me, maybe even surprising herself. Then she was gone.

Twenty minutes later, we were crossing the George Washington Bridge on our way to Jersey and points south when Cliff, reading my mind, finally said, "Don't worry about Peg. She's just a kid in love with music, that's all."

But what I really wanted to know was—when had she arrived at his place? Was it that morning or the night before?

"She came over for breakfast this morning," Cliff answered my unasked question. "That girl has an insatiable curiosity about jazz."

I wasn't sure about the word "insatiable."

But now we were over the bridge, the big V-8 engine was humming and the city was receding. I was feeling a lot more open and free. Who wouldn't feel that way in a yellow Caddie convertible with the wind in your face and the sun blasting down and Cliff with his harmonica making up some toe-tapping traveling blues?

That night we got to Baltimore, where I made some client calls from the hotel. Cliff said he'd sleep in the car and I said that was crazy, there was an extra bed in the room, but when I looked around the lobby and saw that the only colored guys were the ones mopping the floors, I figured there might be trouble.

"The back seat of this Caddie car is more comfortable than a bed," said Cliff. "Besides, soon as we get to Virginia tomorrow, you'll drop me at a bus station and I'll be back in Alabamy in no time."

"I'll be in Alabama in a few weeks, right after the Carolinas and Georgia. Why don't you ride with me?"

"It's different down here."

"That's what Uncle Nate said."

"We won't even be able to eat together."

"We'll eat in the car."

"It's more trouble than it's worth."

"Look, Cliff, I hate the fuckin' South. Last trip I took I was miserable, I was lonely as hell. That's why I didn't want to come back. I wouldn't mind a little company."

"Believe me, brother, it's not going to work."

"I'm back at work," I told John Hampton White over the long-distance wire. He owned the biggest chain of department stores in Virginia. He was what I'd call a rich redneck, a regular prick, but a guy who always bought my bullshit, a good customer.

"Damn, it's good to heah your voice, Daniel. How long has it been, boy?"

"Couple of years."

"So your daddy decided to put you back on the road."

"That's about it, John. How's business?"

"Could be better. But your timing couldn't, I'll tell you, because next week my youngest, Sue Ellen, is getting married."

"Congratulations."

"Now I want you here in time for the wedding, boy, because it wouldn't be complete without a money-grubbing Yankee Jew like you attending as my guest and getting silly drunk with the rest of us. I'm giving a party on Saturday night the likes of which this state's never seen before."

"So you'll be hiring a band."

"Matter of fact, I was going to make those arrangements today. Why? You selling musicians along with your daddy's hats?"

"Now that you mention it, John . . ."

Cliff couldn't believe how good the money was, and I couldn't believe he found a bass player and drummer as quickly as he did. Some friends of friends who lived in Richmond.

Before heading for Virginia we made a couple of stops in Baltimore. Cliff helped me carry the samples into the stores. I wasn't comfortable with him doing that. I didn't want to treat him like a flunkie 'cause he was an artist and maybe even a genius, but he said, "If you can give me a ride, I can give you a hand," and it did make it easier 'cause the storeowners just figured I had a helper.

Far as selling goes, I hadn't lost my touch. The knack came back soon as I pulled the summer line out of the boxes, the sharp-looking straws with beautiful bands in cool shades of light blue, mint green, lemon yellow and watermelon pink.

"They look good enough to eat, don't they?" I asked the storeowners who ate up a quick ten dozen by the end of my first day out.

"You're a wiz, Dan," said Cliff. "You sell better than I play."

"I was just playing around today. Wait till we get to Richmond and you see the number I do on the honorable John Hampton White."

"Before you start selling me," said John, sitting in his office behind his main store in downtown Richmond, "I want to know about this band you're plugging."

White was about forty, former high school football player, handsome in the face, broad in the shoulders, blond hair and flabby round the middle. He liked his bourbon and his bitches, even though him and his wife Annabelle were considered the county's number-one country-club couple.

"Cliff's got the best band around," I assured him.

"Nigger music, I presume."

There was that word again.

"Great music," I said.

"Well, everyone knows that there's nothing better than nigger music. I just didn't think a Yankee Jew like yourself knew anything about music—or niggers for that matter."

Now you know why I didn't want to come back down South. Here I was, biting my lip, fighting my gut instinct to tell the guy to go fuck himself. Why did I have to take this kind of talk? 'Cause John Hampton White was a big customer —that's why.

"The colored are your biggest hat buyers," I reminded him.

"Long as you keep the colors wild. What you got for summer, boy?"

"You'll go wild," I promised him.

In fact, he did go wild; he bought big. But the wild part wasn't his buying; it was his party.

Surviving the South meant playing games. Cliff knew that better than me 'cause he'd been raised down there. Most of the time I hated playing a part. I hated pretending to like people like John Hampton White. I'd rather knee him in the nuts than look at him, which is why it felt so good to sell him so hard. And I especially liked the idea of drinking his booze, eating his food and getting him to pay my man Cliff to play.

I could hear Cliff's piano playing drifting on the afternoon breeze, floating from the backyard garden on the fragrance of magnolia warmed by an early spring sun. It was that kind of flower-smelling day. I'd never been to John's home before, and even though I knew he was rich, I wasn't ready.

This was something out of *Gone with the Wind*. I was looking for Clark Gable and Vivien Leigh. The lush plush setting, the mansion made it look like the South had won the war. A house surrounded by huge white columns—whiter than snow, whiter than doves—white brick and white marble, a house that looked like a library or a museum, with everything white—doors, doorframes, windowframes, guests—everyone was white except the black folks serving and cleaning.

Guests were pouring into the mansion, friendly and smiling, and John and Annabelle were there at the bottom of the winding staircase in the entryway, with chandeliers over their heads and portraits of dead rich white people on the wall, and Annabelle's boobs half out of her bodice, and man, they looked juicy—you could see part of her pink nipples—and John was throwing back the bourbon and beaming like a lighthouse.

"The Yankees have arrived!" he announced, embracing me so tight I could smell the booze on his breath. "Give the Jewboy a kiss, will you, Annabelle?"

Annabelle kissed the Jewboy like she meant it. We'd met only once, several years back, and I remembered that she liked me.

"Welcome, Danny," she said. "Meet the happy couple."

The happy couple looked anything but happy. In fact, the bride and groom looked like wax. They were stiff and nervous, silly smiles plastered across their faces. Sue Ellen was skinny, without a trace of her mama's luscious mounds, while her chubby hubby looked like Porky Pig.

"I see your nigger's missing a couple of fingers," said John, slapping me on the back a little too hard, "but I bet he could tickle those ivories with his dick and still sound good. Grab yourself a drink, boy, and listen to him play."

I headed out, wandering through a dining room big enough to hold a conference of all the Confederate generals, into the enormous garden where a couple hundred people strolled around sipping mint juleps and nipping on slices of barbecued beef. There was an army of white-coated black servants—or slaves, I wasn't sure which—and near the swimming pool was a big wooden dance floor. Close by, Cliff and his boys were playing Glenn Miller favorites in a light-hearted rhythm that had folks doing the fox-trot. When he started singing "Don't Sit Under the Apple Tree," he sounded damn-near white. He saw me and winked with a wicked smile. Maybe he actually liked this silly shit, or maybe he was grinning and bearing. Tough to tell with Cliff.

I scoped the scene for unattached ladies, and being there wasn't none, I kept company with a bottle of vintage French Bordeaux that John's slaves were serving up, the kind of wine that goes straight to your shlong, 'cause to tell you the truth, it'd been weeks since I'd been with Monica or any dame for that matter.

"Do you dance, Danny?" asked Annabelle White.

"I don't dance," I said, "I fly."

"I'm flying a little myself. Let's take off together."

Cliff saw what was happening so he started funking-up the music, putting on a jitterbug backbeat that had me slipping and sliding, twirling Annabelle on my arm, spinning her into my waist, watching her titties bouncing, her mouth opening, her brow sweating, her inhibitions melting, getting mighty moist, I suspected, by the way she was squeezing my hand, getting me horny and real worried, 'cause where in hell was big John?

Meanwhile, the party got wilder. Day had turned to night and the Southern nuts were out in force. Cliff knew just what to do. His music got louder and the rebel yells got shriller and this crazy bitch Annabelle wouldn't let me go.

"Damn, you can dance!" she declared. "'Specially the way you do your hips."

Her lips were practically next to mine while I was still on the lookout for her hubby.

"Don't worry," she said, seeing my concern. "He's passed out by now."

"How do you know?"

She took another belt from her candy-looking liquor drink.

"Some men drink till they must make love. Some drink till they fight. My husband, bless his li'l ole heart, drinks till he passes out. Which kind of drinker are you, Mr. Danny Klein?"

"I fit firmly in the first category."

"I like firm fits," she said, drunk as a skunk, leading me out on the floor for a snakey slow dance.

"My oh my," she whispered in my ear after pressing herself against my hard-on. "You are a friendly one, aren't you?"

I saw what was coming and I wanted to fuck Annabelle not only for the fleshy pleasure, but also to spite her asshole husband. But I still worried about his rebel temper. I knew he collected shotguns. And even though it'd been over an hour since I'd seen John, who knew how long he'd stay passed out?

Meanwhile, the party had loosened up considerably; some couples were even off in the bushes. Mrs. White's bush was much on my mind.

"I love dolls," she said.

"Me, too."

"No," she giggled, "I mean collectable dolls. I've imported them from all over the world—German dolls, French dolls, every sort of doll you can imagine. Would you like to see them?"

"How could I refuse a doll?"

"Let me go first," she said. "Wait a couple of minutes, then follow me."

She walked behind the pool, disappearing down a path. My dumb dick was so impatient I could hardly wait the two minutes. When I caught up with her, we were alone in what looked like the dark woods.

We walked a little distance until we came to this little cottage. "My doll house," she called it.

In the moonlight it did look like a toy, neat and spotless and, naturally, painted virgin white.

Inside she lit a candle and, goddamn, you've never seen so many dolls. Man, I'm telling you, it was spooky in there with their little beady eyes and their waxy hair and their silk and velvet dresses and plastic skin. Weird, too, 'cause all of them were blond and, at least to me, they all looked like Annabelle.

"What do you think, Danny?" she said, holding up one half her actual size, with big boobs shaped like hers.

"Never seen nothing like this before."

"And I've never seen a Jewish man."

"What do you mean?"

"I mean, *really* seen a Jewish man."

No doubt, this dame was loony tunes, the whole fuckin' South was a crazyland, but oh buddy, when she pushed down the bodice and her boobs came spilling out they were even bigger than I'd imagined—fuller, wider, wonderful succulent fabulous fuckin' tits—and I was there, man, I was feeding my face like a motherfucker, and she was reaching for my rod, and she was out of her dress and her slip—nice hips, pink panties—and I was out of my pants and she was looking at my shlong like it was a museum piece.

"Oh, I've heard all about you Hebrew men."

Now I didn't know what the hell she'd heard, but if she wanted to think I was Moses, that was fine with me, 'cause when I felt her crotch, she was wet as the Nile, her delta was flooded, baby, and right there on this big baby bed she lay me down and put a suck on me I'll remember till the day I fuckin' die. That night I thought I'd die fucking, that's how many times we did it, that's how much she appreciated my Hebrew heritage. "I love the way your tip is all shiny and clean," she kept saying, bringing different dolls into bed with us.

"Which doll do you like the best?" she asked.

"You," I said.

"I bet you say that to all the girls. I want to hear about your prostitutes and your strippers. I know you know wild women. How do I compare, Danny?"

"Favorably, baby, very fucking favorably."

I'd been waiting a half-hour outside John Hampton White's office. This was Monday morning after the Saturday night bash, and I was plenty worried. What if his old lady had said something. She was so nuts, who knew? All I knew was that my nuts were on the line. This redneck might have a shotgun waiting for me.

"Come in," he said, finally appearing at the doorway. He seated himself behind his desk. I carried in my samples and sat down. His eyes looked bloodshot.

He cleared his throat before saying, "Sorry I didn't get a chance to say goodnight at the party, but I'm afraid I overdid it. Annabelle assured me you had a good time."

Was he being sarcastic? I couldn't tell. I could only pray.

"Annabelle," he went on, "sure is crazy about you."

I forced a smile.

"Must be that Jew salesman charm," he added. "Now, sir, it's your turn to charm me with your wares. But before you do, I just want to say one goddamn thing to you."

He suddenly bolted out of his chair, his eyes went wide, his fist slammed on his desk.

"What the hell's wrong, John?" My heart started pounding like crazy.

"That gimp nigger of yours, that's what's wrong."

"What are you talking about?"

"If he comes within a mile of my property, I'll shoot the balls off that coon."

"I don't understand."

"You don't have to. I'm just warning you—don't mix music with hats."

I decided to leave the matter alone and sell hats instead. It was a good move. I sold John Hampton White nine thousand dollars' worth.

"You couldn't get him to go for the panamas?" said Pop when I called the news into New York that night.

"It's a huge order, Pop."

"A man like that is emotional. Did you play on his emotions?"

I wanted to tell Pop that I played on his wife, but that wasn't any of Pop's business.

"It was the best I could do."

"To tell you the truth, I was looking for him to spend ten thousand dollars with us."

"Last year he spent four."

"Think big, Danny."

"Let me talk to Mom."

"Your mother's not here."

"Where is she?"

"Playing mah jong, where else? All she does now is play mah jong."

I thought about calling my apartment to see if she was playing with Doc Shotkin, but who needed to know? What I really wanted to know was why John White was so pissed with Cliff.

"He's a faggot, that's why."

"Jesus," I mumbled as we hit the highway out of Virginia.

I hadn't seen Cliff since the party 'cause he'd been staying at a boarding house in Richmond. Now it was Tuesday morning and we were in the Caddie, heading for the Carolinas.

"What's the story?" I asked Cliff.

"After you wandered off with Lulabelle..."

"Annabelle..."

"Whoever—we played another hour and then started looking for our money. Someone said your man had passed out so
I decided to leave him alone. Went back the next day for my
bread. Dig: He's out by his pool, in a little bathing suit strut-
ting around like a bodybuilder, which he ain't. Says the old
lady's in church—probably atoning for the dicking you gave
her—and we're alone and would I mind diving down to the
bottom of the pool to fish out a ring someone dropped. Yes,
I'd mind. Go ahead and do it, he orders me, just strip off your
clothes and dive down there, and I'll tell you what, he says, if
you find the ring, you can keep it. It's a diamond. I don't want
your diamond, mister, and I don't want to do no diving, I just
want the money owed me. Well, he comes over and puts his
hand on my butt and says some shit and I just turn around
and get the hell out 'cause I know if I stay any longer I'll wind
up decking him and they'll wind up lynching my black ass."

"You didn't get your money?"

"Didn't get diddly squat."

"Well, I'm paying you 'cause I got an order out of that redneck big enough for both of us."

"And what about Lulabelle?"

"A doll," I said, not bothering to correct him. "A regular
doll."

When I gave him the details of the doll's house, he laughed
till he hurt, hollering about horny Hebrews.

"All men are horny," I corrected him as a storm broke over
the Virginia countryside, the yellow Caddie cutting through
sheets of rain.

"And women, too," contemplated Cliff. "Especially those Southern belles. They've always wanted what they couldn't have. And found a way to get it."

"I just hope I don't get the clap," I said, scratching my nuts.

"The big order makes it worth it."

"The big order," I said seriously, sounding like Pop, "is what makes the world go 'round."

My head was going 'round from the bottle of bourbon we'd finished off. Bourbon ain't my brew. I'm a Scotch man, but when in the South I figured—do like the Romans do and get sloshed on the local shit. Besides, Cliff was doing a good job of driving despite the fact that he'd downed more booze than me. We'd spent the night in a North Carolina motel where, after dark, I snuck him into my room. He slept on the floor, which made me uncomfortable since he was the artist and I was the salesman but he wouldn't have it any other way. In the morning he was up before me, writing out musical notes on the back of a phone book.

"Think of a song?" I wanted to know.

"Little ideas run through my head," he said. "If I don't jot 'em down, they run right out."

All morning and afternoon, we drove down the Carolina coast. I picked up some cold chicken that we ate in the car, the blue ocean and curves in the highway playing with my eyes like a pretty picture. After sundown, I bought the bourbon and we saluted the sun as it slowly sank into the sea.

The plan was to drop Cliff in Savannah, where he'd catch the bus home. But we were having such a good time I hated to see him go. I hated facing the lonely road alone.

"Ever sleep on the beach?" I asked him.

"Never."

"Used to do it when I was a kid at Sea Gate, right in front of our beach house. All we need is sleeping bags. What do you say?"

"Should be a mild night. Why not?"

I bought the sleeping bags, along with some campfire equipment, at an Army and Navy store. I was a pretty good boy scout before being kicked out for questionable behavior during a picnic with the girl scouts. I'd asked the question "will you?" and the girl scout—foxy Frieda Staenberg—answered "yes," and a half-hour later we were busted. We didn't even have our uniforms off; hell, it was only a little innocent dry-fucking.

"Fuckin's on your mind a lot, Danny," said Cliff, throwing back the last of the bourbon as I told him about my scout scandal. By now we were climbing up a long and nervously narrow bridge outside Charleston. But Cliff had no fear, gunning the Caddie like a Coney Island bumper car.

"Hey, man," I warned, a little worried about his inebriated instincts, "slow down."

"Been over this bridge before, Dan. Know just what I'm doing, man."

He picked up the speed as we reached the tip-top of this tall twisty thing which, from my point of view, started looking like a roller coaster. A mile below I could see moonlight dancing on water. In the windshield I could see red flashing lights behind us.

Red flashing lights!

There were two of them. They parked behind us. One diverted traffic while the other approached the car. Frantically I searched and found two pieces of gum. Handed one piece to Cliff and slipped the other in my mouth, hoping to hide the stink of booze.

"Hey, do you know you're driving this car like you're

drunk?" asked one cop, a tall thin guy with the disposition of a junkyard dog.

"I drive for Mr. Klein," said Cliff.

Cop looked over at me. "This nigger your driver?"

"Yes."

"Is he drunk?"

I tried to say no, but I couldn't help it, I belched instead.

"I think both you guys are drunk. I'm hauling you in."

"Wait a minute," Cliff said. "I'm sober as a saint. I can prove it."

"How you gonna do that, boy?"

"Look," said Cliff full of confidence, "if I can walk that railing up there, wouldn't you have to admit I'm sober?"

I looked at the railing. It was no wider than two feet. I figured Cliff for a dead man. "Don't do it," I whispered while the cop called his partner over for consultation.

"Be cool, Dan," Cliff said.

"Let the fuckers take us in, but don't get up on that goddamn railing."

Cliff smiled as the cop came back. "Okay, nigger," he said. "We're willing to make that wager."

"Ten steps," Cliff said, "should prove my sobriety beyond a shadow of doubt."

"Ten steps it is."

There was nothing above the railing to hold on to—no cables or grids—just twinkling stars above and black ocean below.

"Don't do it," I kept whispering, but Cliff was already out of the car.

Making matters worse, the railing wasn't level; it was on an incline, and when Cliff climbed up there, with me holding my breath, he extended both arms out straight, balancing himself before starting this suicidal stroll down the railing.

I got out of the car, squeezed my eyes closed; I could barely look, hoping it was all just a bad dream. I knew, though, that it was as real as the full moon overhead.

I peeped out of my squint to see Cliff take his first step. He was shakey. The cops were silent, fascinated, hoping and waiting for him to fall. I felt responsible; I prayed to God for his safety. "Let this crazy man live," I screamed silently.

Steps two and three came easily, but on step four it looked like he'd lost it, leaning to his left, lurching to his right—a crazy clown tottering on a tightrope—barely able to bring himself back to balance.

He got through steps five, six and seven with renewed confidence, but on step eight a speeding car coming the other way honked and the teen-aged passengers screamed—"Jump! Jump!"—when my heart jumped out of my chest and Cliff started swaying and I just knew his ass was grass when somehow he caught himself in a crouch position, like a catcher behind home plate, and cautiously, miraculously getting back up, taking those last three steps and then, with a final flourish, jumping off the railing, bowing before me and the astounded disappointed cops.

"Wiseass coon," one of them mumbled.

"Thank you, gentlemen," Cliff replied before asking me, "Are you ready, Mr. Klein?"

Speechless, I got into the car, and we were off into the night.

The night was gorgeous. On the beach you could see all the stars in the sky, each lit by a billion-watt bulb burning behind it. The breeze off the Atlantic was wet, cool and comfortable. The moon was so bright we could see sand dunes far on the horizon rising out of the water like little islands. Happy little sandpipers skidded along the shore. The waves washed up with a big booming beat that relaxed my mind and reminded me of Coney when Sis and I would sleep on the beach and trade secrets about our current crushes.

Cliff and I made a fire. We cooked some burgers, drank some beers, and now, stretched out on a couple of blankets, I felt far away and close to myself, all at the same time.

"I feel like we're eating the stars for dessert," Cliff said. "I can feel them falling in my mouth."

"I still can't believe you, you crazy schmuck. It's a miracle you're alive."

"I told you, man. There's Indian blood in me. My father's grandfather. They say he was Sioux. That's what gives me perfect balance. Didn't you ever notice the guys working on skyscrapers, the ones up the highest scaffolds? They're all Indians."

"I don't like to look up that high."

"You're looking up now."

"And seeing shit I've never seen before. Isn't that the Big Dipper?"

"Slip her the big dipper..." he started singing in a scatty-catty Nat Cole trio kind of groove. "It'll flip her... grip her sweetly... nip her neatly... nice and slow... high and low ... easy flow... go, Dan, go."

"It kills me the way you make up stuff. That's another hit song—"

"It's a hit song here on the beach with God listening and the seagulls applauding."

"It's all a matter of selling."

"I'm sold on this beach thing, Dan. It's your best call of the trip so far."

"I'm hitting Charleston tomorrow, then Savannah, then

Florida. Why don't you come along? Miami Beach will be a blast."

"Our luck's been too good to press any further. Besides, Mama's waiting."

"We'll send her a ticket. We'll have her meet us in Miami."

"You call me a crazy schmuck, but you're the one acting like the South is some easygoing party picnic where folks of different color mingle together like one big happy family."

"The South is my territory. That's what Pop always says. Down South, he says, I can sell anything and anyone."

The dark-skinned waiters were wearing starch white uniforms. Candlelight flickered from the tables which held vases of sweet-smelling gardenias. The joint smelled like a garden. Off in the corner, at the grand piano, Cliff, dressed in a tux, played Gershwin like he wrote the shit while I worked on a snooty piece of ass sitting across from me named Mary Beth Byron.

"The piano player is just *fabulous*," she said.

"All the way from New York City."

"You have marvelous taste, Mr. Klein. And how appropriate to hear Gershwin in a setting only a few blocks from Cat Fish Row. You know about Cat Fish Row, don't you?"

"I know, but I'd like to hear about it again. I like listening to your accent."

"It's where Gershwin wrote *Porgy and Bess*, it's the setting for that gloriously original American opera."

"Glorious," I agreed, trying to figure out the size of her tits beneath her loose white blouse. She wore too much makeup, too much perfume, she was too tall and she talked too much. But I was on the road and the road gets you horny and I picked her up at the hotel where there wasn't another loose female in sight.

"Ah'm from Atlanta," she said, "and in Atlanta we studied Gershwin in the music conservatory like he was Beethoven or Bach. You see, only an educated white man like Gershwin could take the primitive music of the Nig-roes and turn it into something sedate and lovely."

"You mean he stole their music."

"Oh no no," she laughed the way people with too much education like to laugh. "He civilized their music."

"Too bad."

She laughed again. "You are so amusing. But I doubt if you have a formal musical education as I do."

"I thought you said you sold girdles."

"Ladies undergarments, please. But I also sing light opera."

"Look, I'm getting a little light-headed. Let's order."

Over a dinner of flounder, scalloped potatoes and a mess of white wine, I had to hear how smart she was, how talented, how much she'd love to go to the Metropolitan Opera in New York—"Have you ever been?" "Not on your life"—and wasn't it wonderful that I had a Nig-roe friend who came all the way from the Harlem to play—"he doesn't sound at all primitive" —in this charming Charleston restaurant. I explained that was because Sid Gross, my father's friend from B'nai B'rith, a Jewish fraternal organization, owned this restaurant and was easily convinced by Cliff's classy piano style.

Mainly, though, I was wondering whether I was convincing Mary Beth. She was hard to get hold of. The more she talked, the more I undressed her with my eyes, seeing how her long legs could wrap around me twice while I was pumping her.

"Music is my passion," she went on.

Pussy is my passion, I replied inside my head, though outside I couldn't do much more than smile as she went on about

Ravel about Debussy and Gilbert and Sullivan and Rodgers and Hammerstein.

"How'd you get into girdles?" I asked, crashing into her train of thought.

"Undergarments."

"Whatever."

"For years I was buyer at several of Atlanta's better department stores before realizing that the salesmen make substantially more money."

"Unusual for a woman to be working on the road."

"But then again, Mr. Klein, I'm a most unusual woman."

Her last comment made my dick hard. Cliff started playing "Things Are Looking Up" when she looked over at him, her body bending with the music. When I took her hand under the table, she smiled and asked, "Is there any Gershwin song he doesn't know?"

As if he'd heard her, he played "I've Got a Crush on You" and then, turning up the heat, sang a soothing soft-voiced versions of "I'll Build a Stairway to Paradise," "Someone to Watch over Me" and "Do It Again."

Mary Beth Byron was practically swooning. She threw back another couple of glasses of white wine and I figured, with a little musical help from Cliff, I'd scored.

Heading back to the hotel, we strolled along Charleston Bay. The moonlit water was still, the night silent. "That's Fort Sumter," she pointed out to sea. "That's where the Civil War began."

She had a horsey face and narrow hips, but her long legs were driving me nuts.

"Don't you think war is a primitive act, Mr. Klein?"

"I'm against it," I said. "I'm against anything that don't make you feel good."

I took her hand as we neared the hotel. In the lobby—just

to make sure I wasn't rushing her—I took her to the bar where she ordered champagne. I started joking around, saying something like I wouldn't mind seeing her line of undergarments.

"Gershwin," she said, "understood the soul of a woman."

"Me too," I assured her.

"Do you know the song 'A Foggy Day in London Town'?"

"Cliff played it tonight."

"Played it like he lived it, I might add. Played it like a prince."

"So you really think Cliff is something."

"He's fascinating. You mentioned that you've been traveling together. I wonder how's that possible around here?"

"We improvise. Tonight, for instance, he's sleeping in the back of my Cadillac."

"How primitive!"

With that, she finished off her champagne and excused herself, heading for the powder room. While she was gone, I pictured the ways we'd be doing it—from the front and back, on the bed and the floor. I knew she was as needy as me; I knew I'd found myself a wild woman.

One slight problem, though: The bitch never came back.

A half-hour later when I called her room, there was no answer—not then, not all night.

"She was one of these all-night nuts."

"You mean you screwed her in the back of this car?"

"All night," Cliff said calmly as he drove beyond the Charleston city limits.

"That's disgusting."

"She knocked on the window. Said she wanted to discuss Gershwin. Hell, I love Gershwin."

"Man, if someone had seen you, you'd be hanging from the nearest tree."

"That's probably what made it so exciting for both of us."

"You should have heard her talking about your people," I told Cliff. "She's a goddamn bigot."

"Didn't stop you from trying to fuck her."

"She talk about me?"

"She said a bunch of bad things about the Jews. But you would have been proud of me, Dan. Before I humped her, I defended your people to the hilt."

"You're a great guy."

"I try."

"I don't understand. You mean she just climbed in the car and said, 'here I am, fuck me.'"

"I already told you. She had a thing for Gershwin. She made me sing to her. She had to hear 'How Long Has This Been Going On.' She *loves* Gershwin."

"Yeah, but he was a white Jewish guy. Like me."

"Danny, I've never been with anyone like her. She gave me a half-dozen pair of pink panties to remember her by."

"Don't feel flattered. She sells them, she gets them for free."

"And those legs . . ."

"Stop reminding me."

"Where we off to now?"

"Savannah," I said, still pissed. "I'm dropping you off at the bus station."

Cliff just laughed louder and started singing "Bidin' My Time."

GERSHWIN AND JAZZ: AN INTERCULTURAL ANALYSIS
by Winthrop Carrington

Paradoxically and simultaneously, George Gershwin has influenced and been influenced by an infusion of Afro-American music, at once sophisticated, complex and simple. Harmonically, melodically and lyrically, the composer, in synthesizing the subtle sensuality of Negro folklore, struck what seems to me a highly seductive chord.

I took the magazine and threw it against the wall. Fuck Winthrop Carrington. What was wrong with my sister? What was she doing mailing me shit like Modern Music Scholar? Who wanted to read it? Who cared?

"Thought you'd want to read this article by Winthrop," she wrote in a note. "He's really making a name for himself." Yeah, his name was mud as far as I was concerned. Besides, I didn't want to hear nothing more about Gershwin and his "seductive" chords 'cause I hadn't been seducing anyone—not the dames, not even the buyers.

After I had dropped Cliff off at the Greyhound Station in Savannah that morning, I felt bad. I'd been a little grumpy with him, but what the hell; I had to make a living, and with his broads and everything, he was getting to be a distraction, he was getting in my way. Right away, I drove over to Saginaw's, the big downtown men's store which had always been one of Klein's better clients.

"This summer line of straws," I told Harry Saginaw, who looked like a bull dog, "is sensational. Wait till you see the color selection of bands, wait till you see the snappy brims. Harry, these hats are going to walk out of here."

"Glad to see you back on the road, Danny," he said, "but I'm making a switch this year."

"What kind of switch?"

"Benny Pushman was by."

"Benny X. Pushman from Stetson?"

"We're carrying his line on an exclusive basis."

"That's crazy. They don't have the styling, they don't have—"

"Sorry but I'm going with Benny."

Benny was a beanbrain. Benny was a shlep, an old war-horse hat salesman who didn't know shit from Shinola. Benny was the kind of guy who'd sold hats by buying off the buyers with pussy.

"Look, Harry—"

"Next year, look me up next year."

So here I was back at the hotel with Winthrop Carrington and George Gershwin, and it was muggy and hot with the clouds building up and thunder booming and soon it'd be pouring and I was ready to pour my heart out to anyone 'cept there wasn't anyone around which is why I hated being alone on the road. Maybe my family drove me nuts, but at least they took up time and kept me company. Maybe Monica was a nuisance, but I could always count on her to come over whenever I called. Now I called her long distance and no one answered. She was probably banging a stranger. It was too late in the day to see any other customers and what was on tap for tonight except a steak in the hotel dining room and maybe a movie but who likes to see a movie alone? While I was aggravating myself, Benny X. Pushman was probably licking his chops, fingering his order forms like they were females, figuring out how much money he made with his lameass line.

I took a swig of Scotch and tried to nap, but the boom of thunder got louder and the thought of this long road trip got me down and kept me up. Why did I ever leave New York? Why did I ever agree to go back on the road? I loved my family, but the family business was making me crazy.

I finally dozed off, dreaming of tall twisty bridges, though this time it was me, not Cliff, who was falling into the river when the phone rang and woke me up just in time.

"Danny?"

"Cliff?"

"Wanted to see how you were doing."

"Thought you were on your way to Alabama."

"Got sidetracked, man. I'm still here."

"Me too."

"I see. What are you doing tonight, Dan?"

"Just thinking of a little light suicide."

"What's wrong?"

"When a salesman doesn't sell, nothing's right."

"Had a hard afternoon, huh?"

"Lousy."

"Well, why don't you come by the club tonight?"

"What club?"

"Ran into a friend of mine. The guy was arriving in town just as I was getting ready to leave. He's got a gig and said he could use a piano player."

"You're scoring every time you turn around."

"Come on, Dan, you'll come out and have a couple of drinks. We'll have some laughs. This cat's a first-rate horn player. Anything's better than sitting up in the hotel."

"Least you were thinking about me."

"Always. Here's the address . . ."

The rainbow matched the Cadillac and the Cadillac matched my suit. Yellow. It was mainly a yellow rainbow with a row of bright blue just like my blue silk tie and a touch of red which blended with the fire-red wide brim of my straw hat. In the hotel lobby I'd gotten a spit shine on my seamless-toe brown alligators and I wish you could have seen this gabardine suit 'cause it'd been custom-tailored, with the buttons set low and the shoulders extra broad, a double-breasted beauty, yellow as the sun. "The Bold Look for 1948," Esquire was calling it, and I should have been on the cover—that's how sharp I was looking.

Following the directions Cliff had given me, I was riding right into the rainbow. The rain had stopped and the early evening smelled fresh and clean, I smelled of spicey cologne and the city of Savannah was charming as a picture postcard with all the grand old squares and Civil War mansions. It was one of those weird wonderful moments when it was day and night at the same time, the sun and the moon and this high yellow rainbow with pots of glittering gold at either end—I knew they had to be there—and I was happy to be heading out to hear music, happy Cliff had called, even happy when I drove over the tracks to the other side of town where there were shacks instead of mansions and the golden daylight-nightlight was still glowing everywhere, even on this big barn with a beat-up handwritten sign out front—"The Sugar Shack."

Inside it was dark and smokey with sawdust on the floor and rickety chairs and tables and wall-to-wall people, dancers and drinkers, men and women arm-in-arm, gliding and grinding, grinning, grunting, laughing over the loud beautiful music which sounded like Louis Jordan and the Tympany Five 'cause they were playing "Beans and Cornbread" and "Ain't Nobody Here but Us Chickens" and "Choo Choo Ch'Boogie" except it was Cliff banging the piano and his fat friend, bald as an eagle, blowing the sax and no one in the room was white except me.

I'd never been in a situation like this, but I wasn't scared, I was glad, because of the attention I was getting due to my yellow suit and red-brimmed hat and everyone was friendly and the music made me feel safe. Cliff was playing "Saturday Night Fish Fry," and folks looked at me like I belonged. They could see I was a fan. I chased down whiskey with beer, making my way to a table near the bandstand, sitting alone but seeing guys nod to me and a few of the women doing a double-take when the bald saxist announced a dance contest.

"This is gonna be a jitterbug," he said. "I'm the judge, and the winner gets a jug."

I chased down another whiskey while Cliff started stomping out this barrelhouse boogie woogie, the sax man wailing behind, Cliff singing "Let the Good Times Roll," a song which wouldn't let me sit still.

The dance floor was jammed and somehow, whiskey whirling around my brain, I wandered out there, there was no resisting the rhythm, when suddenly this tall leggy lady with a slippery polka-dot dress tight against her tushy joined me, just like that. Her eyes were smiling—she might have been drunk, or just happy—but she grabbed my hand and I twirled her around, pulled her in, pushed her out, spun her all about, letting loose, letting her lead, leaving her room to follow my moves, never missing a beat, right with the rhythm, hands waving, fingers snapping, jumping, jitterbugging, gyrating with as much flair—maybe more—than anyone in the Sugar Shack while the music got louder and Cliff, seeing me, sang even harder until nearly all the couples fell away except three or four which made me and Miss Polka Dots get even crazier. I threw her up in the air, caught her in my arms—she smelled like maple syrup and marmalade—whirled her in a circle forcing the other couples out of our way, they couldn't compete, and we were alone, our feet off the floor, dancing on the moon, weightless and wild, everyone screaming, "Go! Go!" and me beaming, blessed with the beat, crazed by the heat.

"The yellow man and the polka-dot lady are the sure'nough

Sugar Shack winners!" said the sax man. "Collect your jug."

The jug was no jive, the whiskey strong and straight-through to my brain, the whole place cheering me on. "I'm Delilah," she said. "Danny Klein," I nodded. Dazed, dazzled, I saw Cliff coming over during the break, hugging me hard, everyone patting me on the back, fuck Saginaw's, fuck Benny X. Pushman, this was my crowd, Cliff was my man, Delilah was delicious, delightful, outside, rainbow gone, cloud-covered moon, she had a place, a room in a house that was empty, her people back at the Sugar Shack, her mattress lumpy, her eyes lovely, she was twenty or twenty-five—who knew? who cared?—she let me love her, saying, "I like the way you dance . . . oh, Danny, I like the way you dance . . ."

"Why'd you leave the dance?"

"What time is it?"

"Are you alone?"

"What are you talking about?"

"I asked you a question, Dan. What happened after the dance? Is Delilah there with you?" The piano player was pissed.

I fumbled for my Benrus wristwatch. Eight A.M. "Cliff, my head feels like elephants have been trampling through it. What are you doing calling me at this hour?"

"Is she there?"

"Of course she ain't here. I wouldn't take her to the hotel. You think I'm crazy?"

"I *know* you're crazy. Man, you're just lucky to be alive."

"What are you talking about?"

"Cats were looking for you."

"What cats?"

"You shouldn't have left with Delilah. You knew she was my cousin."

"Who knew?"

"I told you."

"I didn't hear you."

"I don't believe you."

"I don't give a shit what you believe."

"I invite you to the gig and you act the fool."

"Because I got laid?"

"Because you could've caused a riot."

"What riot? Everyone loved me. I won the contest."

"You were drunk. You were out of your head."

"What is it, Cliff? I've never heard you talk like this."

"I sent her over to dance with you, just to be nice."

"She was nice. Very nice."

"I sent her over to dance, not to fuck."

"Can I help it if I'm charming?"

"Guys were looking for you, but I talked them out of it. I saved your life."

"Thanks again."

"You risked your life—and my cousin's."

"Where were all these killers? All I saw were smiles."

"You leaving town today?"

"I was planning on it."

"Good. Don't contact Delilah before you go."

"Don't do me any more favors, Cliff."

I hung up, and three hours later was back in the car, heading for Florida.

The Ritz Plaza, the Delano and the National are next to each other in bleached-white downtown Miami Beach.

They're tall hotels with crazy towers that look like Morocco or Egypt.

"It's Art Deco," Peggy said to me. "Some people call it Tropical Deco."

We were across the street at the Surf 'n Sand, which was small but pretty in pink stucco and black tiles and a big pool in the back where, reclining on our chaise lounges, we could look up at the big sun-drenched buildings lined up on Collins Avenue.

"It's cozy here," I said.

"Tell me about Clifford."

"You're not even going to thank me for sending you the ticket?"

"I thanked you once, Danny. Now tell me about Clifford."

"That bathing suit's a little brief, ain't it?" I asked, seeing how she was practically busting out of her two-piecer. The old geezers around the pool were gawking. "And you're letting your hair grow long."

"Who are you, the inspector general? You're worse than Mom."

"You don't know men. I do."

"They've forbidden me to see Winthrop."

"Good."

"How can you say that?"

"You're better off."

"Winthrop's going to be an important critic. He really thinks Clifford is a serious talent."

"Cliff's in Alabama visiting his mother."

"Do you have his address?"

"Why?"

"I want to send him a book."

"What book?"

"A jazz book."

"I got his address somewhere in my suitcase."

"By the way, Uncle Nate gave me a note for you."

I took a sip of my lemonade before looking at my uncle's scribbles on the back of a matchbook from the Second Avenue Deli.

> In a little jam, please wire me
> $500. Will explain later.
> Thanks, Uncle Nate.
> P.S. In Miami, call Betty Wachinsky,
> MI7-8722. She's always ready.

I put the note in my pocket.

"I bet he wants money for the ponies," Peg said.

"Always."

"I don't know why you go on supporting his habit."

"'Cause he supported me. He took me to the ball games when Pop was too busy to be bothered."

"Mom and Pop aren't getting along."

"That's news?"

"It's gotten worse. They took me to dinner last week and all they did was fight. They were so loud I was embarrassed. Mom has no patience with him, and Pop is so moody Mom worries about his health. She sent him to Doc Shotkin for a checkup. Doc says he needs to relax."

"Doc is a dimwit."

"Why do you say that?"

I almost told her, but didn't. I didn't want to think about Mom and Dad and Doc Shotkin and Ida Gruntstein. For the first time, I felt happy to be on the road. "Working my way down from Savannah," I said, changing subjects, "I had a great selling trip."

"You're a salesman's salesman. Always were. Always will be."

"Don't say that. This is my last trip."

"Thanks for sharing it," she said sincerely, spreading sun tan lotion over her neck and arms before sitting back in her lounge chair and starting to read.

"What's the book?" I wanted to know.

"*Notes Toward a Definition of Culture*, by T.S. Eliot. What are you reading?"

"*I, the Jury*, by Mickey Spillane."

"Architecturally, this city is fascinating," said Peggy that night as we drove along the ocean, a salt-water breeze spicing the air. We were headed towards our dinner engagement. "Look at the glass bricks, the Art Nouveau facades, the Aztec friezes, the bas-reliefs . . ."

"You sound like a college course."

"'Twentieth Century Architecture.' Got an 'A.'"

"I think you'll get a kick out of this restaurant," I said. pulling into the parking lot next to the Pink Flamingo.

A pink neon light outlined the long-necked skinny-legged bird. Above, flashing green letters read "Dining and Dancing." Inside, huge murals of giant pink flamingos bathing under white fountains in lush green gardens were everywhere. The tablecloths were pink. So were the chairs and the waitresses' uniforms. We stopped at a table near the bandstand.

"Peggy," I said, "this is Barry Gruen."

"You didn't tell me we were meeting someone," said Peg, surprised.

"You didn't ask."

"Nice to meet you, Mr. Gruen."

"Barry," said Barry, who was in his early thirties.

"Barry's a customer of mine," I said. "A very good customer."

Barry was tall and square-jawed. He'd been a Marine in the war and won medals. Everything about this guy was right, especially his four successful men's stores, which made him the hottest retailer in Miami Beach. He didn't wear glasses and maybe he didn't read too many books, but he knew fashion—tonight he was wearing a raw blue silk suit and a wide basketweave tie—and he wasn't married. I figured Peggy couldn't do any better.

My plan was simple. Put Peggy with Gruen and, a little later, slip off by myself. The note from Uncle Nate was burning a hole in my pocket. I'd called the gal a couple of times, but no answer. I wasn't about to give up, though; not one of Nate's out-of-town numbers had ever failed me.

Barry took to Peggy right away, but Peggy was being Peggy, a little prissy and stand-offish; she was annoyed that I'd fixed her up.

When Barry excused himself to go to the john, though, I set her straight. "He ain't your date, he's my customer. I'm entertaining."

"You're fixing me up and you know it."

"What's wrong with the guy?"

"You'd know that better than me."

"Nothing."

"That's what he is—a big nothing."

"He's successful."

"He smells like a French whorehouse."

"It's expensive cologne."

"I'm bored."

"You'll love the sea bass. Plus there's a band. Be good."

When Barry returned he said to Peggy, "I hear you're in college."

Peggy forced a smile. "I'm at Barnard."

"What are you studying, honey?"

He shouldn't have called her "honey" so early in the evening.

"Sex education," she said.

He smiled. I frowned. "That sounds practical," he said.

"She's kidding," I spoke up.

"I hope not," he answered. "I could use a few lessons myself."

"I'm sure you've had lots of first-hand experience," said sister, "if you'll pardon the pun."

"What pun?" asked Gruen.

"Pompano," I broke in, "they got the most gorgeous pompano here you ever tasted."

"That's what I'm having," Barry said.

"I'm having the time of my life, aren't I, big brother?" said Peggy, who decided to get bombed on some tropical rum-and-bourbon brew.

Dinner conversation didn't exactly flow; it was constipated. Barry Gruen wanted to know if Peggy had been to Hialeah or the dog races. Peggy said dog races were cruel. Barry said only if you lose. Peggy wanted to know if Barry liked music. Barry loved music, especially the band here tonight. Peggy wondered what kind of music they played. Sweet swing, he said, like Guy Lombardo and Freddy Martin. Sweet shit, said Peggy. Barry wanted to know what was wrong with Guy Lombardo. His parents fell in love dancing to Guy Lombardo. Peggy called it milktoast music. Barry called Peggy a snob. I kicked Peggy under the table.

"Why don't you two make peace on the dance floor," I suggested, "while I make a phone call."

The band played "Sweet Sue, Just You" as the unhappy couple joined the foxtrotters.

I made my way through the restaurant, clinging to Uncle Nate's note, when I heard someone call my name. It was Benny X. Pushman, the Stetson salesman, sitting at a booth. Benny's brown wig made him look ridiculous. He was smoking a cigar and thought he was hot shit 'cause of the way his diamond cufflinks matched his diamond tie-bar. Benny was all flash and cash. Here he was, a fifty-year-old trying to act twenty years younger, and just 'cause his dame had drop-dead green eyes and creamy skin and beautiful red lips and the body of a love goddess didn't mean I was impressed.

"Danny," he said, "I been meaning to say hello but I've been keeping a couple of steps ahead of you."

"Or a couple of steps behind."

"Either way, I want you to meet Betty Wachinsky."

I tried smiling, but heard myself sighing as I crumbled up Nate's note and let it drop to the floor.

Back at my table, making matters worse, Barry told me that Peg had left.

"What?"

"She said the music was making her so sick she was taking a cab back to the hotel."

"The crazy bitch."

"That's what I said."

"Look, Barry," I said angrily, "don't talk about my sister 'cause you really don't know her."

Next morning when I got out to the pool Peggy was already eating up T. S. Eliot, his book two inches from her nose.

"You owe Barry Gruen an apology," I demanded. "He's a decent guy."

"He's a customer. And you were doing nothing but double-dealing—setting him up, setting me up. I think you owe *me* an apology."

"I defended you."

"Against what?"

"He didn't understand you."

"Neither do you, neither does anyone in this family. You think I'm going to settle down and marry some regular guy and lead some regular life. Well, I'm not, Danny . . . not on your life."

She slammed the book closed and stormed back into the hotel.

I let the rest of the day pass by before calling her room.

"You feel like listening to some good music, Sis?"

"Well . . . I suppose I wouldn't mind."

"Good. Be ready in an hour."

That night, still barely speaking to each other, we went out alone. In a simple white linen dress with a big black enamel brooch, Peg looked like Mom as a young woman. She looked beautiful. She was happy when I told her that I'd found a hip little jazz joint in Coral Gables. Sitting close to the bandstand, we didn't have to talk; we just sipped our white wine and listened as the brilliant, blistering be-bop brought brother and sister back together before Peggy headed back to Barnard.

Ten dozen to one, I outsold Benny X. Pushman in St. Pete, Tampa and Tallahassee. Maybe I wanted revenge for Betty Wachinsky, or maybe I was just hitting my stride. Either way, my sales pitch caught fire; I was hawking hats like hotcakes.

The coconut palm with a printed puggaree, the pinch-crowned panama, the high-styled porkpie—they were all moving like mad.

I raced into Montgomery on a roll. April showers followed me whenever I went but I didn't care. I didn't mind chasing rainbows. I just wanted to sell hats and get the hell back home. I tried to get Monica to meet me for a weekend.

"Weekends are when I make my money at Minsky's," she said over the long-distance wire.

"I'll double your salary."

"For the weekend or the rest of my life?"

"What are you talking about?"

"Marriage."

"Don't be vulgar, Monica."

"I'll convert."

"To what?"

"To whatever you are."

"I'm just talking about the weekend."

"I'm afraid of flying."

"It's fun."

"For you it's fun. Then when I'm gone, you forget me."

"Have I ever forgotten you, baby?"

"Plenty."

"Forget the whole thing." I hung up, pissed. That's what I got messing with strippers.

By the time I reached Birmingham, horniness had ruined my happiness. I checked into the Greybar Hotel, showered, changed and went out and sold a shitload of straws to Swartz's Dry Goods. When I got through I wanted to celebrate by bouncing on some broad's bones. But go try and find a dame in Birmingham on a Thursday night. I was lucky to find a Rita Hayworth movie. Rita's rear drove me crazy. She was wearing this green fish-tail dress, tight as a second skin, with her tits out to here and that mouth of hers and the way her wavy hair fell over her naked shoulders, me with a hard-on in the dark theater with nowhere to put it and nowhere to go except some lonely bar with a bunch of redneck businessmen talking about the price of pigskins or Birmingham steel. Not a lady in sight.

"What about music around here?" I asked the bartender. "Any jazz?"

"Nigger town's your best bet."

"Which way?"

"Over the bridge and follow your ears. You'll hear something."

Soon as I got over the bridge, I heard piano playing coming out of this dump, a shed more than a bar, with the roof half caved-in and the windows boarded up and a little scrawled sign that read "Woody's."

I parked in front and was hearing this hot boogie woogie— the old-fashioned kind where both hands are going crazy in different directions—and I had a hunch, just a hunch, that I knew the piano player 'cause whoever was playing was fabulous. When I walked inside, though, and squinted through the darkness, I didn't see Cliff but instead an old man bent over the keyboards, his fingers running wild. It was like his head was eighty years old and his hands were twenty. The other six or seven people in there nodded when I sat down and ordered a beer and listened to the concert, thinking to myself that lots of headliners at Carnegie Hall couldn't play as good as the main man at Woody's.

When he was through with "Honky Tonk Train" I told him how much I liked his playing and that I'd once heard Meade Lux Lewis, the boogie woogie pianist who wrote the song, in person. He was pleased I knew something about music.

"You know a piano player around here named Cliff?" I asked.

"The Summer boy?" he asked, showing that half his teeth were missing.

"Yeah."

"I raised him."

"No kidding."

"Grew up right here," he said, slapping his lap.

"He told me he lived around here."

"Raised back in the country. Florenceville. Right next to Yuma. Yuma's my home, it's the county seat."

"Seen him recently?"

"Heard he was back visiting. Someone said they saw him."

"But you haven't?"

"I ain't worried. He'll be by to see his pappy."

"You're his father?"

"Might as well be. Calls me 'Pappy.' He learned every last note from watching me like a hawk. How you know him?"

"From New York."

"Yeah, I figured you for one of those nervous New Yorkers."

"I'm nervous?"

"Ever seen a fish out of water, way it flops around?"

"I'd like to see Cliff."

"You got a car?"

"Sure."

"Well, if you want, you can drive me up there Saturday morning. You drop me off in Florenceville and I'll take you to where Cliff and his mama stay."

"You got a deal . . ." I said, realizing I didn't know the man's name.

"Woody."

"Danny." I smiled, looking into his old eyes and shaking his strong hand.

* * *

"Used to have this little country store in Yuma," Woody was saying as we drove down the Alabama backroads on a breezy Saturday morning. There'd been rumblings of rain earlier, but the clouds had blown away and the day was cool and clear. Little birds twittered in the trees and the further we drove, the further away I felt from the real world. Woody was heavy. He had a big round head, high forehead, Santa Claus stomach, deep bags under his eyes and a rubber ball nose. He talked like he played, slurring his words so that he wasn't finished with one when he was already saying another. He had a wide mouth and a big Adam's apple that bobbed up and down, keeping rhythm for his stories.

"Now in this store," he said, "I had me an old upright, this was years back, and I'd sit and play the hours away, played whatever came to mind and sometimes I'd get to Birmingham and I'd hear a record, but there wasn't anything on any record that I couldn't play and I played shit that's never been on any record, and I don't even know the difference 'tween playing and writing 'cause I'm just playing everything I hear when one day I look down and there's this little kid staring up at me, no bigger than a puppy dog, just sitting and staring and I say, 'Hey, what you looking at?' and he reaches up and starts touching the keys so I tell him, I say, 'Boy, you let me be,' but he stays all the time I'm playing. Week later I'm sweeping up when I see he's climbed up on the stool and there he is tin-kerin' with something that sounds halfway right, so I come over and show him how to do—this finger goes here, that one goes there—and he been copying from me ever since but I don't pay no mind 'cause it's all free, music shouldn't have no money attached to it no way."

"How about your bar, Woody? Don't you make money from your bar?"

"That's what I'm trying to tell you, Mr. New York. There

ain't no money attached to that. Barely enough to open the doors."

"Why'd you move out of the country?"

"Modern this, modern that, everyone talkin' 'bout being modern, just like Cliff, he showed me this modern way of playing that sounds like Chinese music, don't sound like shit, and I wanted to be up-to-date, I suppose, when I left Yuma in the thirties and besides, I met this woman in Birmingham, she's dead now, but she had my nose open for a long spell. Cliff knew her. Fact is, Cliff lived with us for a while in Birmingham but he was too wild, the boy was crazy enough to be playing in bands with white boys and thinking nothing of it until they got to those fancy country club dances where the colored were only good for slicing beef, not beating the piano, but, Cliff, he's hardheaded and stubborn proud. I raised him to a point but then he got away from me."

We drove on, passing little shacky country towns where barefoot black kids chased each other down dirt roads.

"We'll be in Florenceville in no time," said Woody, yawning. He'd been talking for the past hour, telling tales of Cliff's early adventures with the opposite sex. "Soon as he realized what the dick's for," the old man maintained, "he turned into a pussy hound," reminding me why Cliff and I had so much in common.

"How big is Florenceville?" I asked Woody as we drove over a rickety bridge.

"'Bout the right size. Don't expect much."

I didn't. I pictured another podunk country village with Cliff and his mom living in a cabin.

"What's Cliff's mom like?"

"Different. What about you, Mr. New York? How you make your living?"

"Selling hats."

"Straws?"

"Reach in the back and open that top box," I said. "Looks like you're a seven and three-quarters. The porkpie mesh should fit you fine."

Woody put on the hat and beamed. "Damn," he said, "makes me feel rich."

"You're rich in talent, Woody. That's the kind of rich that don't go away."

"You're a funny one, Mr. New York," he said, looking me over, the brim pulled low over his bushy eyebrows. "You sell hats, but you'd really rather be selling piano players."

Fifteen minutes later, he announced that we'd arrived.

Florenceville was a little bigger than I'd imagined. A railroad track overrun with weeds ran through the center of town. There was a main street with six or seven small stores where a few people, who looked like farmers and farmers' wives, were shopping. Stray cats and dogs sniffed around trash cans. I didn't see hardly any cars, just old beat-up flatbed trucks. Behind the row of retailers was a hill where a group of tidy houses framed by white picket fences looked like something out of a storybook. On the other side of the tracks were shacks.

"Which way?" I asked Woody.

He laughed. "You tell me, Mr. New York."

I headed for the shacks. "Which one?" I wanted to know.

"Not here," he said. "They live a ways back in the country."

Oh God, I said to myself, envisioning Cliff and his mom living in a tent. Still, I couldn't wait till I saw Cliff's face when, out of nowhere, I walked in on him with his musical daddy.

My yellow Caddie was nearly too wide for the narrow road which cut its way through the woods as we drove for a couple of miles back into the bush. I needed a jeep. And a jeep, an old army jeep, is just what I saw parked in front of this long cabin made of logs, the kind of place where Abraham Lincoln was supposed to have been born.

We got out and knocked on the door. Cliff opened it up. He looked relaxed in a white terrycloth robe. He looked at me, looked at Woody in his new Myron Klein summer straw, and started to howl. He couldn't stop laughing.

"Mama!" he cried, "you won't believe this. The Martians have landed!"

We walked inside and instead of seeing some dusty primitive cave I was looking at white lace curtains, pretty old-time antiquey furniture and bookshelves crammed with books. The place smelled fresh, like pinewood and flowers.

Cliff hugged Woody. "Pappy," he asked, "how'd you get Klein to give you a free hat?"

"He likes piano players. But lookee here, baby brother, what the hell happened to your right hand?"

"Danny didn't tell you?"

"This is the first time I'm seeing you've got a couple of things missing."

"New York City nightclub. That hat salesman over there saved my life. Got between me and a gangster's gun."

"What's it done to your playing?" Woody wanted to know.

"Made him better," I said.

"I'd have to agree with that." I looked up and saw that the voice came from a woman who'd just stepped out of the kitchen into the main room—I'd call it a reading room with tables and chairs and lamps—where we were standing.

I knew the woman was Cliff's mom because her eyes were just like his. They were peering at me behind round gold-framed glasses that made her look like a teacher. Her dark skin, her tall thin frame, her high cheekbones and perfectly oval-shaped head gave her this queenly air. Her hair was cropped close to her scalp and streaked with gray. Underneath her white apron she was wearing a simple print dress with beautiful blue daisies.

"I'm Marvis Summer. I've been wanting to meet you, Danny," she said before we were even introduced.

Her voice was low pitched, like Cliff's. I felt like we'd known each other for years. "What can I give you to eat?" she wanted to know.

"Whatever you got, baby," said Woody. "I been braggin' on your cookin', Marv, so here's your chance to prove me right."

"Danny Klein!" Cliff smiled as he slapped me on the back. "Brooklyn comes to Alabama."

"Have you heard of Isadora Duncan?"

"Can't say that I have," I admitted to Cliff's mom.

"She called herself the spiritual daughter of Walt Whitman."

"Whitman?"

"The poet."

"Does he come from a chocolate family?"

"No, he was a white man," Cliff kibbitzed.

"I mean, did his people sell chocolate, like Whitman's Samplers assorted chocolates?"

"Mama's always reading about Isadora Duncan."

"Mama," said Mama, "is about to serve up hot homemade bread."

"Mama," said Cliff, "is the Charlie Parker of the pots and pans."

"I see myself more as the Tchaikovsky of the kitchen."

"Mama plays serious piano," Cliff informed. "You'll hear."

It was early evening, and we'd just gotten back from taking Woody over to Yuma. Cliff and I drove over in the jeep.

"Mama bought it from the Army," Cliff told me. "There's a base outside Birmingham where she learned that the supply officer was selling used jeeps dirt cheap to Atlanta car wholesalers. She talked the guy into selling one to her."

Back in the cabin, while Mama was in the kitchen, I looked over the book collection. There were typewritten labels neatly thumbtacked over the shelves—"History," "Psychology," "Philosophy," "Religion," "Art," "Anthropology," "Music," "Dance."

"She a college teacher or something?" I asked Cliff.

"High school. It's a county school for all the colored kids within a fifty miles radius. She's the principal and also the principle teacher. She teaches three grades and five courses. Then she comes home, cleans, cooks, gardens and sometimes reads till three in the morning."

"All her furniture is real pretty."

"Mama's always made money. She saves from teaching, and she's also got something of a whiskey trade going."

"You're kidding."

"You might not think it, Dan, but she's a practical woman. After all, she was a musician's old lady."

"Where's your father?"

"A wandering minstrel, he wandered off a couple of months after I was born."

"And you've never seen him since?"

"Couple of times he sent for me in Dallas where he played bass with a swing band. That was twenty years ago. But between Woody and Marvis, I hardly lacked for musical education. She'd be teaching me 'Moonlight Sonata' in the morning white Pappy'd be showing me 'Jelly Roll's Blues' at night."

"That's why you're such a mess."

"I want you to know, Danny, I almost messed your face up

over my cousin back in Savannah. I was ready to fracture you."

"Sorry about that, Cliff, but that was your problem, man, not mine."

"What problem?" asked Marvis who came in holding the sweetest-smelling cornbread I'd ever seen or sniffed.

"I wouldn't lie," said Cliff. "It ain't rye."

"I know that. What do you take me for, a hick?"

"Ever had cornbread, Danny?" asked Marvis.

"Traveling through the South, Mrs. Summer, I've had a chance to eat a lot of the local food."

But nothing like this lady's cornbread. Now the lunch she'd served me and Woody had been grand—plump chicken, fresh green beans, delicious black-eyed peas. This cornbread, though, was in a class by itself, moist and flavorful with home-churned butter melting all over the top. Biting into it, my mouth got happy fast. I wolfed down a half-dozen pieces and could have had a half-dozen more except I was a guest and didn't want to act like a pig.

Later that night I got to attend another free concert, first row center, sitting in a chair in a little back room in the cabin where they kept the upright piano, a little out of tune but sounding great the way the notes bounced off the wooden logs. Mama Marvis and Cliff shared the bench, and she'd play a little Chopin, and so would he, and she'd tell me, "Listen to Mozart, Danny, it's 'Twinkle Twinkle Little Star,'" and she played so tenderly I thought my heart would break. The way she gracefully swayed to the music, I could tell she loved to dance. The way she hummed along, I could tell she could sing. I couldn't tell, though, how old she was—maybe fifty, maybe sixty—but the way she and Cliff played, the way their four hands blended, I could feel the love between them, mother and son, and the understanding, and the way he kissed her cheek when they were through.

It was after midnight and I was drinking cold milk and eating hot apple pie. Cliff had gone off to bed and I was talking to Marvis at a tiny table in her kitchen. The dishes, pots and pans were cleaned and scrubbed to a shine.

"My sister goes to Barnard, so she's always reading," I told her. "Lots of books make me feel ignorant. They remind me how much I haven't read."

"It's not knowledge that serves the heart, Danny, it's wisdom."

"Of all the characters you've read about, who's the wisest?" I asked her.

She took a sip of hot tea and raised her bright brown eyes upward, as if the answer was plastered on the ceiling. You could tell she loved thinking.

"Probably Aristotle," she said, bringing her eyes back down to me.

"What'd he do?"

"He taught Alexander the Great. He warned him. He said, 'I know you want to go out there and conquer the world, but don't forget who you are, don't forget your limitations, don't forget where you come from.' I like people who talk like that. Tell me, Danny, where do your people come from?"

Marvis was so easy to talk to, I told her about Mom and Dad, and how their parents escaped from Russia and Poland, about Myron Klein Hats limited and my crazy aunts and uncles and how much I loved hats and clothes and jazz.

"I can feel how much you love your family," she said, pouring me a little more milk, "and how much you love music."

"You must love living out here in the woods."

"I love the trees and flowers and the way the grass smells after a good rain. I like being close to the elements."

"You get lonely?"

"Lonely for my son, yes. But I have my students and my friends, my books, my interests."

"The Isadora dame, huh?"

"She inspires me. She was different, but she knew she was right. She believed in her dreams."

Two hours later I thought I was dreaming. Until then my dream had been peaceful. Snuggled under a big woolen blanket, I was asleep on a small bed in the piano room, feeling safe as a little boy spending the night at Grandma's. In my dream, swans were swimming over shimmering lakes with white balloons floating across an ocean-blue sky when suddenly I heard these voices—gruff men's voices—loud and angry, getting closer to me, getting me scared. I opened my eyes, expecting the voices to stop. When the dream gets scary, I can wake myself up. But this time, even though I was up, I was even more scared. The voices were real. The voices were close. The voices were saying shit like, "Niggers! Smart-ass niggers! Fuckin' uppity niggers!"

I pulled back the coarse cotton curtain above my bed, and when I looked outside, my heart stopped:

It was a nightmare worse than any I'd ever dreamed—the men in the robes, the long white robes and the hoods, the wizards of evil—must have been a dozen of those assholes—hooting and hollering, hammering this big wooden cross into the lawn, pouring kerosene over all of it before lighting a match and *boom*, watching the thing burst into a firestone of flames. I heard Cliff and Marvis moving around the cabin. I slipped on a robe and, bent over, afraid a bullet or rock would come flying through a window, I walked from the bedroom to the living room where Marvis was about to open the door.

"Don't," I shouted.

"Let her be," said Cliff. "She knows what she's doing."

As the door opened, the light from the leaping flames poured into the room. Wearing a long black coat, Marvis stood in the doorway, a dark silhouette against a shock of or-ange-red fire. Her voice carried like a preacher's. She wasn't shaking with fear; she wasn't acting; she was real.

"I have no guns in here. I have no weapons. Yet not one of you cowards, hiding behind your clownish hoods, can do me harm. Hasn't anyone told you that love's stronger than fear? If you think screaming and fire will intimidate me, you're wrong. I speak against you in my school, I write letters against you in the newspapers, and, I swear to you all, I will denounce you as long there is breath in this body. Do you hear me?" By now Marvis was practically screaming. "I said, *I will denounce you as long as God gives me the power to be heard!*"

Bam. A shotgun blast went off. I froze. But the bullet must have sailed somewhere over Marvis's head. She flinched, but she never fell. She just stood there in the doorway and, hav-ing spoke her mind, turned her back on her enemies and walked inside. Tears were streaming down her face.

When she closed the door behind her, I heard one of the Klansmen shout, "Fuck you, nigger bitch."

"I need to sit and pray for a while," she said, "Clifford, please bring me my Bible."

When Cliff handed her the book I looked to see whether her hands were shaking. They weren't.

". . . Yea, though I walk through the valley of the shadow of death," she read, "I will fear no evil. For Thou art with me. Thy rod and Thy staff, they comfort me. Thou preparest a table before me in the presence of my mine enemies. Thou hast anointed my head with oil. My cup runneth over. Surely goodness and mercy shall follow me all the days of my life, and I shall dwell in the house of the Lord forever."

I don't know what it is with Jesus, but being Jewish, I'll be damned if I can buy the whole son-of-God story even if the music in the little country church *was* rocking my socks off. Wearing a neatly pressed pretty pink dress, Marvis had taken me—Cliff refused to go—and maybe she expected me to be saved or something, but there wasn't much of a chance, 'cause when the preacher asked for sinners to step forward, I slouched in my seat. I was the only white face there, though it didn't matter 'cause the folks were friendly and being with Marvis, who was obviously the community leader, gave me special status. Everyone was asking her for favors—like writing letters and helping explain details of deeds and laws about their property. She was patient and helpful and kept saying, "We have rights, we must understand that we have rights." There were more people in the choir than the congregation and the songs were joyful and peppy and filled with promise. Even though the building was dilapidated and no one had much money you wouldn't know it by the polka-dot ties and starched white shirts, the billowy blue dresses and beautiful bonnets in yellow and green.

It was Easter Sunday.

"I'm glad you came with me, Danny," Marvis said as we walked through the woodsy path on the way home. Sunshine was pouring through the trees, birds were singing springtime songs, and everywhere you looked flowers were beginning to bloom.

"Clifford is a bit of an agnostic," she told me when I asked why Cliff hadn't come along.

"What's that?"

"A doubter. Do you fit in that category?"

"When those singers are singing, I definitely believe in something."

She smiled. "And you believe in Clifford's singing?"

"All the way."

"Then it's just a matter of adopting a plan."

"I tried once."

"Clifford told me. I know it's rough to make it in music."

"Does he want to come back to New York?"

"I think so. He wants me to come along."

"Why don't you?"

"I couldn't do it, Danny. I couldn't ever leave this," she said, waving to the woods.

"But those woods are filled with nightriders."

"Nightriders are powerful only in the face of fear. I've been scaring them off my whole life."

"I'm still scared for you, Marvis."

"Together," she told me, stopping in her tracks, looking me straight in the eye and taking my hand, "you and Clifford can be strong. Very strong indeed."

I was feeling weak. I woke up in the middle of the night in a pool of my own sweat. I'd been dreaming of red crosses and blue Jewish stars, ghosts and goblins and savage tigers. At first I didn't even know where I was. I was feverish and scared. I was sick. I hate being sick, but at least at home Mom's over there in Brooklyn and she comes running, but here I was in no man's land, in the middle of the woods, and I was burning up, far from the people I loved most. I hadn't eaten one of Mom's meals in two months. I hadn't talked to Dad in two weeks. After the last leg of my selling trip—Nashville was my final stop—I'd be going home but now I didn't think I'd make it. I was sure I was dying. I had the chills so bad that when morning came I couldn't get out of bed. Marvis looked in on me and saw what was happening. Man, I was a mess. She took a damp towel and cooled my brow and said not to worry.

"I need a doctor," I said, thinking that even though Doc Shotkin was a schmuck, I could sure use some of his medicine.

"We've got all the medicine you need."

Marvis kissed me on the forehead and went out into the hallway where I heard her telling Cliff to go in the woods to get certain roots and leaves. *Oy vey,* I thought to myself, *that's all I need.* But I couldn't complain, I couldn't hurt their feelings, I couldn't even move, and I closed my eyes and a few minutes or hours later—I didn't know which—Marvis brought me this big mug of tea which smelled sweet and fresh and powerful and I asked, "Isn't there some kind of doctor around here?" and she said, "Just drink this, baby, and you'll be fine," and you know what, she was right. By late that same evening, the fever had broken. It was another one of Marvis' miracles.

I planned to leave on Wednesday. On Tuesday a letter arrived for Cliff just minutes after Woody dropped by.

"Listen to this," Cliff told us both as we sat in the little piano room while Woody ran his long fat fingers over the keyboard. "It's from your sister, Dan."

"What does she want?"

"Wants me to come back to New York."

"That's what I've been telling you," I said.

"She sent me an article by her boyfriend." He smiled, looking over the newest Metronome magazine. "It says pop music is ruining jazz, but some pure be-bop piano players are getting record contracts."

"That you, Cliff?" Woody wanted to know. "You a be-bopper?"

"He's anything they want him to be," I answered, "long as they pay."

"Now there's a man," said Woody, nodding in my direction, "who understands music."

"You never heard this be-bop stuff, Pappy?" I asked.

"Shit, no," he answered playing an enticing drag-it-out blues.

Cliff joined him on the piano bench. "Move your sorry butt over, Pappy, and make room for youth." Cliff started playing, saying, "This is nothing new for you, it's just a little faster. Couple of new chord extensions, that's all. Now you play one of your beat-up bass lines, Pap, and my right hand will show you how the boys are bopping up in New York."

The two generations got along great. Pappy pushed along this bluesy dance groove down at one end of the piano while Cliff jazzed it up on the upper register. The rhythm had me up and shuffling 'round the room, and when Cliff started singing, even Marvis, who'd been selling corn whiskey to her next-door neighbor, completed the transaction and came in to listen.

"Sing it, son," she said.

"Sounds like a song to me," I said.

Cliff sang from the gut:

> Have you felt the beat?
> Have you heard the news?
> The newest craze is the be-bop blues

The notes are flying
The rhythm's fast
Folks are saying it'll never last

But up in Harlem
Where swing's the king
Be-bop blues is the newest thing

Be-bop blues will get you moving
Be-bop blues so nice and soothing
Be-bop blues will move your soul
Be-bop blues really rocks and rolls
I say, be-bop blues really rocks and rolls

Marvis took my hand and together we jitterbugged up a storm. She was light on her feet, smiling, swishing and swirling, twirling under my arm, both of us caught up in the rhythm. Cliff and Pappy pounded the piano, harder and harder, bleeding those be-bop blues dry.

"Let's record that thing," I said when they were through, me and Marvis both out of breath. "I guarantee you we'll make a million bucks."

"A sixty thousand buck gross is nothing," said Myron when I called him from Nashville. "What have you been doing down there, playing with yourself?"

"This is my biggest grossing trip—ever. I've been selling my ass off."

"I hear you been booking bands."

"Where'd you hear that?"

"Sid Gross in Charleston. He said you had some *schvartzer* playing in his restaurant."

"A friend."

"The guy from the hospital."

"What difference does it make to you?"

"Money—that's the difference. If you're selling piano players, you're not selling hats."

"I told you, my bottom line is fatter than it's ever been."

"With the retail business booming down there, your bottom line should be twice as fat."

"You're not gonna say 'thanks for working your ass off, son,' are you?"

"I'm gonna tell the truth, that's what I'm going to do. And the truth is that you're farting off. Even your mother, your biggest fan, even she's disappointed."

"Let me talk to her."

"She's at Doc Shotkin's."

"Oh God."

"What do you mean, 'Oh God.' She's getting a check-up. What's 'Oh God' about that?"

"I was just worried that she wasn't feeling good."

"Who knows how your mother's feeling? All I know is that she hasn't felt like fucking me."

"Please, Pop, don't tell me about your sex life."

"What sex life? Your mother's become a regular nun while the price of a good piece of pussy in New York is getting out of hand. There used to be a time in this city when the classiest call girl would be tickled pink to tickle your dick for—"

"Gotta run, Pop. Got an appointment."

"When you get to Nashville, Danny, show the straws right and sell them big."

"I'll be home in a week."

"Your mother misses you. You're all she talks about."

"Bye, Pop."

"And Danny, forget this music business. The hat business is

all you know and all you'll ever know. Understand? No more crazy bands."

The hillbilly band was playing "Tennessee Waltz." They were five guys dressed in cowboy outfits. If they weren't making music, they looked like they'd be running around with white sheets and hoods over their heads. You know the type. For all I knew, the whole crowd of crackers could be Klanners. They danced like robots and spastics. But they were happy. Everything, in fact, was pretty normal except for the vocalist-piano player. He was black, and he was singing like a hick. His name was Cliff Summer.

See, courtesy of Myron Klein Hats Limited, I provided the band with not only the western straws, but the singer. That was part of my pitch. It all started when I noticed a card on the bulletin board in the hotel lobby. "Lead singer needed. Must sound like Hank Williams."

I called over to the black boarding house where Cliff was staying while I was selling summer straws to the merchants of Nashville.

"Cliff, can you sing like Hank Williams?"

He answered by chirping a twangy verse of "Lovesick Blues," Hank's current hit. I'm telling you, it was incredible. Cliff sounded white as fresh-fallen snow on the Blue Ridge Mountains.

"That's great," I said. "I'm going to have a couple of drinks and do something crazy."

"Good, 'cause that little bar gig with Woody's buddy fell through. Cat died last year. Now the bar's a garage looking for a mechanic. They aren't too interested in piano players. So I'm sitting here still wondering whether to Greyhound it back

to Alabama or take Mom's advice and follow the supersalesman to New York."

"Believe, me," I said, "the supersalesman has scored again."

At first, the band leader, Horace Gillam, was reluctant.
"Folks won't accept no nigger on stage with us."

"But he sounds whiter than you," I assured him. I wasn't
sure why I was pushing so hard. Might have just been the
salesman in me responding to a challenge—or fact that I
thought the whole thing would be a hoot.

Luck was on my side. Horace was desperate, and besides,
deep down I could see that he really didn't hate anyone.
When I took out a sample western straw with a big beautiful
wide brim, I saw his eyes light up. That was the clincher. Few
men can resist a truly gorgeous hat.

"Bring him by the rehearsal," Horace finally said, "and we'll
see."

They saw plenty. Cliff was such a mesmerizing mimic that
by the time he ran through his Bob Wills and the Texas Play-
boy repertoire—"Waltzing in Old San Antone," "Mean
Woman with Green Eyes," "My Little Rock Candy Baby"—
the boys in the band were ready to join the NAACP

"Damn, that man can *sing*," said Horace. After huddling
together, the band announced that Cliff had the job. It was a
week-long gig with at the Longhorn Ballroom.

Cliff was happy. "No one in New York would believe this"
he said, "but I've always fantasized about singing hillbilly
music. It's sad and it's soulful and I like the shit, I really do."

"I knew you were as nuts as me," I said.

At first, though, the crowd wasn't as nuts about the idea as
us. They pointed and whispered and wouldn't dance. One
redneck called out, "What's the coon doing on the bandstand?"

"Singing," said Cliff, wearing his big western hat. Immediately he went into a version of "Jambalaya," sounding so authentic that I heard one guy swear that Cliff was a white man in black face. Afterwards, even the meanest-looking crackers were applauding. And by the time Cliff was singing "Honky Tonkin'," the folks were doing their hillbilly hop and no one gave two shits about the color of his skin.

"Never been tipped this good in my life," he said after the first night. "Even after you split, I might hang around here a while."

"You're nuts."

"You keep telling me that, but meanwhile I'm making a little jack."

"It's just a lark," I reminded him.

But four days later when I was ready to leave for New York, Cliff wasn't budging.

"They've booked us for another two weeks," he said. "I'm staying put, pal."

"I'm going home," I said, hornier than I've ever been in history. "See you in Harlem."

HOME SWEET HOME

I was back.

It was noon. For some flukey reason traffic was light, and coming in from Jersey I sped through the Holland Tunnel like a maniac. I'd been driving for thirty straight hours and didn't give a damn about sleep or nothing. Just wanted to get home. Wanted to see Peg, wanted to see Pop, wanted to see Mom, wanted to see Monica naked, wanted to plant my feet on New York City concrete.

I was tired, but I was terrifically excited when the tunnel ended and Manhattan began, driving out of darkness into light, blazing New York City light, Canal Street and loading docks and dress plants, warehouses and furriers, meat plants and dairy restaurants. Driving through downtown, I almost cried. It was beautiful to look at the newsstands and see the New York *Daily News* screaming with headlines about "SOCI-ETY SHOOTING AT EL MOROCCO!"—some dame flipped out and shot her old man's mistress—it was beautiful smelling the city with the fruit stands and the flower stalls and I didn't even mind the garbage 'cause it all looked so right and real and made me remember how much I missed seeing masses of people, walking, talking and screaming people, Jewish and Italian and Polish and Chinese people. I'd had my fill of grits and cream gravy and dusty country roads and Main Street U.S.A. where maybe they had one movie theater and not a piece of pastrami or rye bread in sight. So I stopped at Ershowsky's on Houston Street just to taste the tongue and corned beef before making my way through the teeming city with all the factories and candy stores and I stopped again 'cause I was dying for an egg cream, a sweet foamy one, and finally, on lower Broadway, I pulled up in front of Pop's plant —the Caddie was more brown than yellow from the long trip —jumped out, rode up the freight elevator and walked through the door into the arms of my Aunt Bea.

"My Danny!" she squealed loud enough for the whole place to hear. "My Danny is back!"

It was one of those crazy things where everyone stopped working and started clapping, just for the hell of it, especially the women in the trimming room, who ran over to pinch my cheeks and tell me how the Yankees were doing and the Dodgers who had this new rookie catcher named Roy Campanella. "He's another colored guy," said Bea who'd cut her orange hair so short her head looked like a ripe Florida grapefruit, "and he can hit." Thinking about Jackie Robinson, my favorite player, and the fire in his eyes, I couldn't wait to get out to Ebbets Field.

"Get in here!" Pop was yelling at me from his office, but his face was smiling. I could tell he missed me.

"He's so proud of you," said Aunt Bea. "He told us how much you've been selling."

In his office he gave me a hug and a kiss and told me I looked like shit. "What have you been doing" he asked, "driving all night?"

"Yeah."

"You don't know any better?"

"I wanted to give you the Nashville figures," I said, slapping the sales report on his desk. "Pushman came in just as I was leaving and, believe me, he might as well stay in his room and play with himself 'cause this summer Nashville is strictly Myron Klein territory."

Pop looked over the numbers. He couldn't help but be impressed, I tripled sales of the previous spring.

"Not bad," he finally mumbled. "This should make your mother happy."

"What about you?"

"Me, I'm happy if I'm not constipated, I'm happy if I have a decent bowel movement in the morning, I'm happy if I don't have to bail my brother out of jail."

"How *is* Nate?"

"In jail."

"You're kidding."

"Is this something to kid about? Last night they picked him up driving his pirate cab."

"You bail him out?"

"Not this time. This time I'm gonna teach him a lesson. I'm gonna let him sit and rot. And I expect you to do the same. I don't want you to lift a finger in his behalf."

I lifted my wallet out of my coat pocket, found a hundred dollar bill and gave it to the cop behind the desk. It was three o'clock that same day. I still hadn't seen Mom. Pop said she was spending all day with her friend Ida Gruntstein. But what would take all day? I couldn't help but wonder whether that was an excuse. Maybe Ida was covering for Mom and Shotkin. Or maybe today Shotkin was screwing Ida and Mom was the cover. Did Mom and Ida know about each other, I still wondered. Was it like sharing a good butcher, or was it a dark secret on both ladies' part which only I knew? Who knew what?

All I knew was that I was getting a headache from guessing —and I couldn't stand the thought of Uncle Nate being locked up in jail. So I went over to the precinct on Broome Street in Little Italy to fish him out. When I got to the cell he was on his knees, all two-hundred fifty pounds of him, in the middle of a crap game.

"I told you gents I was good for it," said Nate, looking up at me and soaked with sweat. "Here's my banker."

Lemme tell you—my uncle was very relieved to see me.

"Hey, Danny," he said, "you're looking great. Do me a favor, though, and straighten me out with these guys. I'll take care of you later."

I shelled out another eighty bucks to his cellmates—"the dice are freezing cold in here," said Nate—and we were on our way.

"Your father tell you what happened?" he asked as we drove out of Little Italy over towards the Brooklyn Bridge. I was taking Nate home to Flatbush.

"Something about your pirate cab."

"A bum rap. Nothing but city politics, with me caught in the middle. The little guys always get caught in the middle."

Looking over at Nate, it was hard to see him as a little guy. It was also hard, in spite of his losing ways, not to love him and remember how much I'd missed him. He had these big fat cheeks and this sweet smile and when he talked his eyes smiled too.

"So tell me about the South," he said. "I know you got a couple of war stories for me."

"I'm a little worn out right now. Been driving for days."

"And you took the time to fish me out of the slammer? Now ain't that something! Tell you what, Danny, I'm paying you back . . ."

"Don't worry about it, Uncle Nate."

"I feel terrible about your having to come get me."

"Weren't you the one who came to get me when the principal caught me smoking and making book in the bathroom?"

"I taught you how to make book. I remember how you made a killing—and you were only in the ninth grade."

"Pop would have killed me. But you came down and pretended you were my father."

"That was nothing, Danny. I'm the one who owes you, not just for the dough you sent from Miami and not just for the help you gave me today, but for being the best goddamn nephew any uncle could ever hope for. I'm paying you back by giving you the tip of a lifetime."

"A nag?"

"A store."

"What do I want with a store?" I asked as we started up that beautiful bridge constructed with crazy crisscrossed cables. What a thrill to see the East River, the skyscrapers behind us and Brooklyn ahead.

"A store is the only way out for you," said Nate.

"What are you talking about?"

"Somehow, kid, I gotta protect you from my brother. He's getting worse."

"That's what he says about you," I said.

"The store makes sense. And it's a steal."

"What are you talking about, Uncle Nate?"

"Your future," he said, raising his hands towards the

heavens as the sky darkened and the twinkling lights of the city, one by one, came to life.

"He's getting worse," said Mama after hugging and kissing me like I'd been missing for decades not months. She was letting her black silver-streaked hair grow long. She still smelled like Bonwit's perfume counter and was wearing a red silk housecoat with peacocks running all over it.

I'd just dropped off Uncle Nate and was back at my parents' apartment on Ocean Parkway, the place where I grew up.

"Who's getting worse?"

"Your father."

"That's what Uncle Nate says."

"Don't listen to Nate. Nate's a bum. Nate should listen to his brother Myron."

"You just said Myron's gotten worse."

"Myron's going crazy, Danny. Last week he fired Harry Talbot."

"The West Coast salesman?"

"Harry was in New York. Like you, he'd just come off a good selling trip, but Myron swore he was stealing. I said, 'Myron, this man is a jewel, this man is a crackerjack salesman, why must you shoot yourself in the foot?'"

"'Like the dame who shot her husband's mistress at El Morocco?' he asks. 'What in hell does that have to do with anything?' I ask. 'Because you're driving me to it, Anita, you're driving me into the arms of other women.'"

"Mom, that's strictly between you and Pop."

"Don't think you're not in the middle of this mess, Danny, because you are. With you gone and me and Doctor Shotkin in your apartment—"

"Don't tell me."

"You and me, Danny, we've always been very close. I tell you everything."

"I don't need to know everything."

"I may wind up marrying the man."

"You're already married."

"Louis Shotkin is practically begging me to divorce your father. He says he'll leave his wife in a minute. My heart is torn in two, but I'm seriously thinking of doing it, Danny, I really am."

"I'm thinking of marrying him," said Peggy.

"Don't."

"Why?"

"Mom and Pop will never forgive you."

"Mom and Pop can go to hell."

"That's no way to talk, and on top of that, he's a creep."

"You say that, but you don't know Winthrop."

We were sitting at the Automat eating macaroni and cheese, our favorite since childhood. Peggy's hair was up in a bun, sort of like Mama's old hairstyle from when we were kids. On Peggy, the style looked sophisticated, especially 'cause she was wearing these pleated high-draped linen trousers which showed off her tushy a little too much for her own good.

This was only my second full day back in the city and already I was snowed under by domestic dilemmas. I hated them and I loved them. Hated them 'cause everyone depended on me, everyone confessed to me, everyone used me as the man in the middle. Loved them because they made me feel important and wanted, like I was pulling the strings although I knew I wasn't. Either way, it was part of being back in the thick of things, like walking through Times Square and seeing the marquees blasting the names of the new movies— "Key Largo" with Bogey and Bacall, "The Paleface" with Jane Russell, whose tits towered over me as I glanced up at the twice-the-size-of-life color cutout photo of the long-legged lady. *The World Telegram* was all excited about Howard Hughes buying RKO and Robert Mitchum getting busted for marijuana while his new movie, "Blood on the Moon," was playing a half-block from the big clock at the Astor Hotel, which was where I'd met Peggy before taking her to the Automat. The city was really buzzing.

"I've decided to go to graduate school," Peggy announced.

"Great," I said. "What for?"

"Columbia's offering a new master's degree in American Civilization."

"You mean studying old Indians and stuff like that?"

"I mean modern art and modern music. I may actually get to study jazz. They've given Winthrop a lectureship. He'll be one of my teachers."

"Oh God."

"He'll also be writing for New Urban magazine."

"What happened to Metronome? They fire him?"

"Metronone loves him, but he's decided to expand his readership beyond music fans. That's why New Urban is so important. Intellectuals should be the natural supporters of modern jazz. And they will be, once they know more about it. Winthrop is dedicated to spreading the word."

"I'm going for another macaroni and cheese. Want one?"

"I'll eat part of yours."

"Look," I told her, returning with the goods, "I don't think your timing is right."

"Why?"

"You'd do better to wait."

"Wait for what?" she asked, scooping out a huge forkful of macaroni.

"Wait for some common sense to return to your brain."

"You'll be happy to know, Danny, that Win is prepared to help Clifford."

"Cliff's in Nashville."

"He'll be here next week."

"How do you know?"

"He called me yesterday."

"What's he calling you for?"

"He'd been trying to get you, but you haven't been home. I convinced him to come to New York."

"*You* convinced him? Who are you, his manager?"

"He's coming to New York because Winthrop's got him a recording session."

"I thought there was a recording ban."

"Winthrop got around it. I told you he's brilliant. He's organized a session out in Jersey. The musicians won't be able to use their real names but they'll all be paid. Winthrop's producing the date. He's gotten some of the most advanced beboppers on the East Coast to play, and I've convinced him to include Clifford on the date. What do you think of that?"

"I think you've pigged out on the macaroni and cheese. You haven't even left me a taste."

If I don't get a taste of Monica tonight, I thought to myself, checking my watch, *I'll wind up fucking one of Pop's call girls just out of desperation.* But now I'd called her at least a dozen times, but the dizzy dame was nowhere to be found. I'd even tried Minsky's but they said she quit. Where was she?

"Gotta make a quick call," I told Peg.

I dropped in my nickel, dialed her home number and heard even worse news. Disconnected. No further information.

"So what do you think about Win finding work for Clifford? He'll get as much as three hundred dollars."

"What do I care?"

"I thought you cared a lot."

"Three hundred dollars ain't shit. What Cliff needs is a hit record, not some highbrow record session for college profs."

"You think you can do any better for him?"

"I know I can."

Back out on the street, walking up Broadway, Jane Russell's tits made me think of Monica, every shapely sharpy I passed made me think of Monica, Monica on my brain, Monica on my nuts, Monica was mad for me but I knew she was playing hard to get and I couldn't get any harder. There were other dames, dozens of dames I could have called but no one put out like Monica, no one gave it up with such a beautiful and friendly attitude, no one had Monica's moves. Monica was a pro and I was practically willing to pay for her services.

"Monica!"

I looked up and there she was on the cover of the Police Gazette. I couldn't believe it. She was modeling some racy story about sleazy swindlers and white slaves, but she looked gorgeous, her red hair flowing, her green eyes flashing.

I bought the rag and dashed to a phone booth where I called the magazine and asked for the guy in charge of the models. I gave him some bullshit and in two minutes got the number of Monica's new modeling agency. I gave them some bullshit and told them I'd be by tomorrow morning to look over their ten top models and I wanted this girl on the cover of their current issue to be included in the lineup.

"What for?" they wanted to know.

I said I was a producer in from Hollywood.

The next morning I made my move. I hardly slept all night because Mom had changed around my East River penthouse in little ways that made me crazy. She'd bought new towels, sheets and pillowcases. She'd also placed a photo of herself as a young woman on my nightstand. She looked beautiful, but I didn't know whether she'd put it there for me or Shotkin. Plus, I swore I smelled ether or some other terrible doctor's smell all over my bed. I dreamt of puke green hospital hallways and pale yellow operating rooms.

But bright and early I was at the modeling agency over on Eighth Avenue. I had on this coffee-and-cream-colored silk suit and kelly green tie that matched the broad brim of my spring straw. No one could doubt that I was a million dollar producer. Making matters even more convenient, the agency had a two-way mirror where I could look at the girls but they couldn't see me.

The girls were gorgeous. Four blondes and four brunettes made appearances. But Monica was different; Monica was dazzling. When she came out my shlong practically stood up and saluted. She was wearing this low-cut tight top and a snug skirt that hugged her hips, giving her a tantalizing hourglass effect. My heart was deeply affected, but my head was having fun so I told the boss to bring Monica into my private screening room.

I pulled down my hat over my eyes and asked her, "You have objections doing nude scenes?"

"Danny Klein!" she screamed. "You fake! What the hell are you doing here?"

"Just looking for a lunch date, baby."

After slipping the agency twenty bucks for their trouble, I took her to the Savoy Plaza where I acted like a bigshot and tipped Paulie and maitre d' a fin for a good table. Big tips always impressed Monica, who I could see was angry and happy at the same time. I knew she'd missed me, but I also knew she was determined to stay away until she was sure she could count on me—forever.

"Men don't like pressure," I said, softly caressing her arm as she sipped champagne. "And to tell you the truth, sugar, my family's driving me nuts."

"You use your family as an excuse. They drive you nuts only because you let 'em drive you nuts. But I don't care. I'm getting good work without your hat ads and without Minsky's. I'm getting high-class stuff."

"I was proud when I saw you on the Police Gazette," I said sincerely.

"Ever hear of the Lucite-barreled Parker 51 fountain pen?"

"Something new?"

"Yeah, and they want me to model for it. See, I'll be holding this pen and writing something romantic, like a poem."

"You're a poem, baby, you really are. I missed you, I swear I did."

"While you were gone I got my own career going, Danny. That way I don't need you. That way you can't hurt me."

"Why would I want to hurt you? And besides, I'm the one who needs you."

"For a night."

"For lots of nights."

"And then what?"

"Who can read the future?"

"A palm reader on Tenth Avenue. She told me, 'Be careful of a man wearing a felt hat.'"

"This is straw, and what does she know from hats?"

"She knew my mother worked in a button factory."

"Your mother works in a zipper plant."

"Yeah, but it's still a factory."

"Lots of mothers work in factories."

"I never want to work in a factory."

"You'll never have to. You're with me, Monica, and I promise, honey, I'm going to treat you right."

"You're talking this way 'cause you haven't seen me in so
long. Can't you see I've changed?"

"Right now I see you in that black-lace see-through thing I
gave you last Christmas."

"I left it at your apartment."

"Let's go find it."

After I slipped Mom's photo in my top drawer, I found it. I
also found that Monica, despite her change of attitude, was as
hungry and horny as me 'cause she'd hardly seen any other
men while I was away—that's how much she liked me—and
we found all our old hot spots, we wound our way around the
world, loving, licking, sticking together, picking up where
we'd left off, pushing it to the limits, lapping it up, letting it
loose, nothing to hide, dick deep inside, Monica moaning,
groaning, grinning and spinning around 'cause she liked it
from the back, my finger flicking her clit, sucking her tits,
fucking so sweet, riding high, sliding low, hammering her
home until she screamed so loud I was proud of staying in the
race, pacing myself to satisfy her so strong and long that afterwards she was so weak with pleasure I figured she was too
tired to talk. I was wrong.

"You really love me, Danny, don't you?"

"Didn't I show it?"

"You showed it today. But what about tomorrow?"

"Tomorrow I'm going back to work."

She started crying.

"What's wrong now?"

"I'm thinking of all the women you had down South."

"I didn't have any."

"Why are you lying?"

"Why do you have to cause trouble?"

"'Cause you don't make me feel safe."

"I'll give you a teddy bear."

"Now you're talking mean."

"Look, Monica, we just had beautiful sex, so why mess it up with a lot of yap?"

"You're scared of making a commitment."

"I'm not scared of nothing!" I yelled as I took off for the bathroom.

"You don't like commitments, do you?" asked Myron Klein, lighting a cigar as we sat across from each other in the Myron Klein mirrored showroom on lower Broadway.

"Why do you ask me such a thing?" I asked, wondering whether he'd been in touch with Monica. We were going over the fall and winter line. I'd picked out a piece of green felt and drawn a design which I considered pure dynamite. I pictured the hat with a good curl to the brim, a slick tapered crown and a welt edge to keep its shape. The felt was soft-finished and smooth as pussy fur, the kind of hip hat that'd go great with tweed jackets and open-necked sport shirts. "This number will take us into the fifties," I'd told Pop, "where fashion is going to get more casual."

"I asked you to do one job," said Pop, ignoring my fashion statement, "and now you're doing another. Is that commitment?"

"I'm committed to help us sell hats," I explained. "And that means staying ahead of the competition. And I'm telling you,

Pop, this green felt number is a killer. Look, I've made a half-dozen sketches so you can see it from all different angles."

Myron didn't even look at the sketches.

"You're a salesman, Danny, not a designer."

"What are you talking about? I even designed an ad for this thing." I showed him my little thumbnail layout.

"Advertising is *my* department," said Myron.

"It used to be mine."

"You've been away."

"You sent me away."

"We already got an ad campaign for the fall."

"What is it?"

Pop reached into a drawer and pulled out a half-dozen mock ads. They all featured a picture of Pop wearing different styled hats. The headlines were all the same: "Myron Klein, King of Quality Hats."

Shocked, I said, "I thought our slogan was 'Where Quality Is King.'"

"I hired a new ad agency and they switched it around. What's wrong? You don't like it?"

"No offense, Pop, but I'm not sure the buying public really cares that much about seeing you. They'd rather see a young male model with some good-looking broad, the way we used to have."

"This was what the new ad agency wanted. They kept saying, 'Myron, you're the company. It's your name, your hats, and it's wrong not to put your picture in the ads.'"

"Well, I think they're wrong."

"All of a sudden you're telling the experts that they're wrong."

"I'm entitled to my opinion."

"I'm telling you, Danny, you're a salesman. Stick to selling," he said, fingering his diamond tie pin. "I'll do the designing, I'll do the advertising, you'll do the selling."

"You really don't like this green felt number?"

"You and green. Ever since you were a little boy, you were in love with anything green just because it matched your eyes."

"Come on, tell the truth, Pop. Don't you think this is a gorgeous hat?" I asked, pointing to my sketches.

"It's too flashy. Maybe for the niggers, but—"

"Why do you have to talk that way?" I snapped. "The colored keep us in business."

"The colored got you thinking like them—that's what's wrong with you. I'd never do business with the colored."

"But you don't mind selling them."

"I don't mind selling anyone, but you, Danny, you're a better salesman than me. You're a better salesman than anyone."

"I'm sick of hearing that."

"Because you won't make a commitment to sales."

"What does that mean?"

"I want you to take over the California territory—that's what it means. And I'm giving you a raise to boot. A fatter commission base. You'll wind up making more money than you're worth."

"You actually want to send me out to the West Coast?"

"Who else do I got? I had to fire Harry Talbot."

"Why?"

"Because he was slipping. Besides, when I saw what you were doing down South, I knew no one could handle California like you. You're going to sell the shit out of our fall line in L.A. and Frisco. I know you are. So why don't you take off a couple of weeks and just relax? Maybe you want to go to the

Catskills, maybe the Jersey shore. Let me know and I'll foot the bill, just because I want you to know what a good job you did down South."

"How come you never told me that when I was calling you from the road?"

"Motivation, Danny. Motivation's something the president of a firm has got to understand. I gotta keep my people motivated."

"Well, I ain't motivated to go to California. I've already put in my time."

"Here we go again. Commitment, Danny—why is it so hard for you to understand commitment?"

"Why is it so hard for you to understand that someday someone is going to have to take over this firm—and that someone is going to be me."

Pop pulled the cigar from his mouth and narrowed his eyes. His teeth were clenched when he said, "Over my dead body."

Some people may like it, but to me Newark, New Jersey, is the asshole of America. I hate the place. It's paint plants and gray skies and crummy brick buildings. It's nowhere. To get there, you're always smelling oil refineries and pig shit from Secaucus and, all the way over to the Pulaski Skyway, we were stuck behind trailer trucks farting in our face. I wasn't happy. Winthrop was driving his dumpy roadster—he thought having a foreign car was hip—the trip was bumpy as hell, and making matters worse, he drove like a girl.

With Sis in the front seat with Winnie, him in his bow tie and college-prof suit, and me and Cliff in the back, we were on our way to the session.

We'd picked up Cliff at the train station—he'd come in from Nashville—and naturally I was glad to see him. Even though it'd been only a couple of weeks since I'd been with him, I missed the guy. I wanted to hear more about the hillbilly band. Win and Peg couldn't believe that he'd play a gig like that, but his pockets were bulging with money and he looked great. I could tell that he was happy to see me, but I wasn't thrilled that he was being so goddamn nice to Peg and Winnie, like they were really doing him a big favor. When I found him jobs—like the country-and-western thing—they paid good. Far as I was concerned, today's session was off-track and out-of-the-way. I was just along for the ride.

The truth is that I was still feeling fucked-over from my meeting with Pop. I hadn't decided how to respond or what to do, but, believe me, my mind was working overtime. Battles with Myron Klein never got you anywhere. But there were other ways.

Seeing Cliff, though, was good for me. Being around him always made me feel creative. He was that kind of guy. And I couldn't help but think that the real reason he was back— beyond this jivey gig in Jersey—had to do with me. Marvis must have spoken on my behalf.

"You talk to Mama before you left?" I asked Cliff.

"Called her last night. She said to say hi and give you her love."

"She's a doll," I told Peg and Winnie. "And a regular scholar. The woman's got guts you wouldn't believe." I explained how she backed down the Klan and they thought I was bullshitting.

"You tell 'em Cliff," I insisted. "Tell 'em about Marvis."

"You have to see her to believe her." He smiled, content to let Win and Sis think whatever they wanted.

"Now let me give you my analysis of today's session," Winthrop said to Cliff.

"Doesn't that analysis shit come afterwards?" I said.

"Let the man talk," Cliff insisted, shutting me up and making me mad.

"To be candid," said Win, "my first pianistic choice was Thelonious Monk. But Monk's in Chicago, and Peggy, whose taste is developing quite nicely, insisted you could fit the bill. I'm taking a bit of chance because harmonically this could be an enormously taxing session. The other players are extremely advanced and prepared to push structure to the limit."

"Cool," is all Cliff replied, sticking a Camel in his mouth and lighting up.

The session was at a place called Savoy on Market Street in downtown Newark. Downstairs was a jazz record store where a few eggheads were hanging out and upstairs was a small studio. The cats hadn't arrived yet, and immediately Winnie started eyeing his watch. He took out his clipboard and started going over the list of songs with Cliff, who was so relaxed I wondered whether he was stoned.

When the cats arrived—a thin young trumpeter called Miles, a tall saxist named Dex, Klook the drummer and Benny the bassist—there were smiles and salutations all around. They all knew Cliff. Benny had the boo and had no hesitation about lighting up. That sticky sweet smell stunk up the session, now floating on a cloud of pot. I myself took a small puff. Peg looked at me like I'd committed adultery, but mainly she was looking at Cliff.

"Perhaps it would be more prudent," Winnie said, "if we held off on the stimulants until after the session."

But the cats—with their berets and goatees and funny-looking sunglasses—acted like they didn't hear him. Talking their own private language, they started rolling more funny cigarettes.

"Really, gentlemen," Winthrop insisted, "I strongly suggest—"

"I strongly suggest," said the gruff-voiced Miles, "that you tell the engineer to turn on the juice and then shut the fuck up."

The cats obviously had their own program, regardless of what was written on Win's clipboard.

"Now the first song," said Winthrop, ignoring Miles, "is 'Steeplechase,' which suggests a uncompromisingly brisk tempo, wouldn't you agree?"

No one said nothing. They just took out their instruments, tuned up, got a sound level and played. Miles, a silent dark-skinned dude, was cool—he had this light airy tone—Dex was hot and Cliff filled in all the empty spaces, his eight fingers dancing like fifty Rockettes. They might be on grass but damned if they didn't play great—six songs, one after another, no rehearsals, no nothing, just a nod from Miles to Dex or Dex to Cliff to indicate who should play which solo.

Now this ain't popular music, I said to myself, sitting in the control room with Win, Sis and the engineer. *This ain't money-making music. But it sure as hell blows like a hurricane and burns like a bonfire. Maybe you can't follow the melody, maybe there's not much melody, but maybe that's not the point. You can't dance to it, you can't hum it, but you gotta respect the cats for playing it 'cause it's as complicated as the classical shit they play up in Carnegie Hall.*

Five songs later, the session was over and the guys were celebrating when I got an idea. I walked from the control room into the studio with Peg and Win following.

"Hey, gents," I said, "I want you to hear this song Cliff wrote down in Alabama. Remember that thing, Cliff? Remember 'Be-Bop Blues?'"

Cliff laughed. "Yeah, it was cute, but who could remember the words?"

"Me," I said, fumbling for a piece of paper in my back pocket, "I even wrote them down."

"The session is over," said Winthrop, obviously pleased with what the cats, Cliff included, had played.

"Wait a minute, Winnie. Just listen to this."

Cliff started playing the tune on the piano while I whispered the words in his ears. The melody came right back to him:

> *Have you heard the beat?*
> *Have you heard the news?*
> *The newest craze is the be-bop blues*
>
> *The notes are flying*
> *The rhythm's fast*
> *Folks are saying it'll never last*

The musicians picked up their instruments and joined in, jamming on the spot. Klook the drummer laid on this ballsy beat-back which really made you want to dance.

"Turn on the mikes," I called to the engineer. "Let's record this thing."

"Keep those machines off," Winnie said, waving his hands. "This has nothing to do with what we're doing here today—"

"Lighten up, Winnie,"

"Stay out of my business!" Winnie's horn-rims were steaming up, his veins bulging out of his forehead.

"Cat's got a cute little song," declared Dex, the long-legged saxist. "Let him sing it, man."

"I'm producing this session," said Winnie, "and some inane pop song has nothing to do with what we're creating here."

"Please, Danny," whispered Peg, pulling on my sleeve, "don't get Winthrop upset. He's responsible for this session."

"I'm just interested in making money," I said.

"Now there," said Miles, pointing right at me, "is an honest white man."

"Money's got nothing to do with it," I said to Mom. "It's the idea that he's always throwing me out of town. I feel like he's always kicking me out on my ass."

"Darling," Mama murmured softly as we wandered through Bergdorf-Goodman, her diamond dome ring flashing, "you shouldn't look at it that way." We were in the middle of one of our rituals—clothes shopping. Anita would help me pick out mine and I'd help her pick out hers. We'd been doing this since I was old enough to know the difference between linen and silk, which happened before I was ten. I got my taste from Mom, not Pop, who never made a fashion move without first consulting his wife.

"Your father's going through a bad period—don't I know that better than anyone?—but he's right to say that you can outsell anyone out there."

"I'm not going back out there."

"What do you think of this dress, darling?" she asked, holding up a balloon-skirted puff-sleeved scarlet red affair.

"It's not you."

"Why not?"

"Too racy."

"My doctor says I look fabulous in red."

"The hell with what your creepy doctor says," I said, "we were talking about Pop."

"What about this one?" asked Anita, pointing to a white-and-purple polka-dotted design by Pauline Trigère.

"I like it."

"Good. Write down the style number and we'll pick it up on Thirty-ninth Street."

That was also part of our ritual—find it on Fifth Avenue but buy it in the garment district. Seemed like we knew every clothing wholesaler in the city. Never in the history of our family had I heard of anyone buying retail.

At Saks we looked for stuff for me. Anita had an eagle eye for fabric and style. Summer was almost upon us, and I could always use a couple of lightweight suits. Mama picked out a cool dozen. Naturally, she consulted me, but her instincts were dead-on.

Make no mistake, I'm a fashion maven. I know sharp from square; but no one can match Anita Klein for picking eye-popping threads. Glen plaids and pinstripes, double-breasted and double-pleated, chocolates, greens, slate grays and pure whites . . . in a matter of minutes she helped me put together a hot-weather wardrobe that would make any man proud.

Meanwhile, a trio of snotty salesmen looked us over, wondering why I was writing down all these lot numbers. Since I was a little kid, I'd been trained by Mama not to care about such scenes and, believe me, being here with Mama made me feel like a little kid again. The truth, though, is that I liked it; I liked when Mama took care of me.

From Bergdorf we drove over to Thirty-ninth Street and Sixth Avenue, which is the heart, liver and guts of the garment district. There the streets were teeming with trucks, guys pushing racks of pants and skirts through the gutter, cabbies caught in traffic screaming bloody murder, cigar stands squeezed next to luncheonettes, me and Mom going up freight elevators and walking through warehouses to find our friends who'd give us the goods at cost or just a little above. This wasn't easy work, but finally by five o'clock the shlep was over. Watching Mom wheel-

and-deal was always a treat and at the same time a humbling experience. She was the champ. At day's end she had a half dozen new dresses and I had at least four summers' worth of suits.

Afterwards, over egg creams at a candy store on Thirty-third Street, Anita finally got to the point.

"You got what you wanted today?" she asked.

"More than I can use."

"My treat."

"You don't have to do that, Mom."

"I don't have to do anything. I do what I want because I know that in this world there are very few people who I do for who will also do for me."

I could feel it; I was being bought. This was another part of our family ritual—give so you can get.

"What do you want me to do for you, Mom?"

"Take Peg with you to California before she marries this gentile."

"But I'm not going to California."

"You say that now, but I know you, darling, I know you'll change your mind."

"I'm not changing my mind and besides, I can't control Peg. No one can. She wants to stay in New York and so do I."

"A change of scenery will do you both a world of good. Have you heard of Beverly Hills? They have such beautiful flowers out there, flowers like you wouldn't believe. It's like they spray the air with perfume. Myron took me there. When was that, three years ago?"

"Let him take you again."

"Don't talk nasty to your mother," said Anita, puckering her lips as she spread on a fresh layer of ruby-red lipstick.

"I'm saying this in all sincerity," I said. "I think you should pay more attention to Pop. He needs you."

"Of course he needs me, and he needs you too, my darling Daniel. Myron is a man who needs all the help he can get. That he functions outside an insane asylum is nothing short of miraculous."

"You used to tell me how it was time for me to take over the company. But now you're not talking that way. What happened, Mom?"

"I have a plan. All good business people have plans. By the time you get back from California—in three, four months— the company will be in better shape. You'll help me by increasing sales out there, Danny, you really will, and by the end of the year the timing will be perfect. By then, I'll have your apartment redecorated—"

"I don't want my apartment redecorated. I don't want you in my apartment anymore."

"Now listen to how you're talking to your mother."

"I'm through talking, Mom, I'm through talking to everyone about everything."

"We gotta talk," said Monica over the phone.

"This ain't the right time, baby. I'm on my way out."

"Just as I thought. You have a date with another woman—"

"Yeah, my Aunt Bea."

"On a Friday night? You expect me to believe that you're taking your old maid aunt out on a Friday night?"

"She's not all that old and she's got tickets to the Dodger-Giant game at Ebbets Field."

"Look, I know I didn't go to Barnard or nothing like your sister, but how gullible do you think I am?"

"If you don't believe me, come to Ebbets and see for yourself."

"Is that an invitation?"

"I wish I had a ticket for you, baby, but the game's sold out."

"You've sold me out for the last time, Danny Klein. Next time you want some quick satisfaction, go beat your own meat 'cause *this* girl is too uptown for you. You hear me, Danny, *I'm too goddamn fuckin' uptown for you.*"

"Why are you talking that way, Monica? What the hell's wrong with you?"

"You, you're a bastard. *That's* what's wrong."

With Monica's shrill still ringing in my ear, I drove over the Brooklyn Bridge on this warm night in late May, figuring that Aunt Bea would take up where Mom left off. I'd put up with it, though, only 'cause I'd put up with anything to sit behind home plate and watch my Bums play ball.

See, Ebbets Field ain't no ball park; it's more like a person, a real live living human being who breathes and smells and smiles, an old friend, a close relative. Ebbets Field has personality, squeezed right into a cozy Flatbush neighborhood, where Sullivan, Bedford, Montgomery and McKeever Streets meet. It's this funny-shaped place, with weird windows, angles and arches, with flags flying on top and a Stahl-Meyer frankfurter stand across the street. It ain't big and rich like Yankee Stadium, it's modest and friendly like the people pouring through the turnstiles, people of different colors 'cause the Dodgers, unlike the Yanks, have colored players and the colored people love that and, to tell you the truth, so do I.

At the main gate I spot little Aunt Bea wearing her blue Dodger jacket and waving to me like crazy. Her bright orange hair is tucked under her Dodger cap, and she's even more excited than I am. She pinches my cheek, takes my hand and makes me feel like I'm six. I don't care, I'm happy to be six again, happy 'cause now we're inside, hurrying through the marble rotunda with the guys hawking scoreboards and toy pencil bats with pictures of Duke Snider and Gil Hodges, the vendors screaming "Dodja souvenirs, get ya' genuine Dodja souvenirs!"—and the smell of peanuts and beer in my nose, and my eyes darting every which way, my heart beating fast as, hunched over, me and Bea walk up one of those huge ramps, higher and higher we climb until finally we find ourselves in the stands, under the magic night lights—the green of the grass, the dirt of the outfield, the Schaeffer beer sign in right field, the big black scoreboard, the billboards for Bulova watches and Old Gold cigarettes, the players themselves warming up—Pee Wee Reese, Billy Cox, Carl Furillo. This is my first game of the new season, and I'm excited, I'm anxious to see the Dodgers' rookie catcher Roy Campanella. "Preacher" Roe is pitching and even before the game is under way, even before Gladys Gooding plays the national anthem on the organ, pinochle games have popped up all over, skinny guys playing gin rummy, fat women waving flags that say, "Kiss Me, I'm From Brooklyn!" and the sad-sack Dodger Sym-Phony band beating out "Roll Out the Barrel and We'll Have a Barrel of Fun."

The first five innings are brutal. Giant pitcher Larry Jensen bleeds the Bums dry. We can't get a hit. Meanwhile, Whitey Lockman belts an empty-bases blast into dead center field. Giants 1, Bums zip.

"We'll get it back," says Bea, chasing down her hot dog with a beer.

"You can count on it," I agree, though in the seventh, when the Giants score another run and we're still scoreless, I start worrying. Without too much interest down on the field, Bea starts talking turkey.

"Your mother says you're upset with her, Danny."

"Let's see if we can score this inning," I say, changing subjects.

We both cheer as Jackie Robinson rips a single to center, steals second and then, with George Shuba fanning on an inside fastball, takes off for third. It's a dazzling, dirt-kicking smooth-sliding steel . . . but oh, shit, he's called out.

"Ya' got ya' eyes up ya' ass!" Bea informs the ump.

In the eighth inning, the Giants score their third run. The game may be gone, but it's a measure of Brooklyn loyalty never to leave before the final out, and we ain't going anywhere.

"Pressure, poor Danny, everyone's always putting pressure on you," Bea sympathizes as she lights up a Lucky Strike, blowing the smoke out towards the mound where Dodger reliever Hank Behrman is warming up.

"I'm fine, I really am, Aunt Bea. I just have to make some decisions."

"You're telling me. That father of yours is about to run everyone out, including your own mother."

"I wouldn't exactly call my mother a cream puff," I say taking up Pop's part. After all, Anita's doing all kinds of double-dealing that Bea doesn't know nothing about.

"I know my sister Anita better than you think I do. I'm not saying she's a saint. How do you think I got cross-eyed?"

"No one ever told me."

"Well, I'm telling you. Your mother pushed me off a swing in the playground of P.S. 181, our elementary school on Delancey Street. She pushed me because I was swinging next to little Harold Swartz and *she* liked little Harold and *she* wanted to swing next to him and when my sister Anita wants something—I don't have to tell you this, Danny—my sister gets what she wants."

"But how 'bout what *I* want, Aunt Bea, doesn't that count?"

"Of course it counts, Danny dear. Your mother lives for you. She worships the ground you walk on. What you want, she wants. We all want to see you in Myron's office. None of us has any doubt that you'll be the boss. From the boys in the mail room to my girls in the trimming department, it's what everyone wants. And it'll happen. With patience, Danny, you'll get what you want."

"Look at this, another walk," I say, turning my attention back to the game. Bottom of the ninth, Dodgers still down 3–0, but after two out, Jensen's walked the second straight Dodger.

With the game on the line, Pee Wee Reese stands at the plate. On the first pitch he surprises everyone; the runners are going as he squares up and drags a perfect bunt along the third base line, beating the throw by inches.

Everyone safe. Bases loaded.

Now here comes the rookie, squat stocky Roy Campanella. He's got a funny stance; he waves the bat like a wand; he looks steady and strong; he digs deep into the batter's box; he waits. Jensen winds, pumps, kicks and delivers.

Swish!

The fast ball is ferocious; Campy swings late and misses.

"Imagine the pressure on this guy," says Aunt Bea.

Campy knocks the dirt out of his spikes and digs in for the next pitch. Camp swings way out in front of the floating change-up. He looks bad; Jensen's fooled him again.

"The true test is how you do under pressure, Danny. That's what separates winners from losers."

From where we're sitting, I can see determination in Campy's eyes. He grinds his teeth; muscles move up and down his neck; I can feel how bad he wants to connect.

Here comes the pitch, over the plate and a little low, it hangs there and, oh boy, does Campy connect!

The whack of the bat, the solid smack of wood on cowhide, and there it goes.

Thirty-two thousand Flatbushers leap to their feet.

"Go!" screams Bea.

"Go!" I scream even louder.

The ball's winding dangerously close to the left field foulpost . . . oh, God, it's going to be close . . .

"You can do it, Danny," Bea hollers, like I'm the batter, like I'm the ball soaring through space, "You can do it!"

The ball's got the distance, but will it clear the post, will it fall fair . . . will it? . . . will it . . . ?

It does.

It makes it.

Grand slam home run!

Dodgers win 4–3.

The Bums have a new hero, this smiling plump lovable Campy fella trotting around the bases while all of Brooklyn goes nuts.

"Told you you could do it, Danny," Bea cries as real tears run down her face.

Afterwards, on the juke box in the gin mill, Billie Holiday is singing "Do Your Duty" while Aunt Bea throws back several Rheingold beers. She has her eye on a tough guy sitting on a stool at the end of the bar. He looks like a wrestler. His sleeves are rolled up, his muscles big and his arms tatooed with anchors and hearts. I see him wink at her. It's time for me to leave.

"Gotta go, Aunt Bea."

"Don't leave till Billie's through singing," she orders. "To me she's the greatest. Remember when she sang with Artie Shaw?"

"Not exactly, but I remember you telling me about her when I was a little kid."

"Have I ever steered you wrong?"

"Never."

"I'm telling you, Danny, it's pressure that brings out the best in you. You'll come through for us. I *know* you will."

"Thanks for the tickets, Aunt Bea, it was a beautiful ball game."

I kiss her cheek as Billie finishes the song and Aunt Bea moves towards the brute at the end of the bar.

Pressure. I was thinking pressure, I was feeling pressure when the next morning, back at my apartment, there was no hot-water pressure. Just what I needed. There I was, sticky and soapy in the middle of my shower and figuring it was probably Doc Shotkin who screwed up the plumbing because he had no business using my fuckin' shower and fucking my mother in my apartment while I'm trying to sell straw hats in Podunk, Mississippi, for Myron Klein who's gotta see his mug in every fuckin' ad the company ever does.

The phone rang while I was trying to sponge off the soap. I threw a towel around me and picked up the receiver in the hallway.

"Where are you?" Pop wanted to know.

"Where do you think I am? I'm at home talking to you."

"I need you to go to Jersey today. We got an emergency at the body plant in Nutley. Something's wrong with the felt, I been seeing too many imperfects and I gotta get to the bottom of it."

"Send Sam. Sam's quality control, ain't he?"

"You've forgotten more about hats than Sam ever knew. Besides, Sam's out."

"What happened to Sam?"

"He's out, that's all. What, I gotta explain to you? Sam's a wise guy, he talks back. I'm through with backtalk, I'm telling you that right now."

"Pop, it's Saturday morning and no one's going to be at the felt plant on Saturday morning."

"They opened special for you. I made them. The plant manager's waiting."

"The last thing in the world I wanna do is drive to Jersey. Besides, I got plans."

"Cancel them."

"I can't."

"What plans are so important that they can't wait?"

What the hell; I figured I might as well tell Pop the truth. "I promised Uncle Nate I'd spend the day with him."

"What? To bet on the ponies?"

"I don't know what we're going to do, except I promised him 'cause I really haven't seen him much since I've been back."

"Far as I'm concerned, you never have to see that bum."

"I love him."

"You would. You love everyone except the one guy who's paying your bills."

"I earn what I make."

"Then get your ass out to Jersey or forget the whole thing."

"Fine, I'll forget the whole thing," I said, slamming down the receiver in my father's ear, something I'd never done before.

The phone started ringing again—it had to be Pop looking to have the last word—but I didn't answer.

Five minutes later, though, when the doorbell rang, I had to answer. I was glad I did. It was Cliff. He was wearing a wide-brimmed straw—one of my own designs, a gift from me—a white shirt, white pants and black sneakers. He looked terrific.

"Hey," I said, slapping him on the back, "I've been trying to get in touch with you but that hotel in Harlem said you checked out."

"Checked out last week. I've been ripping and running. Your people have been keeping me busy."

"What people?"

"Peggy and Win. Peg found me a little cafe in Morningside Heights, up around Columbia, where I've been working weekends. Win got it mentioned in the New York *Times* so business has been pretty good."

"And no one called to invite me?"

"Sorry, man, but I didn't figure it was your kind of scene."

"What does that mean? College kids and eggheads?"

"Mainly."

"Are you singing? Will they let you sing your blues?"

"Ain't that kind of gig, Dan. I'm playing progressive stuff— Bird lines, Bud Powell riffs, Monk changes. I mean, these people are serious about modern music."

"Is the money serious?"

"Barely enough to pay for a room in the boarding house up on 140th Street. For the time being, though, I'm cool. I just stopped by to say I missed you, man, that's all."

"The feeling's mutual, Cliff."

"I know you're going through some rough times."

"Who told you that?"

"Peg, for one. But she didn't have to tell me. I know how it is between you and your old man. You've got a lot to deal with."

"Look," I said, changing subjects, "I haven't given up on you, Cliff, I really haven't. And I still don't think that this modern jazz shit is ever gonna make you any money."

"It isn't about money, man. It's about advanced music. It's a challenge, it's a kick to play it."

"But deep down, Cliff, is that stuff really you? What I heard back in Alabama when you were with Woody and Mama, the gutbucket blues with the big beat—you were singing that from your heart, man, that was powerful, that was the kind of music everyone loves."

"It's all powerful, it's all part of me."

"But don't you see, Cliff, marketing and management are the keys, the difference between playing some artsy fartsy college club and having a record on the radio. That's where I come in."

"Haven't we heard this song before, Danny?"

"Yeah, but this time I'm dead serious."

"Listen, Dan, I didn't come over here to get you to hustle me work. I just came by to say hi. I hope everything's going along for you like it should, 'cause I care about you, man. I really do care."

"And they're off!"

The Belmont announcer called the race in his high-pitched hysterical voice.

"You're nuts," said Uncle Nate, sitting next to me in the grandstand, "putting that kind of money on a horse named Felt."

"Just a dumb hunch," I said, trying to enjoy some Saturday afternoon sunshine. But Pop was on my mind. I was tempted to jump in the car and drive to Nutley just to keep the old man quiet, just to prevent another shouting match.

"Goddamn!" shouted Uncle Nate, jumping to his feet. "Your horse is making a move."

My five-to-one shot came in. Despite Nate's losses, I was five hundred bucks up for the day. Suddenly I wasn't worried about Pop any more. I had my own Felt working for me.

"My brother's working you pretty hard I hear," said Nate in the clubhouse where I ate a light dinner and he put away a couple of two-pound smoked whitefish. Every time I saw my uncle he seemed to get bigger. Today his double-extra-large pink and white cabana-striped shirt was pulling so tight against his gut, the buttons were about to pop. But under his big bushy brows he had these twinkling eyes that made you forget his size.

"I don't know how much longer I can last."

"Ain't I been telling you that for some time?"

"But I had to go down South. I had to make that last trip."

"Well, you made it and it's done and now he wants more, doesn't he?"

"I suppose."

"He'll always want more. Which is why you gotta get the hell out. Remember that store lease I mentioned?"

"The one off Times Square?"

"It was a prime location for a man's hat store, but you didn't move quick enough, kid. Someone scooped it up. It's gone. Now Pepper Katz calls me—the guy you met who owns that nightclub—well, Pepper also owns some real estate and he calls me and mentions a tenant of his who's gone belly-up and lost his lease."

"Pepper Katz is an asshole."

"Maybe, but he's also a guy with a deal you ain't gonna get anywhere else. The only problem with this store is location."

"Where is it?" I asked.

"Harlem."

"Where in Harlem?"

"125th Street. Down from the Apollo."

"Are you kidding? That's a fabulous location."

"Thought you might be interested." Uncle Nate took a giant-sized forkful of whitefish, chewing and smiling as the food slid down his throat into his big belly.

GRAND OPENING

I couldn't sleep. Figures danced inside my head—the price of a twelve-month lease, the cost of inventory, help, fixtures, insurance, bookkeeping. A storeowner's gotta think of everything. And that's how I was starting to think—like a storeowner. And why not?

Pop was always calling his brother a bum, but Nate wasn't altogether crazy. A store would make me feel like my own man; a store, once and for all, would let me fly out of that nasty nest of family problems. Let Myron figure out his own felt problems in Nutley. Let Mama take over the company and run it herself. She didn't need me; Doc Shotkin was all she needed. And if Peg wanted to spend the rest of her life with some moldy fig tight-ass jive-ass jazz critic, that was her problem. I just wished that she and her Winnie the Pooh professor would leave Cliff alone. They were hurting his career where I was sure I could help it. But how?

Ideas started shooting off in my brain. I kept seeing that

green felt hat that I'd designed. That was it. I'd get a green neon sign made in the shape of a big hat that'd be flashing off and on. Man, would that stop the shoppers on 125th Street! Better yet, I could give Cliff a day job in the store selling hats. I'd train him. He was a people person, he had a good enough personality. But what a minute . . . Cliff didn't give two shits about hats. What Cliff cared about was music. What about selling music? How 'bout selling records? 125th Street was a great location for a hat store, but, right down the street from the Apollo, it was also a perfect place to sell records. Why not combine the two? Sure, it might sound crazy, but so what: They called Marconi and the Wright Brothers crazy. But those guys knew what they were doing, and so did I. One side of the store for hats, the other for records. Buy a straw hat here and a Basie tune there. The two would complement each other. The customers would love it. What an idea! But what if it all failed? What if I fell on my ass? I'd never been out there alone, not without the help of Mom and Pop. Could I do it? Did I have the balls? All night long, my doubts and determination were waging a full-scale war. I was too excited to sleep, and early the next morning—this was Sunday—despite the fact I knew him to be a first-class schmuck, I had Pepper Katz on the phone, promising to meet me at the location at noon.

A sleepy Sunday in Harlem, and the world finally seemed at peace. Families decked out like royalty calmly strolled back from church. Some cats and chicks were just getting up from Saturday night, moving real slow, talking real quiet. Driving up Eighth Avenue under the El, shafts of sunlight poured through the grids. It was beautiful. I felt like I was heading towards my destiny as suddenly a subway train roared over-head, breaking the morning silence.

125th Street was practically deserted. The stores were closed. I was a little early so I drove around, checking the

location of other record shops and hat shops in the neighborhood. Shit, there was plenty of competition. I passed the
Apollo, where the marquee advertised a big summer show
starring the Ink Spots, Pearl Bailey, Illinois Jacquet, Eddie
"Cleanhead" Vinson and "Pigmeat" Markham. Next door at
the Braddock Hotel, where Cliff said Charlie Parker liked to
hang out, a sign in the window of the bar said, "Two Drinks
for the Price of One."

I parked my Caddie and walked down the street, looking
for the shop that had lost its lease. When I found the place my
heart started thumping. Was this me? Was this my future?
Peeking through the metal grating, I saw it was a nice-sized
store, not too narrow, not too wide, a twenty foot frontage,
maybe fifteen hundred square feet of retail space. The place
was empty of everything but scattered piles of garbage. I
couldn't tell what kind of goods they'd been trying to sell.

"Men's hats," a voice said from behind me.

I turned around and saw Pepper Katz. He was tall enough
to be a basketball player with a nose the size of the basket. He
had big bug eyes and a moustache that looked like a hot dog.

"That ain't too encouraging," I said as Katz unlocked the
grating and opened the door.

"I ain't here to encourage you," he informed me. "I'm here
to rent you a store if you want it. If not, there are plenty who
do."

"With salesmen like you, it's no wonder the hat shop went
under."

"Look, kid, I ain't no salesman, I don't kiss no one's ass, and
I don't like being dragged out of bed on a Sunday. But I know
there's money in your family and I said to Nate, I told him
that this one time I'd give you a break. So we're talking five
hundred dollars a month with the first two months' rent and a
five hundred dollar security deposit on a year lease which

means you bring by a check for fifteen hundred dollars tonight
or tomorrow it goes to the Primadora Havana Cigar stores
who know this is the Times Square of Harlem where empties
come up only once in a blue moon."

"What time tonight?"

"Eight. You bring it by the Park Sheraton. I operate out of
the Park Sheraton."

"What about your jazz club over on Lenox Avenue?"

"I sold it. Jazz ain't selling worth a shit these days."

"Mind if I look around a minute?"

"Hurry."

My eyes surveyed the scene, trying to envision where the
displays would go—which side for hats, which for records.

"Any idea why this hat store didn't make it?" I asked Katz.

"The guy didn't sell enough hats."

Pepper Katz reminded me of Pop. Is this the man I wanted
for a landlord?

"There's nothing wrong with the space," he told me. "It's
just whether you wanna run a business in Harlem."

"Why, what's wrong with Harlem?"

"Nothing. You can do good business in Harlem. I have a lot
of property around here, I do very well in Harlem. I grew up
in Harlem before it turned. Many, many years ago Harlem
used to be Jewish. Did you know that?"

"I knew that."

"So it turned and it changed and there's still money to be
made, believe me, money in real estate, money in retailing,
even money in music if you can figure out what the
schvartzers will pay to hear."

Schvartzers meant blacks in Yiddish, but it had an ugly ring
to it. It hurt me to hear Katz use the word. I thought of Cliff's
mom and the Ku Klux Klan and decided that there were

probably as many ignorant assholes up here as down there. Pepper Katz was one of them.

"Anyone ever call you a 'kike'?" I asked him.

"My whole life. Especially the Irish."

"Then where do you come off calling people *schvartzers?*"

"What are you, a spokesman for the Communist Party or something? Look Mr. Self-Righteous, I live, eat and breathe with these people. They respect me because they know I'm a man of my word. Ask around. Ask the colored what they think of Pepper Katz. They'll tell you. Meanwhile, you'll tell me tonight whether you want this place. Tonight by eight."

Back at my apartment, it was still early afternoon, and my head was still whirling. I wanted to do it, but I was scared— scared of losing money and pride, scared of pissing off Mom and Pop. It would be like resigning from the family. I needed advice, but who could I call? While I was trying to decide, advice called me.

"If you know what's good for you," said Pop, "you'll be here bright and early tomorrow morning—and with an apology. I had to go to Jersey by myself, which was a good thing since I wound up with a ten thousand dollar credit. That's the kind of damaged goods they were sending us. In this company, I got to do everything by myself. I want you to know that if it wasn't for your mother, you'd be out on your ass right now. She says 'no,' she says, 'Danny's a good boy, give him another chance.' Last chance, Danny, I'm telling you, this is your last goddamn chance. Now talk to your mother."

"Danny, darling," said Mama, "your father's a little excited right now, but there's really nothing to worry about. You and him, you're both tired. You'll come in the office tomorrow

morning and we'll sit down over a cup of tea and talk. It's
getting hot in New York and you'll be cooler out in California
anyway. What's today? The second of June? You'll take your
time, sweetheart. You'll leave in a week or so. Myron and I
are thinking about coming out there to visit you and Peggy at
the end of July. Have you talked to your sister? We'll get a big
bungalow at the Beverly Hills Hotel. Like one happy family.
It'll be a beautiful summer for all of us."

I didn't say anything; I didn't have to; a half-hour later my
sister called.

"If you was me," I asked Peg, "would you open up a combination hat and record shop in Harlem or go sell Pop's fall line
out in California?"

"The Harlem store is a wonderful idea. It's absolutely perfect for you. Do you have enough savings to finance it without
help?"

"It would take most of the money I got socked away."

"I have some money of my own, you know. I'd go in with
you, Danny. I trust you. I'd help you, I'd help run the record
department. Besides, who wants to go to California?"

"Mom's expecting me to take you with me."

"What! What would I do in California?"

"Get away from Carrington the Creep."

"We're engaged."

"Oh God. Have you told Mom?"

"Have you told her about your store?"

"Are you kidding?"

"Then we're even. Have you thought of a name for the
store?"

"No, but I thought of a sign. A big green hat in flashing
neon."

"That's fabulous. What about some musical notes under the
hat—some blue neon notes to contrast with the green. That

would let passersby know that you're also selling records."

"Great. Maybe I should just call it 'Danny Klein's.'"

"Maybe you shouldn't. That sounds like something Pop would do. Be more creative. How about 'Blue Notes Under a Green Felt Hat'?"

"That's crazy, Sis. There ain't no stores with names like that."

"That's what makes it so good. It's original. Look, the competition up there must be fierce, but you've come up with an original concept, hats and records in one store. So why not have an original name?"

"You might have something there."

"How much financing do you think it would take to keep the store afloat for a year?"

"I'd have to get out a pencil and paper and go over the numbers. My head's spinning, things are moving a little fast." I told her about Katz's ultimatum—money by eight.

"Do you think he's serious? . . ."

"I know he's serious," said Uncle Nate, who had dropped by to see what I thought of the store. "125th Street is prime location. It's one of the hottest strips in the city, especially for the stuff you wanna sell."

"I'm a little nervous about the whole thing."

"You're a natural-born merchant. I don't gotta tell you that. But do you got the dough?"

I went into my bedroom and opened the wall safe behind the wedding picture of Mom and Dad. For some reason, I'd always kept that photo in my bedroom, hanging there like some holy shrine. Uncle Nate was at the doorway looking at me. I stood in front of the lock so he couldn't see the combination. It wasn't that I didn't trust him, but I knew gamblers.

They were as bad as junkies, maybe worse. I went through the few stocks and bonds that Mom had given me (to ease her and Pop's tax bite) and came to my emergency cash. I counted out three thousand dollars, a lot of that my bar mitzvah gifts from eleven years ago.

"Danny," said Nate, eyeing the cash, "before you close the safe, if you could slip me ten fins—I'll have it back to you tomorrow—I really would appreciate it."

I gave my uncle fifty dollars and sent him on his way, figuring that was a cheap enough price to pay for a hot real estate tip.

By five o'clock my stomach was doing dips; I was really getting nervous. I needed something to calm me down, to help me think straight. I thought of sex. I thought of Monica.

"I'm thinking of changing my life, baby, and I'm looking for someone to talk to," I told her.

"Bullshit. You're looking for someone to screw."

"I haven't heard from you in so long, I wanted to call and see how you're doing."

"Doing just fine. There's a producer who wants to put me in a movie."

"With or without your clothes?"

"You're just jealous."

"Who is this producer?"

"He's out in Hollywood. He wants to fly me out."

"That's where I'm supposed to be going."

"For what?"

"For Pop's business. He wants to send me back out on the road."

"He can't do that to you, Danny," Monica said quickly, acting like she used to act—concerned for me.

"I'm having a hard time figuring out this shit," I admitted.

"What's to figure? Tell him to buzz off."

"But he's my father and everyone's counting on me over there—Mom and Aunt Bea and all the ladies in the trimming room—"

"How many of those ladies have you trimmed?" she asked, jumping back into her jealousy bag.

"Their average age is sixty and not one of them has their real teeth. They're just nice ladies, that's all."

"Your problem, Danny, is that you're too nice to everyone. You oughta be nice to yourself. You oughta be nice to *me*."

"You come over and I guarantee you I'll be nice—"

"You haven't changed, Danny Klein. You'll never change."

"You're a hundred percent wrong. I'm on the verge of making the biggest change of my life."

"If you're not talking about marriage, I'm not interested."

"Come on, Monica, this is a big deal. I'm about to—"

"Forget it, I'm tired of being conned."

Click . . . then a dial tone.

Five o'clock and what was left to do? How was I going to decide? Take out paper and pencil and do some figuring: Basic inventory, rent . . . I'd been over the items a hundred times. I could afford it—at least for a while. I'd sell the Caddie, buy a Chevy and pocket the difference. If Peg helped, that'd make it all the easier. I didn't lack for nothing except the guts.

"May I speak to Daniel Klein?"

"This is Danny."

"Hello, there," she purred in a sugar-coated Southern accent, "this is Annabelle Hampton White from Richmond, Virginia."

"Jesus, Annabelle," I said, feeling a quick rise in spirit, "where are you? You sound so close."

"The Park Sheraton Hotel."

"You're kidding. I was just thinking about coming down to the Park Sheraton."

"Well, don't think, run, because I don't like waiting and I'm all alone."

The doll looked like Annabelle.

"I bought her yesterday at F.A.O. Schwarz. That's always the first place I visit in li'l ol' New York City. They have the most gorgeous dolls."

The doll had blonde hair, like Annabelle's, and was sitting up on the dresser, staring down at us. Annabelle had put on a couple of pounds since I'd seen her last, but that was okay. I liked women a little round. She was already modeling this red see-through nightie she'd bought at some naughty lingerie shop on Times Square.

"I got it with you in mind," she told me. "Chills ran through me when I thought of you looking at me wearing this."

"How's John?" I asked, knowing I only had an hour to decide whether I was going to see Pepper Katz, knowing that this woman had a pair of the most delectable tits on either side of the Mason Dixon line.

"John's back in Virginia. This little shopping trip is an anniversary present."

"Isn't he worried about you traveling alone? Isn't he jealous?"

"John and I have little in common, Danny boy, other than a mutual interest in certain male attributes."

So Cliff was right, I remembered, *John was queer*.

"We have an understanding," Annabelle continued, her eyes fixed below my belt, "that allows us both a long, large measure of enjoyment."

Nervously, I looked at my watch.

"You have somewhere to go, dahlin'?" she asked.

"Not for an hour."

"Then we don't have a second to waste, do we, pumpkin?"

I knew I was hungry, but Annabelle was downright famished. Her pussy had a mind and mouth of its own saying "Come on in, the water's fine!" I complied. I dove in. I slipped it in and flipped her over, I banged and bumped and boned her down until she could hardly breathe. But then, with a second wind, she came on like a wild person. She called me a cowboy. "Saddle up and ride, ride me rough." With her ass up in the air, I went through the backdoor, I went in deep, strong and steady, humping and pumping until she screamed and squeezed and shook all over... but me, there was no release for me. Hell, I wanted to give it up, wanted to let loose, wanted to explode, but nothing happened till I closed my eyes and thought about my Monica and then —just like that, I was home free.

"Damn, Danny boy," said Annabelle afterward. "I've never had a man like you before."

I smiled. I felt sure of myself. I told her I appreciated the compliment. I said I'd call her tomorrow. I got dressed and took an elevator to the tenth floor. At five to eight, I rang Pepper Katz's bell. At five after eight, I threw twelve hundred dollars in cash on a coffee table in his sitting room.

"Two months' rent at four hundred dollars a month," I said, "plus a four hundred dollar deposit. Take it or leave it."

He took it.

"I can't take it!" Pop was screaming. "You invite him over here only to aggravate me. Why must you aggravate me?"

Peg and I were sitting on the beach outside our house in Sea Gate. Mom and Pop were arguing inside. They were yelling so loud you could hear them in Far Rockaway. It was ten days after I'd put down a deposit on my store. Only Peg and Nate knew I had done it, but I hadn't been at work for a week and the freeze between me and my folks had gotten frostier. Mom had been calling me but I refused to say much. My position was that I hadn't quit, I'd been fired by Pop for not going to Nutley—and that was that.

"But I changed his mind," Mom had insisted.

"Yeah, but you can't change his personality. Besides, I don't care what anyone says, I ain't going to California."

"It's only for two months, Danny dear."

"I don't care if it's for two days. I'm not going."

"Then where does that leave you?"

"I'll figure out something," I'd said, lacking the nerve to tell her the truth.

Then the next Friday she'd called again. "Your father and I will be at Sea Gate on Sunday and I'm cooking for the whole family and you can't say no. Peggy's coming. You'll pick her up and you'll bring her and that's that."

"I'm telling them," Peggy had told me on the drive from the city. "I'm telling them that I'm getting married in September."

"Why don't you let me tell them about the store first?"

"That'll get them too upset."

"And your news won't?" I still hated the idea of Sis marrying Winnie the wimp, but she'd invested one thousand dollars with me and was being so terrific about the store I didn't have the heart to give her a hard time.

"I know my engagement is going to make them crazy."

"My store might make them crazier."

"Let's just play it by ear," Sis suggested.

The minute we arrived, Pop asked me, "Where the hell you been for the last week?"

"You kids go for a walk," Mom broke in. "Your father just got up. He's always a little irritable after a nap."

That had been an hour ago. Now we were back from our walk but weren't about to go into the house, with Pop still screaming.

"You'll act like a human being," Mom was yelling back, "because they're your children, they're your own flesh and blood, and they need you."

"*Your* children, *your* flesh and blood. They need *you*. I'm nothing but a checkbook to them, a guy who gives and gives but never gets."

"You get plenty."

"From who? From *you?* That's a laugh. From you I get, 'I'm tired, Myron,' from you I get, 'leave me alone, Myron, I got this headache, Myron.' From you I get blue balls—that's what I get."

"For God's sake, Myron, will you stop screaming? The children might be listening."

"Good. Let 'em know their mother's a fuckin' nun. Let 'em know their father has good reason to be aggravated."

I wanted to put my hands over Peg's ears like I used to do when we were kids and Mom and Pop were at each other's throats. Peg would start crying and I'd tell her not to worry, I'd say Mom and Pop were just playing a game. Now, fifteen years later, the game was still going on except I was tired of playing.

I looked out at the waves crashing against the shore. I felt like crashing my head against the side of the house. A half-hour later we were all sitting around the table eating baked chicken. Mom's potato kugel made me feel a little better, but I still wasn't feeling great. I loved the seaside, but I never did love our beach house. Mom had decorated it in Chinese modern. Strings of beads were hanging down everywhere, the furniture was black and green, the place was always dark. Mom was wearing this housecoat with Chinese emperors running around waving big swords. Her perfume was too strong and she thought Peggy's bathing suit was too skimpy. I agreed. Anita made her daughter wear one of her own housecoats—this one had giant yellow tulips—Pop was wearing a white terrycloth robe and I had on this blue-striped seersucker matching shirt-and-shorts outfit which I'd picked up down in Miami.

"Seersucker's gonna be the season's biggest dog," said Pop, ripping into a chicken leg. "Everyone thinks it's hot, but it's not. It's not a good-feeling fabric."

"It's cool and its comfortable," I said. "It's already a big item this summer."

"Down South maybe," Pop answered. "Not in New York, not in California."

"I wouldn't know about California."

"We don't have to talk about California," said Mom.

"Why not?" asked Pop. "What else do you got to talk about? I thought that's why everyone's here, to talk about California."

"I have no interest in California," said Peg.

"We're all making a mountain out of a molehill," put in Anita. "We're talking about a very enjoyable trip. Consider it a pleasure outing."

"Consider it dead," I said.

"I have something else to say," said Peg.

Silence.

"What is it, dear?"

"I'm getting married."

Silence.

Mom looked at Pop; Pop looked at Mom; Mom looked at me; I looked at Peg.

"I'm serious," Peg said. "I'm getting married in September. Winthrop and I want you to be there. We're having a private ceremony at City Hall with a small party afterward at the Savoy Plaza."

"And what about a rabbi?" Mom asked weakly, already knowing the answer.

"Winthrop's not Jewish and I'm not religious, so there's no need for a rabbi."

"Listen to her talk!" Pop exploded. "Listen to the big shot! 'No need!' Just who do you think you are, young lady! Who do you think provided for your needs the first twenty-one years of your life? You think you know it all, but you don't know nothing! And what about your children? Are you going to raise a family of *goyim?*"

"Better not to discuss this now," Mom advised.

"You were the one who wanted this discussion," Pop yelled at Mom, "so now you've got it. And you, my college-educated daughter, just what are you going to do for the rest of your life? Live off your rich Christian husband?"

"You don't even know the guy!" Peg fired back. "He's a perfectly wonderful man. He's a writer and a scholar with an encyclopedic knowledge of jazz. He's encouraging me to go on with my studies. He wants me to go to graduate school and I'm going in September."

"On his money, I hope," said Myron.

"On my own money and the money I'm going to make working with Danny in his store..."

"What store?" Mom and Pop asked at the same time, all eyes turning on me.

"I'm opening a store," I finally found the nerve to say.

"What kind of store?"

"A hat store."

Anita turned pale, Myron turned pink. "That's the craziest goddamn thing I've ever heard, even from you. What the hell do you know about retailing?"

"I'm a great salesman, you told me I was."

"Selling's one thing, managing's another. You're only twenty-two years old—"

"Twenty-three."

"You're wet behind the ears. I guarantee you, you're going to fall on your face."

"That's encouraging."

"Oy, Danny," said Mom. "You're gone too far this time. Both my babies have gone too far."

"*Out!*" screamed Myron, first pointing to me and Peg and then to the door. "*I want you both out of my sight.*"

"Don't say that, Myron," Mom pleaded, but by then he had already thrown a plate at my head. I ducked, and the dish crashed against the wall, chicken juice and moist chicken skin working their way down the black-and-gold Ming Dynasty wallpaper.

"I'm feeling sick," Mom said, running from the room. "I'm calling Doctor Shotkin . . ."

Maybe the shock was good for me. Maybe I needed the separation to concentrate on the Grand Opening. I peeked in on Annabelle one last time for a good-by poke, and that was it. Monica was still on the top of my mind—especially when I was on top of Annabelle—but Monica was nowhere to be found and I didn't have time for her or any other romantic bullshit 'cause August 1 was only a month away and August 1 was my Grand Opening.

I swung into action like a drummer for Duke Ellington. I was banging the tom toms, beating the snare and riding the high hat—all at once—running around town, buying fixtures and setting up my inventory. I put Sis in charge of records and didn't even mind when she wanted Win to help. After all, the guy knew something about jazz. Besides, I saw him and Peg as buyers offering their services for free.

Cliff loved the whole idea and said he'd work both sides of the aisle—hats and records—he didn't care, the Columbia jazz-joint gig was paying his rent and he and Peg were busy making in-store signs. Meanwhile, the big sign was my own personal assignment.

I found a neon place way the hell downtown near the Holland Tunnel. I walked in with my sketch—this big wide-brimmed hat covering a bunch of musical notes. "Make the hat green," I said, "and make the notes blue." He said it'd take six weeks; I promised him an extra five fins if he delivered in three. I was rolling.

Rode out to Allentown and bought some goods from Stetson. Back in the city, I did some super-shrewd buying from Adams and Dobbs. I was determined to put together the most fabulous fall line in Harlem.

Naturally the guys I bought from were old competitors. At first they didn't believe me. At first they figured it was some sort of spy scheme. But I showed them my lease and I showed them my money. Of course they all wanted to know one thing: "You gonna carry Myron Klein hats?" "Hell, yes," I said. Some of Myron's models were my own designs, and I was determined that this store was going to handle the best of everything...

"He'll handle my merchandise over my own dead body," Pop told Mom to tell me. "Why should I help a kid who's busy cutting his father's throat? Tell him I wouldn't sell him Myron Klein hats if he was the last customer on earth."

"Fair enough," I told Anita. "A clean break."

"This whole thing's breaking my heart," said Mom. "It's a terrible mistake, Danny, and it's not too late to change your mind. Your father's a very sick man."

"Don't I know?"

"I mean physically sick."

"He's got Doc Shotkin taking care of him."

"I don't appreciate your sarcasm. And besides, who's taking care of your books?"

"Sis. All those summers she helped you up at Pop's place, you taught her right. She's a math wiz like you."

"If you want help . . ."

"I'll call you, Mom, I promise I will."

"I'm giving you back the key to your apartment."

"Thanks. That'll make it easier for me."

"And your sister's wedding date, I don't want to know from it. Don't tell me. Act like it's never going to happen, and when it does, and if it does, act like it didn't."

Meanwhile, something did happen. I found out that Billy Eckstine was opening at the Apollo the same date as us—August 1. Through Pepper Katz I learned the name of Eckstine's manager and talked him into having Billy make an in-store appearance during our Grand Opening. How could he refuse? Mr. B roll-collared shirts were all the rage, and ever since Eckstine dropped his be-bop band he'd started making big money singing pop songs like "I Apologize" and "Everything I Have Is Yours." I got Arrow to pay for a promotional display on their shirts, I got MGM records to ship me a ton of Eckstine sides, and I even got the neighborhood newspapers to do articles so I wouldn't have to buy ads. I could see the customers already lined up around the block. Everyone loved Billy Eckstine.

"Eckstine was far more respected when he had his jazz

band," said Winnie. "As a pop artist, he'll be attracting the wrong crowd."

"Any crowd is the right crowd," I informed my future and schmucky brother-in-law. "We just need warm bodies coming through the door."

Peg and Winthrop were buying too heavy into bop, so I had to limit their budget and do some ordering myself. I was sure to secure an amply supply of Nat Cole's "Nature Boy," the smash hit of 1948, and Dinah Washington's "It's Too Soon to Know."

It wasn't too soon to see that the store was going to be gorgeous, with the walls painted a cool mint-green and the linoleum floor jet-black and the hat posters of homburgs and derbys and the poster of Fats Waller and Louis Jordan and dark wood display-cases and brand-new brass-plated light fixtures and the biggest cash register—all shiny and silver—that National made with the prettiest-sounding ring you can imagine.

The Friday morning before our Saturday opening the big sign arrived in a flatbed pickup truck and you should have seen the crowd it attracted. Cliff, Peg, Uncle Nate and me had been unpacking merchandise. At the last minute I decided that in order to compliment the Mr. B dress shirts I would carry a few lines of neckties. So we were displaying hand-painted Signets and Wembleys—gorgeous wide ties with fruits and flowers— when we heard the honk. We ran outside. You could see the giant hat and the happy musical notes floating underneath. I thought I'd explode with excitement. It took five hours for four men to put up the sign, and by the time they did it was dark. Thank God, 'cause then we could turn on the electricity and stand underneath and watch the green neon—when I say green, I mean green like money, green like grass, green like a pool table top—with the royal blue musical notes dancing under the hat, flashing on, flashing off, flashing on again, and then a long line in letters, alternating green-and-blue letters that read, "Blue Notes Under a Green Felt Hat." I felt so proud, especially when passersby stopped to stare, wondering what it all meant, looking in our window and seeing the Stetsons and the swing records and the big announcement about Mr. B who'd be there tomorrow at noon to sign shirt boxes and record sleeves with me in the middle, conducting the whole operation. It might have cost me most of my savings to get to this point, and sure, my reserves were low, but it was worth it, I knew it was, I knew it was going to work.

I must have stared at that sign for an hour before going back into the store and attending to last minute details. I personally washed the windows for the third time that day. Nobody minded working late. It was after midnight when Uncle Nate brought out a bottle of champagne. We raised our glasses and I got toasted. "To the boss," they said, and man, did that feel good! Until the phone rang. Who could be calling this time of night?

"Danny."

"Mom."

"I been calling your apartment, I been calling your sister's apartment, I been calling everywhere. I couldn't find the name of your store. Who knew it had this crazy name? Luckily I remembered you gave me the number but I didn't find the slip of paper until—"

"Mom," I interrupted her, "you sound terrible. What's wrong? Is Pop all right?"

"No one is all right. My sister Bea is dead."

I didn't get to meet Billy Eckstine. I heard all about it from Cliff and the three clerks I hired to help out. Cliff was in charge of the cash—there was no more honest man in America—and he promised to take pictures. I showed up at the end of the day when sales had shot over a thousand dollars, twice as high as my highest predictions. People really had been lined all up and down the block. I was happy, but mainly I was dazed. I'd spent the day with my mother picking out a casket and making arrangements for the burial. I couldn't believe that Aunt Bea was gone. Even harder to believe was the way she went.

Mom wouldn't tell me. All she said was that it was a freakish accident. "Why do you need to know any more?" she asked. When we got back from the funeral home, Mom went in her room to be alone and cry. Pop was sitting in the kitchen table over a cup of tea. He seemed approachable. For the first time in his life, he spoke softly. I felt like he needed to talk, like he needed to tell the story. "Your Aunt Bea was a little crazy," he said, "but she was a devoted worker. She'd never do to me what you're doing. She'd never dream of it. She had quirks. She liked to drink, but she was loyal. But it was those men, those truck drivers and dockworkers. Why she fooled with them, I don't know. What she saw in them, I don't understand. Last night she got drunk and went to see one of them. Which one, I don't know. He lived on Empire Boulevard and she went to visit him but he didn't hear his doorbell —he was asleep, maybe he was also drunk, I don't know—and she rang and rang and when that didn't work she decided to climb through his bedroom window—he lived on the ground floor close to the front door, I can't even tell you this guy's name—so there was your Aunt Bea climbing along this narrow ledge and you wouldn't think any harm could come of such a thing except she lost her footing and fell and cracked her head on one of the big stone lions. She cracked her head open and fractured her skull and was dead by the time the ambulance took her to the hospital. This is how your Aunt Bea died, Danny. This is what your mother must live with."

"She'll live in the kind deeds she did on earth," said the rabbi the next day in the funeral home. "She'll live forever in the hearts of those who loved her."

I loved her, I cried inside my heart. *I loved her because she loved me, because she loved jazz and the Dodgers and took me to prize fights in the Garden and she was the one who made me feel the most wanted at Pop's place, she was my biggest fan, she never deserted me, even when she found out about the store she called and said,"Look, I wouldn't lead my life the way you're leading your life, but you're you and I'm me and I can't help but wish you well, Danny, I know you'll succeed because of your wonderful personality and the way people love you. I'll be out to see the store soon, I promise. As soon as things settle down for your mother and father, I'll be out to see you." But now you can't come out, Aunt Bea, and I can't see you, I can't visit you in Coney Island and ride the Wonderwheel and taste the fries at Nathan's and feel like a kid and see you winking at those big guys, 'cause those big guys killed you, those big guys and those goddamn winks . . . why . . . why couldn't you be a little careful? . . . why'd you have to go drinking all the time? . . . I know you were different, no husband, no kids, you just did what you wanted to do, but you could have called me, you could have worked at my hat store instead of working for Myron in the trimming room and hearing him yell all day long except you didn't mind, you were happy, look at how all your girls are crying for you, everyone from Pop's place is here crying for you and coming over to me and hugging me and saying, "We miss you, Danny, we truly do," like I died or something, which is just how Pop is treating me, he'll always treat me that way until I come back crawling on my hands and knees. I can't do that, Aunt Bea, I can't do it for Mom or Pop or you or anyone else, I got to be out there alone or else I'll never know who I am or what I want, I know I want you back, I want you alive in your apartment listening to Billie Holiday records like you used to do, you taught me to love all this music, you loved me like you loved the music, no questions asked, no need to explain, just the beautiful music and the way you were a little crosseyed that gave you a funny little look but I didn't care, I loved the way you looked, I loved how you weren't scared of nothing, but maybe you were a little scared, maybe deep down you needed something that none of us could give . . .*

"She gave so much," the rabbi continued, "to those she loved."

In the limo to the cemetery we were stone silent—Mom, Pop, me and Peg. Not a word uttered. Pop kept a cigar in his mouth, unlit, I suppose, out of respect to Aunt Bea. Mom alternated from soft sobbing to outright crying. I held her for a while, then Peg held her, then even Myron held her hand.

By the side of the grave, when the casket was lowered in the ground, Mom lost control. "Bea! Bea! Didn't Mama tell you? Didn't Papa warn you?" Tears were running down her cheeks, down my cheeks, everyone crying, everyone sweating from the terrible heat and the sticky muggy air and the sadness. On the walk back to the limousine Ida Gruntstein and her husband Bernie came up and embraced Mom. Behind them were Doc and Evelyn Shotkin. Shotkin avoided looking at me before kissing my mother on the cheek.

"It was good of you to come, Louis," said Myron, patting Shotkin on the back. "You're more than a doctor, you're a real friend."

"BE-BOP BLUE$"

The first month in the new store wasn't easy. One minute I was thrilled—just to be there, mixing with the customers, fixing up dynamite displays of records and hats—and the next minute I felt like a traitor.

"If you really leave your father like this," Mom had said on the phone a few days after Aunt Bea's funeral, "then I'm leaving him too. The only reason I stayed with him is for you and Peggy."

"I don't think that's done us much good."

"Why are you talking that way to me? You used to be respectful, you used to—"

"Mom, I'm in the middle of waiting on a customer. I'm trying to run a business."

"What if you had your father's business to run?"

"No one will ever run Myron Klein Hats Limited except Myron Klein."

"I could change that. I'm *going* to change that. I'm going to convince Myron to retire and let you run the place."

206

"It's too late, Mom. I got my own place."

"It's never too late for me to help my children. Never."

Anita was making those kinds of calls to me at the rate of one a day. I tried not to be mean 'cause I knew that Mom, like me, was still suffering over Aunt Bea. But I also tried to explain that I had my own life to lead. I couldn't look back. Instead I was looking around the store and liking what I saw. The crossover concept was working.

Say, a cat came in looking for King Cole's "Hit That Jive, Jack." "Sure thing," I'd say. "Got it right here." Meanwhile, on the big in-store Victrola, I'd have Earl Bostic blowing "Hot Sauce Boss." "Sounds good," the customer would say. "Who's the horn player?" "I'd tell him, and while he was listening we'd wander over to the hat side of the store, where I'd show him a beauty of a blue-tone rough-felt snap-brim. "It's the sharpest thing for fall," I'd explain. He'd try it on while the automatic turntable changed over to Bull-moose Jackson jawin' 'bout "Big Fat Mamas Are Back in Style." The guy might walk out with four records and two felts. The atmosphere was right for buying, the goods were right for the neighborhood, and the sales were ringing up sweet and steady.

"It's because of your personality," Cliff would tell me when he came in to work at the store part-time. Cliff wasn't a super salesman; he was the low-key effective type. He liked that I had the balls to quit Pop's place. Cliff was the kind of guy who liked challenges.

"The place is a reflection of you, Dan," he said. "No wonder it's taking off. You've put your heart into it, and the people around here can feel that. You're a natural. They appreciate that you're sincere about what you sell."

* * *

"I think you're selling too much commercial music," Peg complained after we closed one night in late August.

"Now that's a fucked-up thing to say," I said to her. "This is commerce. How could anything be *too* commercial? That don't even make sense."

"True jazz fans resent their music being bastardized. I don't even know why you carry these jump 'n jive records."

"People like them—that's why. They dance to them."

"It's our obligation to promote the art—"

"Look, Peg," I cut her off, "those jukebox jump-songs you hate make up ninety percent of our record sales. I ain't arguing that the pure be-bop jazz isn't cool. It is. But be-bop isn't easy for the guy in the street. And the guy in the street is who we gotta sell—not some overeducated Ivy League critic living off his father's blue-chip stock—"

"Winthrop doesn't like you any more than you like him, Dan. That's why he hasn't been coming around here."

"I'm glad, he's the worst salesman I've ever seen. A customer asks him for some record and he gives 'em a fuckin' lecture on the history of music."

"I don't care what you say, the wedding's still on for next week."

"Did I say anything about the wedding? Have I been trying to talk you out of it?"

"Ever since I started dating him."

"But not recently. My new policy with you and Mom and Pop is live and let live."

"I resent your putting me in the same category as Mom and Pop," she said, sounding more off-the-wall than ever.

"I got a new business here, Peg. I'm just trying to make it work."

"It's working great, but it's also partly *my* business, and I have a right to express my views about the kind of music we sell."

"Your views, not Winnie the Pooh's views."

"There you go again . . ." Her eyes started to tear.

"Look, Sis . . ." I started to apologize.

"I'm marrying him . . . I don't care what you say, or what Mom or Pop say, or what anyone says . . ."

"No one's saying nothing. You sound like you're arguing with yourself."

"Furthermore," she said, before storming out, "I don't even want Clifford Summer to play at our reception. I don't want to see him there. I don't want to see you either. If I have to have a wedding party attended by strangers, that's just fine with me, because I love Winthrop, I love him and no one can tell me otherwise!"

Two days before the wedding and I hadn't heard a word from Peggy. I wasn't complaining because I was concentrating on work, designing a small ad featuring a few loss-leaders, sale items that might cost me some money but would generate traffic. It was ten in the morning and the store was empty when who should walk through the door but Benny X. Pushman. He had a new black rug on his head and a sleazy smile on his face.

"I already bought direct from Stetson," I told him as he surveyed the shop.

"Not bad, Danny, not bad at all. You got a sweet little operation here—with what the records. Clever, very clever."

"Look, Benny, I'd love to shmooze but I'm busy."

"Who came to shmooze? I came to sell."

"I already told you that I bought direct."

"I'm no longer with Stetson."

"This is news. Who hired you anyway?"

"Myron Klein."

I felt a long cold knife pierce through my heart. "I don't believe you," I said.

"I didn't believe the commission rate your old man offered. Highest in the business. How could I refuse? I'm making a small fortune. So I just wanted to stop by and let you know that I convinced Myron that if you want to carry our line, I'd be happy to write up the ticket. I got the samples out in the car..."

"Don't bother."

He left, but for the rest of the day I was plenty bothered. Jealousy and anger bubbled up inside my brain. When Annabelle Hampton White called to invite me to meet her for a weekend in Miami I didn't tell her that the idea made me sick, but it did. I just politely refused. I'd had enough with Annabelle and her dolls. There was a certain doll named Monica who I wanted to see, but she was on the *Twentieth Century Limited* in a private car with some producer rolling out to Hollywood. Before she left, she'd promised to come see the store but she broke her promise. Then at the last minute Peg changed her mind. She called on a Friday and apologized like crazy, making me promise to come to her wedding on Saturday. "You'll be my only relative there. You have to come."

"Okay," I said, "I'll come." But, believe me, I didn't want to.

I hate judges, I hate City Hall, I hate caviar, I hate prune-faced Protestants who look like they got a permanent case of constipation. I know I'm being unfair, but that's how I felt the day of Peg's wedding. I hated the whole fuckin' thing.

The judge looked like an undertaker. He sounded like he was pronouncing a death-sentence instead of uniting two people in holy matrimony. I wouldn't exactly call myself super-religious, but it still bothered me that no one mentioned God. And to tell you the truth, I wasn't thrilled that my sister wasn't being married by a rabbi. I could feel Mom and Pop's icy absence.

No matter, standing next to Sis, I was the sole representative of our family. I guess you could say that I gave her away. Standing next to Winnie were his parents, stiff as their son, who looked like they'd come over on the *Mayflower*—tall, straight-backed, blue-eyed, giving me small tight smiles and looks like I was a pushcart peddler.

The reception at the Savoy Plaza was small and boring. I knew a couple of Peg's friends from Barnard, but no one else. I felt out of place. Instead of a band, they had a chamber music quartet. Instead of a spread with chopped liver and rare roast beef, they had wimpy crackers and caviar. They didn't have enough champagne and the wedding cake was half the size it should have been. I imagined my mother saying, "Typical gentile wedding." There were pink doilies and a couple of pale-faced waiters who looked like they were doing you a favor refilling your glass. It was all real sophisticated with lots of snotty chit-chat and everyone saying everything with perfect pronunciation.

Peg had her hair up and she looked beautiful except she wasn't wearing a white wedding dress, she was wearing a navy blue suit with pearls and matching blue pumps because I guess that was also supposed to be sophisticated. She kept coming over to me and squeezing my hand kissing my cheek and asking me if I was happy for her and I lied, I said I was. But I didn't see happiness in her eyes; I didn't feel joy; I didn't see her looking at Winnie with love or even passion. I just saw the whole thing as a way for her to escape Mom and Pop and Brooklyn and the cornball Chinese modern decor in Sea Gate.

It wasn't a happy wedding. No one got loud. No one got drunk. No one danced. No one hardly smiled. I was back at my place by five o'clock. I tried to listen to Drew Pearson presenting "This Is Your FBI"—my favorite radio program— but couldn't concentrate. From my living room I stood and stared at the East River, thinking of Aunt Bea, thinking of how life just flows by—people live, people die, murder, marriage, getting rich, going broke, it all just flows by.

I don't know why, but that same night I decided I no longer wanted to live in that apartment. I decided I wanted to move, to be closer to the store and the people who were giving me my livelihood. I decided to get a place up in Harlem.

By the end of September I was on Riverside Drive near 135th Street. I still had a view of a river—this time it was the Hudson—my apartment was a little smaller than on the East Side but decorated to my taste, not Mom's. I framed a bunch of record posters the promo guys gave me for the store. It was beautiful coming home and seeing Billie Holiday on my wall —she always made me think of Aunt Bea—and Jack McVea, Slim Gaillard, Hazel Scott and Rose "Chi Chi" Murphy. A photograph of the front of the store on opening day hung in my hallway, greeting you just as you came through the door. The furniture was simple and comfortable, not big and fancy like Mom liked. I sold the grand piano and bought an upright so Cliff would have something to play when he came over. And he came over a lot, especially after his gig near Columbia dried up. Winthrop was busy setting up different recording sessions, but most of them never materialized and those that did didn't pay shit.

Peg was busy at graduate school. Once in a while she came by the store just to see me or chat with Cliff, who was now working there nearly every day. Sis said that she and Winnie were living down near Gramercy Park. I never did go see their apartment. I no longer liked Win coming around the store, and he knew it. I supposed he didn't want me around his apartment.

Living in Harlem had me happier than I'd been in a long time. Being around the colored all the time made me feel secure. It was like living in a foreign country, but a country where I felt more comfortable, where I belonged, where no one made any demands of me and I always felt wanted. I was offering people things *they* wanted—swinging music and sharp-styled hats.

Sure, I'll admit I was a little lonely. With Monica in California and me working in the store night and day, I hardly had time for the ladies. All my energy went into the business, which was paying off. Sales were growing. I was even making a small profit. I was months ahead of my projections. I was proud of myself, although once in a while something ugly might happen which would set me back for weeks.

Example:

Five o'clock on a rainy Tuesday afternoon and I'm alone. Cliff's off today and the woman I got helping me has gone home a little early. Guy comes in. Big guy with broad shoulders and hard eyes. He's dressed to kill. I could feel he has an attitude, but I also figure he might be good for a big sale.

"Heard the new Ella side?" I ask him.

"Ella who?"

"Ella Fitzgerald, who do you think?"

"You talk like you know the lady."

"I haven't had the pleasure."

"But you sure as shit don't mind making money off her, do you?"

"What are you talking about? She makes money when I sell her records. We both make out."

"Only difference is, you and the record companies make out like bandits. Fuckin' exploiters, that's what I'd call you."

"Hey, wait a minute, buddy. I don't exploit, I sell."

"You Jewish, ain't you?"

"What does that have to do with anything?"

"Ashamed to admit it?"

"Hell no, I ain't ashamed of nothing."

"I'd be real goddamned ashamed if I was you."

"Look, pal—"

"I ain't no pal of yours. I ain't no pal of no Jews who buy up our neighborhoods and sell us back our own music at twice the price it should be."

"Get the fuck outta my store," I shouted, coming around the counter, not caring how big the bastard was.

"Fuck you," he spits.

"Fuck *you*," I spit back.

And before I know it, he rips me with a right to my jaw.

I wish I could tell you otherwise—that I flattened the bum —but the truth is he was out of the store before I came to.

It was weird. He didn't steal money or merchandise—it was just hit and run—but I didn't care; I wanted to find him and press charges anyway.

"Don't," Cliff advised me when he found out what had happened. "You'll just stir up a hornet's nest. Stay cool. Chalk it up to experience and remember—assholes come in all colors."

Cliff was a comfort. Along with Uncle Nate—who was doing a little light delivery work for me—Cliff was really my only pal. When I went down South, he'd been with me. When I came back and opened the store, he'd been by my side. He'd helped my career, and I felt bad that I hadn't been paying enough attention to his. It's just that the shop, like a new baby, needed lots of tender loving care. Cliff understood. Cliff helped me care for the baby. Besides, he had a feeling— and so did I—that our fates were hooked up. We were brothers. Ever since he came back to New York he seemed more patient, less angry about the music scene. "Things are working out," he liked to say. Cliff knew that I loved his company, but he also knew I was never deep-down happy with him working as a salesman. After all, the guy was a genius, and ever since I heard him last December—it'd been eleven months—I wanted to help him any way I could.

This is why the record side of the store helped a lot. By the end of October I had a good feeling for what was selling and what was stiffing. It was a tailor-made market-test situation. Meanwhile, my cash flow was improving and I promised my-self—and Cliff—that if the Christmas selling season met our projections, Danny Klein was going to make another move— this one upstairs.

See, from time to time Pepper Katz dropped by to sniff around. Naturally he was pleased with what I'd done, though he'd be the last guy on earth to ever tell me. Instead, he complained about all the tenants moving out on him. He mentioned the insurance firm on the second floor above the store. He said that their lease was up and they weren't renewing.

I got to thinking. I got to remembering. I remembered that record store in Newark where Sis and Win had taken me and Cliff. Above the store was a studio. *How about that?* I asked myself. *How about investing a little money in a small recording studio where not only Cliff could record, but we could find some other talent and maybe start turning out hit records?*

"Lousy idea," said Uncle Nate, shaking his head. "Out and out lousy."

It was a chilly Sunday morning and we were down on the Lower East Side having breakfast in the back of Nushky Binder's butcher shop. Nushky was also a bookie and an old pal of Nate's. His wife made us a beautiful plate of scrambled lox, onions and eggs and a fresh pot of coffee. The bagels were piping hot. Nushky treated us like royalty which wasn't surprising since over the years Nate—and indirectly me—contributed heavily to this guy's financial well-being.

On the subway coming downtown I'd read through the *World-Telegram*, which was filled with predictions about next week's presidential elections. I was pulling for Truman—if he was good enough for FDR, he was good enough for me—but the pollsters were picking Dewey. I was awfully glad, though, to read at least one piece of good news: the record ban was about to end.

"See," I explained to Nate, "everyone's gonna start recording again. I'm telling you, there's lots of money to be made."

"I don't see you making it."

"Why not?"

"You're a *shmatah* salesman, not a music man."

"Are you kidding? I'm grossing nearly as much with the records as the hats."

"But now you're talking manufacturing, you're talking about making records, not just selling them. That's risky, kid."

"Not if you got an ear for what the public's buying."

"The public's fickle. I don't see you taking what little money you're making and throwing it away on that colored guy. That's your plan, ain't it?"

"I'm not planning on throwing anything away. I believe in that guy."

"Look," said Nate, putting away his second serving of lox, onions and eggs, "I got something, a better proposition for you. I got a sweet little situation right around here on Eldridge Street where we can both make a fortune."

"What's on Eldridge Street?"

"A linen store—sheets, pillowcases, towels, chenille bedspreads, the works. This guy's in debt up to his ears. He's willing to sell for a song, inventory and all."

"I don't want a linen store. Besides, how would I run a place up in Harlem and a shop downtown?"

"That's the beauty part—you wouldn't have to. I'd run it for you."

I saw this coming; I would try to be gentle but I knew it wasn't going to be easy.

"I don't think it's the right move for me, Uncle Nate."

"Didn't I put you into your hat store? Didn't I pick a winner? Well, this one's even better. I can smell the profits."

"I don't want to argue with you 'cause you're probably right. But I figure it like this—I gotta believe in what I sell."

"This guy carries only top quality. What's not to believe?"

"I gotta do more than believe, Uncle Nate. I gotta care about what I'm doing and what I'm selling. You taught me that."

"I just thought we'd be good partners, that's all," he said, his head hanging down like a big bulldog.

I felt like shit, even though I also felt like I was being manipulated by another relative. I loved Uncle Nate, but maybe I loved my new-found independence more. I'd fought to be free from my family, and I didn't want to give in now. I also knew that this linen shop business would drain me dry. I hated hurting my uncle's feelings, but self-preservation came first. I felt myself getting tougher, which, when it came to my family, was definitely something new. First I turned down my father, now my uncle. Was this really me? The more we talked, the more convinced I became.

"I'm sorry, Uncle Nate, I really am. But I got my own program now. I'm turning my store into a success, and I'm going to do the same thing with this recording studio. I know what I'm doing."

"I wish you luck, kid. I just hope you ain't biting off more than you can chew."

He slurped down his coffee and kissed me on the cheek before getting up to leave. His breath didn't smell great. "Put it on my tab," he said to Nushky on his way out. I couldn't help but think that this was the first time in ages he hadn't hit me up for a loan. That made me feel good—and also bad.

Leaving Binder's butcher shop, walking around the Lower East Side, I still felt bad. Feeling bad, I guess, 'cause Uncle Nate just turned and left like he no longer needed me. Well, wasn't that what I wanted? Wasn't I happy not to be in the middle of all this fuckin' family fighting? Didn't I want to avoid the endless world war between Mom and Pop? Wasn't it good that I could finally tell Uncle Nate no?

I didn't know. This old Jewish neighborhood was changing my mood, was making me think of all my relatives, the women in the trimming room, the people who really cared for me. Wasn't family a precious thing? And wasn't I throwing it away? Old women shlepping home bags of groceries, dark-haired schoolgirls who looked like my sister—playing stoop-ball, jumping rope—junkmen and jewelers with the same voice as Pop, women with the same eyes as Mom. I was a long, long way from Harlem.

I decided to walk. The sky was charcoal gray, and the day was growing bitter cold. The paper said it might be the first snow of the year. I liked winter. Chilly weather got me moving faster, working harder. I was looking forward to the holidays, to big sales and new challenges. Walking through Greenwich Village, I felt free. I didn't need Mom, didn't need Pop. Sitting on a bench in Washington Square Park, I watched a potbellied artist painting a skinny sparrow. The bird in the picture looked so lonely. The guy must have felt sorry for the sparrow. I got up and walked on, feeling a little sorry for myself. Being cut off from everyone wasn't easy. Many was the time I was tempted to show up at Pop's place and ask what I could do for him, just like I used to ask when I was a kid. Many was the time I was tempted to call Mom and see if she was all right. It had been two months without a word, but I intended to keep it that way. After all, they'd never even been by to see my store. It was like I had this newborn baby they were ignoring. They'd never seen the green neon hat and the blue musical notes. They didn't even know I was making a go of it. They hadn't talked to Peg since her marriage. I suppose they blamed me for that too.

I stopped to look at the Flatiron Building. Little flakes of snow started falling on my face. It felt good. The weather was raw. I felt raw. The weird shape of the building made me wish I had a camera. It was almost like the building was talking to me, saying, "I'm different, you're different, we're all different."

It's okay to be different, I thought as I wandered over to Gramercy Park. It was such a tiny park, so quaint and pretty, like something out of a storybook. In the back of my mind I remembered Peg's address. It was right off the park. I stopped at the apartment building and saw that, sure enough, "Carrington" was apartment 6C. But what did I want with Peg? What did I need to see my sister for? Maybe I felt bad for putting down Nate; maybe I just needed a little family contact. I started to ring the bell but stopped myself. I walked away, but then I walked back. This time I pressed the buzzer. What was wrong with wanting to see my sister?

"Danny, I'm happy to see you," she said when she opened the door. "We were just having a little brunch."

"I see you got company. I don't want to crash your party."

"Don't be silly. Come on in. I've been thinking about you, I've been meaning to call."

Her apartment had all these modern paintings, abstract stuff showing women with three eyes and four mouths. There were books everywhere and strange-sounding jazz playing on the phono.

"Thelonious Monk," said my brother-in-law, who coldly introduced me to their friends. Win said that the black-bearded guy was a writer with a magazine I hadn't heard of, much less read. The women were smoking cigarettes. One of them was thin, the other had full lips and curvy hips. Her name was Joyce and she made me think of Monica even though Monica wasn't a professor of psychology at the New School for Social Research and Joyce was.

"What do you do?" asked Joyce, who couldn't have been older than thirty. She had wavy brown hair that fell to her shoulders.

"Sell hats."

"Oh," said the skinny lady, acting like I'd just cut a fart.

Joyce, though, looked interested. I was interested in her healthy-looking chest.

"Danny also sells jazz records," Peg chimed in. "My brother has his own store with an original name, a terrific sign, and a fabulous record department."

Sis was trying to sound chipper, but deep down I thought she looked sort of lost. She was serving a nice lunch, she had her hair down and was wearing an artsy outfit—a soft gray cashmere sweater over black slacks, a silver necklace and long dangling earrings—she was keeping up with everyone's conversation, but somehow she didn't seem to belong in her own house.

"I hear you have a book contract," one of the writers said to Win. "Something about a history of jazz."

"It's a major work," Peggy answered for her husband. "We're very enthusiastic about it."

"Peg's pleased because she'll be helping me with the research," said Win, like he was throwing the dog a bone. "Emphasis will be placed on the last decade, the period of jazz that I consider absolutely crucial and woefully misunderstood. There must be a line distinguishing true jazz from what passes as jazz in the popular press—the sub-par products pandering to the public's basest taste."

That's when I knew it was time to leave.

"Aren't you going to eat anything, Danny?" Sis wanted to know.

"Just wanted to stop in and see your place, baby. It's real pretty, and so are you."

"I'll be up to the store soon. Say hi to Cliff."

"Will do."

Walked some more till I got cold and took the A-train home. The minute I walked out of the subway station into the rhythm of Harlem, I felt better. White snowflakes were falling on black New York. The minute I walked into my apartment and heard Cliff playing the piano, I was happier. The minute I smelled the scent of sticky sweet reefer, I knew I wanted to get fucked-up myself. I wanted to forget the family shit and just fly with the music, just sit back and watch Cliff's eight fingers flying over keys.

"Still remember 'Be-Bop Blues'?" I asked him.

"Got the melody, got the beat, but you got the words."

"Not only that, my man," I said, "but I got the plan."

I didn't wait till the end of the holiday selling season. Truman surprised Dewey and all the wiseguys, and for the first two weeks of November my sales surprised me. Customer traffic was so heavy I had to hire more help. Business was so good I called Pepper and told him that, come December 1, I wanted to lease the space above the store on a month-to-month basis.

"What are you gonna use it for?"

"Recording studio."

"What do you know about a recording studio?"

"You know, Pepper, every time I want to give you more money, you find a way to make me feel bad about it. What is it with you?"

"I'll be happy to take your money, but the music business happens to be something I know particularly well. You don't got the teeth for it, Klein."

"We'll see," I snapped, and then proceeded to cut a sweetheart of a deal.

I planned the session for December 5. I had a good feeling about that date, not just because it was my twenty-fourth birthday, but because that was the night, a year ago, I'd heard

Cliff play for the first time, the same night Joe Louis jolted Jersey Joe.

It didn't take much time to convert the insurance office to a basic studio. We put in sound-proofing and bought ourselves a Webcor tape recorder with a decent mike. Cliff found a guy who knew something about sound. Cliff also found a bass player, guitarist, drummer and tenor saxist. I wanted a slick rocking sound. I was convinced that "Be-Bop Blues" was a hit.

See, I had the upright piano taken from my apartment to the store before moving it upstairs to the studio. While it was in the shop I'd have Cliff play "Be-Bop Blues" for the customers. Everyone loved it. Everyone said, "Where's the record? I wanna buy the record." Which was all the proof I needed.

The day of the session was a little strange for me. It was my first birthday outside the family. Mom called, but she was cool as ice. We were on and off the phone in less than a minute.

"I haven't forgotten you. I'll never forget you," she said, sounding like I was already dead. Far as my personal life or Peg's, she didn't ask a single question.

Hadn't heard from Pop. Not even from Uncle Nate. They were pissed that I'd pushed them out of my life, but at least they could have sent a card. Peg's silence surprised me the most. She was always with me on my birthday, just like I was with her on hers. It was a tradition that we'd told each other we'd always honor. But here it was, six P.M. and I might as well have been an orphan for all the family attention I was getting.

Then at six-thirty Sis walked into the store. Man, was I happy to see her! She was all bundled up in this little fur coat and I was surprised that instead of Winnie she had her friend Joyce with her.

"We were over at Columbia," said Sis, "and I couldn't let the day go by without seeing you."

She gave me a big hug, and Joyce was all smiles. Joyce had

this wavy brown hair and those full lips and when she took off
her long trench coat I refamiliarized myself with her fantastic
figure.

"I'd heard so much about your store," she said, "I had to see
it for myself."

"Glad you came by," I told her. "You're both just in time for
my birthday party."

"Here in the store?" Peg asked.

"Upstairs in our little recording studio."

"What time are you recording Clifford tonight?"

"How'd you know about that?"

"Clifford told me."

"When?"

"Last week. Is there a law against our talking?"

"He didn't tell me he told you."

"Well, are we invited to the session or aren't we?" asked Sis.

"Sure, you're invited. But if you hate commercial records,
then you've come to the wrong place, 'cause we're making
this one as commercial as commercial can be."

"Clifford said to be open-minded."

"And I'm easy," said Joyce, letting me know that, even
though she was a psych prof and I owned a hat store, she liked
my style.

"Before I forget," said Peg, "let me give you your present."

She reached in her purse and pulled out a little box wrapped
up with a green bow. A little note on top read, "To the best
brother in the world." Inside was a tie pin in the shape of a hat.
The hat was outlined with a dozen sparkling diamonds.

"I'm wearing it every day," I promised her. "I swear, I'm
wearing it every day for the rest of my life. It's gorgeous."

It was going to be a happy birthday after all.

*   *   *

The musicians were already upstairs tuning up. They were black, we were white and the engineer was Chinese. A regular United Nations. Cliff was warming up the piano. The minute he saw Peg his face lit up. They gave each other a kiss, and I could tell he'd probably sing and play a little better 'cause Sis was around. The way they hugged used to bother me, but now I saw that if Cliff had become a brother to me, Peg had become a sister to him. Anyway, I was sure glad she left Winnie the Pooh at home. He'd hate this session.

Joyce loved it. Sis whispered that she'd been asking about me ever since we met at Peg's place. She told Sis that I was "terribly cute."

The Chinese engineer knew what he was doing, adjusting the level and placing the musicians for the right blend. We were doing two songs—"Be-Bop Blues" and a "B" side, a pretty King Cole-styled ballad Cliff had written called "Stars in Your Eyes."

First, Cliff ran down "Be-Bop" for the boys. He had an arrangement already worked out in his head. Nothing was written down. I was a little worried, but the cats were such quick studies they had the tune down in a hot minute And believe me, it *was* hot—the tenor honking, the guitarist riffing, the bassist thumping, the drummer back-beating.

"All right," said Cliff, taking command, looking especially dashing in a red shirt and loose-fitting blue-pleated trousers, "let's knock this sucker out."

He sang:

> *Have you felt the beat?*
> *Have you heard the news?*
> *The newest craze is the be-bop blues*

The notes are flying
The rhythm's fast
Folks are saying it'll never last

But up in Harlem
Where swing's the king
Be-bop blues is the newest thing

Be-bop blues will get you moving
Be-bop blues so nice and soothing
Be-bop blues will move your soul
Be-bop blues really rocks and rolls
I say, be-bop blues really rocks and rolls

I loved the first take; I thought it was fuckin' brilliant; Cliff's voice was rough and smooth, silky and scratchy all at the same time; the tune jumped like a jackrabbit. You couldn't help but pop your fingers and tap your feet.

But Cliff wasn't satisfied.

"One more time," he told the sound man.

The second time was even better. The tenor saxist played a break that sounded like a roaring lion. Cliff was on fire, all grits and guts.

When they were through I said, "I know it's a smash."

"Are you sure you want to use the term 'be-bop'?" Sis asked. "This really isn't a be-bop song at all."

"That's the point," I said. "We just use 'be-bop' like a funny phrase, something that sounds hot and happy. Maybe critics think of be-bop as some pure artsy thing, but the average guy just hears the word and thinks, 'Hey, that sounds cute, that's jazzy.'"

"I think Danny has a point," said Joyce. "We academics can get awfully pedantic sometimes."

"What does that mean?" I wanted to know.

"Preachy and teachy," said Cliff, winking at Peg.

"Now for the love song," I said. "Wait till you girls hear the love song."

The tenor player switched to alto as Cliff switched gears, going from a rockin' rhythm to a sugar-sweet love-you-down baby ballad.

"Stars in your eyes," he sang, "glowing like gold . . . stars in your eyes . . . so soft yet so bold . . ."

By the way Joyce and Peg were listening, I could see that the man was making his point. Cliff was one fine crooner. I pointed out, though, that this was the "B" side, but the girls were convinced that the love song was the winner.

"The way he sings," said Joyce, "just melts my heart. He's so sincere."

"I sincerely think that the money song is 'Be-bop,'" I insisted, happy the session had gone so well.

I paid the sidemen and Chinaman and offered to give the girls a ride home.

"I live out in Forest Hills," said Joyce. "I hate to bother you."

"No bother," I insisted, secretly surveying her shapely legs and deciding what else I wanted for my birthday.

"I've gotta run down to the Village," said Cliff, sensing my plan of action. "I'll take Peggy home."

Rather than run out to Queens right away, I took a chance and asked Joyce whether she'd like a little birthday champagne back at my place.

"Why not?" was her reply.

I was ready, but also a little worried. Joyce was something new for me. I didn't have much experience with college girls, much less college teachers. Besides, she was probably five years older than me. But Joyce was careful to make me comfortable. Driving over to my apartment, she let me know how much she was enjoying the evening. "Never having seen a recording session before," she said, "this has been a treat."

Thinking of treats, uncorking the bottle in the kitchen, eyeing Joyce sitting on my living room couch, I realized that I'd underestimated her legs. They weren't good; they were sensational. Her fleshy calves had just the right curve. Beneath her tight-fitting dark knit dress I could see the sweet swell of her hips. Her nose was a little on the large size, but that didn't bother me because her brown eyes were beautiful, her skin silky smooth. Her little dimples seemed to be smiling at me. I also liked the beauty mark on her left cheek. She wore square-shaped glasses that gave away her profession, but when I came in with the champagne she took them off. That got me excited.

We toasted my birthday and started sipping. She quickly drained her glass dry and I quickly poured her more.

"What prompted you to open your own hat and record store?" she asked.

"A guy's gotta make a living somehow."

"It's such an interesting combination, though. Do you think it's a reflection of your own personality?"

"You trying to get psychological or something?" I asked.

She laughed. "I'm sorry if I sound stuffy. It's an occupational hazard. I wasn't really trying to analyze you."

"Lemme ask you a question, then. How'd a nice girl like you wind up teaching college when you got the body of a model?"

"Why, thank you," she said, smiling broadly. "I've never been asked that question before. I suppose the answer is that I'm interested in human behavior, so psychology was a logical major. The interest lasted through five years of graduate school. With a Ph.D. in psych, my occupational options were limited. A teaching job came up, so I took it."

"Do you like it?"

"I'm the only female on staff, and I definitely feel resentment from my male colleagues. But I manage."

"They resent you 'cause you're smart. Smart women make men nervous."

"You don't seem nervous."

"That's 'cause you can't look inside me. Inside I'm pretty nervous."

"Why would that be?"

"'Cause I figure you got me figured out."

"And why would that bother you?"

"You'd know what was on my mind."

"And why would that bother me?"

"You ain't supposed to know."

"But what if I told you that the same thing was on my mind?"

"See, that's why you make men nervous. You're too smart. You ain't supposed to say things like that."

"I'm not supposed to be sincere?"

"Sex doesn't have to do with being sincere," I said.

"Who said anything about sex?"

"I did and you did. Haven't we been talking about sex?"

"Is sex on your mind?"

"We were talking about your mind, not mine."

"But I don't consider sex mental. I consider it instinctive."

"Yeah, that's how I look at it too."

"And yes, I do have strong sexual instincts."

"No lady has ever put it to me like that before."

"No lady has ever told you that she finds you sexually attractive?"

"It ain't anything to really talk about with a lady. It's just something to do."

"Well, then, let's do it."

"Just like that?"

"Just like that."

Just like that we were in my bedroom and Joyce was in my arms. Kissing her mouth, her tongue felt on fire. The prof was steaming hot. I loved running my hands over her sheer nylons, I loved unbuttoning her buttons and feeling her bra, feeling under her bra, feeling under her dress, feeling her moist, feeling her flow, feeling her feeling me, feeling and smelling and losing myself in her perfume and her panties and the way she arched her back and gave it up so easy—God bless women who give it up easy—no pretending, no games like Annabelle, no demands like Monica, just letting me love her, letting me know that I was doing it good, so good and so long-lasting, wide open and soft moaning, no screaming or scratching but steady encouragement and ready for more, hotter and harder and higher and lower, backwards and forwards and geared up to get up and stay up till I let loose with the juice—damn did I come!—with Joyce happy to have me so deep inside.

"Happy birthday," she said.

"You made it happy."

"You made it better than anyone ever has before."

"That's music to my ears."

Music was playing on the radio, Sinatra singing "Night and Day" and Joyce taking her time getting dressed.

"You can stay if you want . . . I mean, I'd like you to stay."

"Is this someone you know?" she asked, pointing to a picture of Monica from a Hollywood paper. It was an ad Monica had sent for the B movie she'd made, *White Slaves*. She wasn't wearing much.

"Monica Montgomery. Yeah, she's a friend."

"I hate to make you drive me all the way to Queens, but if you wouldn't mind . . ."

"Wouldn't mind at all."

Going over the Queensboro Bridge I broke the long silence between us. "This is a funny thing to say, Joyce, but I don't even know your last name."

"Palmer. What was that actress's name again?"

"Monica."

"Monica Montgomery. Is that her real name?"

"I'm not sure," I said, amazed at how dames have this way of smelling each other out. "Why do you care?"

"You seem to care enough to keep her picture next to your bed."

"I haven't seen her in months. She's living in L.A."

"She cuts quite a figure."

Broads, I tell myself, *even brainy broads start getting jealous after one friendly fuck.*

"That's all right," she said when I drove up to her Forest Hills apartment building, "you don't have to walk me to the door."

"I don't mind."

"It'd be better if you didn't. It's three A.M., and there's a good chance my husband might be looking out the window."

"Why didn't you tell me the bitch was married?"

"Where do you come off calling her a bitch? She's a professor and a close friend of mine and Win's—"

"You set me up with her. She told me she thought I was cute. You were practically pimping for her."

"I was doing nothing of the kind," Peg protested over the phone. "We were at a lecture together, I told her I was going to see you, she said she found you fascinating so I invited her to come along. You took over from there."

"I was sandbagged."

"If it was painful I'm sorry."

"It wasn't painful, I just hate being tricked."

"Look, you're both adults. And the truth is that she's in the middle of a miserable marriage."

"Which I ain't interested in getting in the middle of myself."

"Let's just forget the whole thing."

"I don't like being used."

"Remember in Miami Beach when you set me up with that greaseball salesman?"

"He wasn't a greaseball and he wasn't a salesman. He owned his own store and he wasn't married."

"It's the same principle. Only Joyce is a quality person."

"Barry Gruen's the guy's name and he carried quality goods."

"I don't exactly consider Monica Montgomery a high-quality actress."

"How do you know? You've never seen her act."

"Why are we fighting?"

"'Cause you're doing what Mom does. You're grading my girlfriends, you're telling me which ones are good for me and which ones aren't. I hate that."

"And what about your attitude toward Winthrop?"

"You're right. We shouldn't be fighting. We should be staying the hell out of each other's hair."

And with that, I hung up.

I heard the record in the mastering studio and suddenly my mind was clear, my anger gone.

Cliff was standing next to me, listening carefully to the sounds of his own making.

"Are you as sure as I am?" I asked him.

"Baby brother, I don't see how we can miss," he said, his mouth breaking into a broad smile.

The week before Christmas, the day the actual record arrived, I'd already bought big-ass blaring loudspeakers to hang outside the front door of the store. I was prepared to blast the neighborhood. I also had a list of the New York disc jockeys and appointments to see every one of them. Not only that, I'd hired a salesman to help me sell the side to area record stores. See, I was setting up my own little label—Green Felt Records. (I'd wanted to call it Blue Note, but someone was already using the name.)

We were set for sizzling sales in every department. I merchandized the store with special tie-and-scarf displays. Wreaths and holly were hanging everywhere. I even moved the upright piano back into the record department and had Cliff, sounding smoother than Bing, singing swing versions of "White Christmas."

Then at high noon I heard the honk of the delivery truck and ran out to meet it. Out in the freezing cold, I unloaded the cartons myself. Inside, me and Cliff unpacked the boxes like little kids ripping open Christmas presents. Inside were five hundred copies of "Be-Bop Blues." I picked up the weighty 78 RPM shellac record and kissed it; I held it in my hand like a precious jewel. The green label with the hat in the corner—designed by me—looked like a million bucks. "Be-Bop Blues," it read, "vocal by Clifford Summer." Man, this side was something to see!

I immediately put it on and cranked it up so you could hear Cliff singing—"Have you felt the beat? Have you heard the news? The newest craze is the be-bop blues"—all up and down 125th Street. By five o'clock I'd sold fifty copies. The thing was taking off like a rocket.

In the next six days, with the store jammed with Christmas shoppers, we sold another three hundred sides.

"It's a goddamn miracle," Pepper Katz had to admit, Pepper Katz who doesn't have a good word to say about anything. "Look, kid, you better let me distribute this record for you before you get burned. I've done this kind of thing before."

"Got it all under control, Pepper," I told him. "Got five thousand copies out in New York City alone."

"But what about Philly and Chicago? What about L.A.? How you gonna take it national?" he asked, his long skinny fingers scratching his billiard-bald head.

"Do I look like a schmuck? I'm already talking to Decca about that. I'm gonna break it locally, though, so I can make a sweeter distribution deal."

"Watch out," warned Katz, his big bug eyes widening. "This business is run by barracudas. A little guppy like you don't stand a chance."

"Thanks for the encouragement."

"I ain't being discouraging, I'm just being real. If I didn't know your Uncle Nate I wouldn't care. But I told him I'd look out for you."

"Look at this radio play report," I said. "Three more big-time deejays are playing it."

"You got yourself something," Pepper admitted. "Just watch out it don't bite you in the ass."

HAPPY NEW YEAR!

I decided to throw a party, a wing-dinger. I had to do it on short notice but it didn't matter. I was moving so fast I could have planned a king's coronation in a couple of days, which is what it was: Cliff's coronation. We'd sold over three thousand units and had ordered another five thousand from the factory.

I was flipping out, running from record stores to radio stations back to my own store where I was selling hats and hustling on the phone and watching the miracle mushroom. Everyone'd been telling me that I didn't know what I was doing, and here I was setting the world on fire. I almost called Mom and Pop, just to let them know, but why did I need to brag? They'd find out in due time.

The New Year's Eve blast was all set. I told my best customers and friends to come by my place any time after nine. I was ringing in 1949 in a big way. I'd bought myself a double-breasted bottle-green flannel suit and rousing red tie just for the occasion. I didn't have a date, but who needed one? I was still the host with the most. I'd taken a chance and changed my life and, goddamnit, I was making it.

"Glad you could make it," I told Horace Austin, my neighbor from down the hall, a black social worker with degrees from Howard University and the personality of a prince—smart and sincere.

Cliff arrived next with a letter from his mom in Alabama. She'd gotten the record and was thrilled. "Tell Danny," wrote Marvis, "that the Lord's light is shining on him. I'm so proud of you both."

A couple of fine foxes who owned their own beauty salon around the corner showed up ready to party wearing high white feathers and white mink. Everyone was bringing in bottles. Cliff was already at the piano when the musicians walked in, the same cats from the "Be-Bop Blues" sessions. Naturally that was the tune everyone wanted to hear—and hear it they did—over and over again, no one got tired of it 'cause it was the hottest hit on the street, you could hear the record playing from other people's parties, you could feel the excitement as more party people poured into my place, everyone getting shit-faced, me included, so that at eleven-thirty when Peg showed up with Joyce, I was already pretty plastered.

"Welcome, ladies," I said. "Where are your husbands?"

"Home," said Sis, looking real down and avoiding my eyes. "Hope you don't mind us showing up like this."

"Have a drink, have a dance," I offered. "New Year's Eve ain't no time for fighting and frowning. You both look like you lost your best friend." It also looked like Joyce's white silk sheath was a size too snug.

"Can I talk to you a minute, Danny?" asked Peg.

"And when she's through," Joyce joined in, "I want to apologize."

"Goddamn, you girls sound serious. Relax, will you?" Who could hold a grudge on a night like this?

"I need to see you alone," Sis insisted.

We went into my bedroom and sat on the bed piled up with winter coats. The smell of fur was everywhere. I was sipping Scotch while Sis looked sober as a judge. She was holding a newspaper.

"What's this?" I asked.

"Tomorrow's New York *Times*."

"I'm not interested in tomorrow's New York *Times*."

"You will be when you read this."

"I'm too wrecked to read. Read it to me."

"I just want you to know that I had nothing to do with it. I argued against it. I swear I did."

"What the hell are you talking about?"

"'The Bastardization of Be-Bop,' read Peg, 'by Winthrop Carrington.'" She cleared her throat and swallowed hard before going on. "Once again, crass commercialism has reared its ugly head. The most important musical innovation of the past decade, the only original avant-garde movement in any American art form, has been undermined by a trivial and tasteless tune which, unfortunately, has been gaining airplay on certain area radio stations. I refer to 'Be-Bop Blues,' which is neither a blues nor a genuine be-bop composition, but rather a weak blending of both."

"Hey," I said, "I thought newspaper guys are supposed to give the facts, not personal opinions."

"This isn't a story, it's a review. Let me read the rest."

"I've heard enough. He's just jealous 'cause when he recorded Cliff nothing happened and my record is a hit. It's a personal attack on me—that's all it is—and next time I see the wimp I'm gonna put my fist through his face. You understand that?"

"I feel terrible about it, Danny, I really do." Her eyes glistened with tears. "I tried to persuade him not to publish it but—"

"Look, Peg, it's what I've been telling you all along. The guy's a creep, he's no good..."

"But he's my husband."

"There's no law against leaving him."

"I can't."

"Why the hell not?"

"Because..."

"Because why?"

She closed her eyes when she said the words. Tears were running down her cheeks. "Because I'm pregnant. I'm due at the end of May."

"Geez..." The idea of baby—a niece or a nephew—was beautiful, but this was breaking my heart.

"Just tell Clifford I'm sorry," she said. "Will you do that?"

"Peggy..."

"I'm going home now. I just wanted to tell you about the article before someone else did. I wanted to explain. Now there's nothing more to say."

I was too stunned to argue. I finished off my Scotch and walked her to the door.

"You don't have to go, you know."

"I know what I have to do," she answered. "I've got to go home."

"What about Joyce? Isn't she going with you?"

"Joyce is a big girl. She's on her own."

Joyce was on her third drink before I got back upstairs after finding a cab for Peg. I was still shocked by the news, but there wasn't any time for tears. The radio was tuned to the celebration at Times Square, the countdown had started, and before I knew it three dozen people in my apartment were yelling, blowing whistles and kazoos, screaming "Happy New Year!" hugging and kissing everyone in sight.

I was being hugged and kissed by Joyce.

"I'm sorry," she whispered, her boobs crushed against my chest. "I'm truly sorry."

"Lighten up," I advised, my mood all mixed up. "This is supposed to be a party."

The party was over about three A.M. All the guests were gone except Joyce.

Cliff had been next to last to leave. He trotted out with both of the white-feathered foxes, one on each arm.

"Did I see your sister run in and out of here or was that just my imagination?" he asked on his way out the door.

"She was in a hurry. She said to tell you 'Happy New Year.'"

There was no reason to ruin Cliff's night with news of Winnie's rotten review.

"Want me to help clean up?" asked Joyce when we were alone. Confetti and empty booze bottles were everywhere, dirty dishes and ashtrays overflowing with butts.

"I'll help *you*," I said. "I'll put you in a cab and send you home to your husband."

She looked at me with dewy half-drunk eyes. "I've left him."

The phone rang at eight in the morning, New Year's Day, with Mom saying, "I've left him."

"Who?" I asked, thinking I was still dreaming.

"Your father. I've left him for good."

Still asleep, Joyce reached over and let her fingers slide down my chest, massaging my balls with her hand. Suddenly my dick was more awake than me.

"Can we talk about this some other time?" I asked Anita.

"I'm shaking, I'm half-hysterical, and you want to talk about it some other time?"

"I got to bed late."

"I got a deal on your old apartment."

"What?"

"Your old apartment on the East Side. I'm moving in tomorrow."

"I'm moving back. I hate Hollywood. They're nothing but a bunch of phonies out here."

"Monica, is that you?"

"Who else do you know in Hollywood?"

I looked at the clock. Noon on New Year's Day. Joyce was still asleep. I peaked under the cover. Her bare ass looked like a work of art.

"Are you alone?" Monica wanted to know.

Quickly I covered up Joyce. "I'm alone and I'm sleeping."

"I want you to pick me up at the airport. I'll be coming in tomorrow and I want to see you, Danny. Since I've been gone, things have really been changing."

"You can say that again," I said.

Mom's long lacquered nails, red as apples, had me thinking of the Wicked Witch of the West.

She'd called me over to the beauty salon on Park Avenue where every week a womanly man named George did up her hair and a manly woman named Myrtle filed and polished her daggerlike nails. Today—January 4, 1949—she might have been a general dressing for battle. Her silver-streaked hair looked like a helmet; her long-lashed eyes were steely strong. I hadn't seen her in months, but she acted like there was nothing wrong between us. As George combed and Myrtle polished, Anita spoke nonstop:

"He's in retreat. He's in hiding. But I know the game he's playing. Believe me, I know. You don't live with a man for thirty years and not know. I told him, I said, 'Myron, if you don't take Danny back, if you don't make him president—and I mean put it in black-and-white—I'm leaving you, I swear I am . . .'"

"But Mom, I don't want to be pres—"

"Then he says, 'over my dead body' and I say, fine, if it takes your dead body to let my only son have what's rightly his, then fine, from my mouth to God's ear let it be known that my husband needs to die before he can give to his son. 'That's how you talk to the man who's provided for you your whole life?' he wants to know. And I tell him, Daniel, this time I tell him the truth, I say, 'I know how every penny of this company is spent, I know where the bodies are buried—because, believe me, without a little creative bookkeeping Myron Klein Hat's Limited would have gone limp years ago, just like you've gone limp.' 'Who you calling limp?' he asks. 'You, my darling husband, you who've had an impotence problem for ten years.' 'You're frigid as an iceberg,' he says, 'and you call me impotent? You've got the goddam nerve to'—"

"Mom, please, lower your voice, everyone's listening."

"George and Myrtle?" she asked, looking up at the man and woman busy primping over her. "George and Myrtle know more than you."

"That's just it, I don't want to know."

"It's time you knew."

"But you've told me before."

"I never left him before. I never told him about Louis before."

"Oh, God..."

"I looked him in the eye and said, 'Myron, I know about your women. I've always known, I've always put up with them, I've always stayed because of the business and the children, but I have needs too. You call me frigid, but Dr. Shotkin wouldn't agree with you.' 'What does Shotkin know from women's problems?' Myron wants to know. 'Shotkin's a family doctor,' he says. 'Louis is my lover,' I say. 'You're lying.' 'I swear on my mother's grave.' He turns white, he turns red, I think he's having a coronary right then and there. I wonder whether I should call Shotkin. But he does it for me. 'I'll kill that no good son-of-a-bitch,' he says, dialing the number. 'He wants to marry me,' I say. 'He's dying to marry me.' 'I'll ruin the bastard!' Myron is screaming. 'I'll call every one of his patients! I'll throw him in bankruptcy!' 'You impotent bastard!' I yell. 'You frigid bitch!' he yells back. 'Give me Dr. Shotkin,' he says to Louis' secretary. 'The doctor is in Bermuda with his wife.' 'As soon as he gets back,' Myron tells me, 'I'm killing him.' 'As soon as he gets back,' I say, 'I'm marrying him.' 'You have to divorce me first!' Myron's still screaming. 'I'm divorcing you,' I say, 'and I'm taking your business and I'm giving it to Danny—that's what I'm doing.' So one-two-three, I pack up and leave and rent your old apartment. It's been empty since you left and the decor is unchanged. It's still as gorgeous as ever. The minute he gets back from Bermuda, I tell Louis. In an hour I have a meeting with my attorney. That's why I'm fixing myself up. What do you think of the color of my hair, Daniel?"

"Mom, I want you to know that things have changed. I've got my own business now. I'm making good money. I'm doing what I've always dreamed of doing. I've put out a record."

"With your colored friend?"

"Yes, with my colored friend, and it looks like the record's a bit hit."

"So what's to stop you from keeping all that *and* Myron Klein Hats Limited? One shouldn't cancel out the other."

"Listen to me, Mom—I don't want to be in the middle of your marriage."

"My marriage is over."

"But your divorce has just begun. For my own sanity, I need to stay clear."

"And your sister, how will she feel about all this?"

"You haven't talked to her?"

"Until I finally found the nerve to leave your father, I haven't been able to talk to either of my children."

"Peg is pregnant."

"By the gentile?"

"Of course by the gentile. The gentile is her husband."

"I never thought the marriage would last."

"I didn't either."

"Is she happy?"

"You tell me. You talk to her."

"It's too painful."

"Talk to her, Mom. She's your daughter."

"She's my mother, Danny, but I can't talk to her. She's so prejudiced."

"You sound so unhappy, Peg. You need to talk to someone. Maybe you need to talk to your mother."

"I need to take care of myself during the pregnancy. I can't afford to get upset. Mom will only upset me. It's better that I just stay with my studies and be with Winthrop. Researching his book will keep me busy."

"I don't understand how you can do that creep's dirty work."

"You're starting up again, Danny. For the sake of the baby, please don't start up."

I hang up and step out of the phone booth in front of Grand Central Station. Mom's on her way to the attorney—she asked me to go with her and I said never in a million years— and I'm on my way back to the store, my head about to explode with a dozen different emotional bombs. Once I get home I'll be okay. Back on 125th Street, the world is easier to take. There, far from everyone, I know what I'm doing—the store, the record, everything is working out. What do I have to worry about? Didn't I pick up Monica at the airport and take her back to my place where we fucked our brains out? Didn't I admit I'd missed her something awful? Monica had changed. She said again that Hollywood was run by phonies, and that I was no phony. She was impressed that I was living with the real people up in Harlem. I'm glad, though, that I told her she couldn't stay with me. But I was nice enough to help her find an apartment in Chelsea—I didn't want her any- where near Harlem—and remind her that I still couldn't make a commitment 'cause of so much going on in my life. This time she understood. She wanted to help in the store, she wanted to do anything to stay close to me, and sure, I like her, maybe I even love her, but being with Joyce last night, going to the ballet for the first time in my life, well, I gotta admit it was pretty to see all the girls in those tights and frilly little skirts and afterwards we loved like there was no tomor- row and I'm wondering if I'm crazy or just a normal man to like laying Monica one night and Joyce the next, thinking of one while fucking the other and having a ball with both.

I was tired.

Crossing Fifth Avenue, a nasty little Nash nearly ran me

down. Maybe I'd been distracted by the headline from the *Daily News* about Evita Peron taking over another newspaper down in Argentina and thinking about Anita Klein—the Evita of Ocean Parkway—going after Myron's balls. I felt like warning Pop, but then I'd be in the middle of the mess.

Walking up Fifth towards the subway station I decided to make a quick stop at a record store on the corner of 49th Street to see how "Be-Bop Blues" was doing. Inside, traffic was light and the manager was on the phone. I was looking through the bins when I started hearing the first strains of our song. *Great*, I thought, *they're playing it right here in the store.* But suddenly my heart started thumping and my throat went dry, 'cause it wasn't Cliff's voice on the record, it wasn't Cliff's voice at all, it was this white puny pukey voice, this pale-faced putrid voice, some no-count white-bread singer with a milktoast half-ass arrangement and the words changed around, this guy singing not about 'Be-Bop Blues" but 'Be-Bop *News*." What the fuck was happening? When the record was over, I ran over to the phono and looked at the 78. Sure enough, it said, "Be-Bop News" vocal by "Johnny Jones." Then I noticed the label. It had a little picture of a cat chewing on a peppercorn. "Pepper Katz Records" it read.

"Where'd this thing come from?" I asked the manager, by then off the phone.

"Came in late this week, but I can't keep it in stock. The thing's walking out of here. They're playing it all over the radio."

"But it's a fraud! It's a fuckin' fraud! It's just a watered-down copy of Cliff Summer's 'Be-Bop Blues,' the song I shipped you last month."

"You mean the race record?"

"What race record? It was a regular record, a regular hit."

"Maybe up in Harlem and with some of the colored who

work in midtown. But this 'Be-Bop News' sounds like it's going to be an across-the-board hit."

"It's against the law. I'm tellin' ya,' they flat-out copied our song. They can't do it!"

"They do it all the time. How long you been in the record business, buddy?"

"Can I use your phone?'

"Long as it's local."

I dialed Katz.

"I'm suing your ass," I said.

"Fine," he answered, tone flat.

"It won't be fine when they put your ass in jail."

"Fine."

"And I'm breaking my lease. I ain't paying you another cent in rent."

"Fine."

"And I'm going to the press, I'm breaking the story, I'm exposing you for the low-life slime that you are."

"Fine."

"How the hell could you do such a shitty thing?"

"I told you I wanted to help. I warned you, but you wouldn't listen."

"Then you go and fuck your own tenant."

"Fucking and business are two different things."

"Not to you, they're not."

"Look, I don't got time for your bullshit, Klein. You wanna sue, sue. But I'll tell you right now, you don't got a leg to stand on."

"I'm afraid that you don't have a leg to stand on," said David Berg. He'd grown up down the street from me in Brooklyn, gone to Harvard and was considered a genius by everyone in the neighborhood. At twenty-seven he had a job with a high-powered Wall Street law firm, knew both my parents and spoke with a deep soothing voice. It didn't hurt that he looked like John Garfield.

"How can you say that?" I said. "I played both versions for you. Don't they sound alike?'

"You can see distinct differences in the lyrics and hear distinct differences in the music," he said. "Certainly your competitor set out to imitate you, but he was careful to make certain changes—"

"But they *sound* the same, don't they?"

"A court won't decide on sound. The decisions will be far more technical and, in my judgment, you won't be able to sustain your charges."

"You call this justice, David?"

"No. I call it reality. The music business isn't known for its ethics."

"But what if I asked you to take the case anyway, David? Would you do it as a favor for someone from the old neighborhood?"

"I'm afraid I can't, Danny. Beyond the fact that I wouldn't want to take your money in a no-win situation, there's the fact that I'm already representing your mother in her action against your father. Candidly, Danny, one Klein case at a time is all I'm emotionally equipped to handle."

My own emotions had sunk to a new all-time low. Harry Truman was being sworn in as President while I was swearing that somehow someway I'd get Pepper Katz. Thanks to him, our song had stopped selling. Thanks to him, I couldn't even get a national distribution deal. And what was I going to do? Move out of the store, which was making me good money?

Change locations when the location had turned out to be a gold mine?

So there I was—feeding the mouth that had bit off my balls. I was mad enough to chew glass. I was mad enough to bust up the store and leave Katz with the bills.

Cliff was more philosophical. Cliff kept cool. At first he was as pissed as me, but after a couple of days he started taking the long view. He proved to be the best friend I could have. See, he believed in me, just like I believed in him.

"Fuck Pepper Katz," he said. "The guy's a goon, a two-bit show-biz gangster. But why out of spite hurt yourself by giving up the best business you've ever had? That's crazy. Why waste money by suing him when smart lawyers say you'll lose? If you look at it the right way, Dan, you'll see that we've won. We've proved to ourselves that we can do it. Mama was right. It was a matter of confidence—and you had confidence, Danny, you really did. You went out there, you sold me and my song and you created a hit in New York City, the toughest town around. That's no mean accomplishment, man. At the least, you've broken even. Maybe even made some bread. Am I right?"

"You're right . . ."

"So I say, let's build this church on a solid foundation. Let's write some more songs, let's promote some more hits."

"You sound so good, Cliff."

"I sound the way you sounded when I lost my fingers. You were telling me the same sort of shit. I lost a couple of fingers but I didn't lose my talent. You lost a coast-to-coast hit, but you didn't lose your guts. I can sing, you can sell and, far as I'm concerned, the world better watch out."

* * *

It was easier said than done. My worst fear—that creating a hit tune was no easy feat—proved all too true. While Mom was whacking away at Pop in court, while Peg was taking prenatal classes, while Winnie the Pooh was jacking himself off with high-brow jazz reviews, Cliff wrote dozens of different songs, dance numbers and ballads, none of which broke out of the starting gate. I was using the hefty store profits, growing fatter by the month, to invest in musicians and manufacturing. But even with extra-hard effort we couldn't do what we'd done the first time with ease— spark a local bonfire. It was frustrating. And making it worse for me was the non-stop sideshow produced by the family Klein.

Example:

"I'm suing Shotkin." This was Mom phoning me a week after we'd met at the beauty shop.

"Why?"

"He refused to leave his wife."

"That doesn't surprise me."

"How can you say that?"

"I'm a man, Mom. I know men. They might mess around, but when they're caught they run home to Mama."

"He swore on a stack of bibles that he'd marry me."

"Why don't you try talking to Pop? He called me last night. He sounded like he really missed you."

"What's he calling you about?"

"He wanted to know whose side I was on."

"And what'd you say?"

"Nobody's. Kids want their parents together. I'm no different."

"It's no good. Myron and I are like sugar and salt. I try to be sweet but the man is so bitter."

"You work well together. You've always worked well to-gether."

"I'm working to depose him, that's what I'm working to do. I need your help."

"Don't even ask."

"Why must you hurt me? Why must you put a knife through your mother's heart? Ever since my sister Bea died—"

"I got a customer, Mom. I gotta go."

The customer was Uncle Nate. I hadn't seen him in months. He looked older and sadder. His eyes had lost their twinkle.

"Store looks terrific, kid. Sorry I missed your birthday. And sorry about Katz screwing you in the tush like that."

"Where you been, Uncle Nate?"

"Miami. Remember Betty Wachinsky?"

"You tried to set me up but Pushman got her first."

"Yeah, well I'm marrying her mother Rose."

"You're kidding."

"Would I kid about such a thing? She owns a laundry and she needs help. Besides, she's madly in love with me. Plus I like the climate. I've been having good luck with the nags down there so I figure, what's to lose?"

"I don't want to lose you, Uncle Nate."

"You'll come down to visit. I was getting to be a pain in your ass anyways. My nephew is going places. He don't need no leeches."

"Stop talking that way."

"I'm proud of you, Danny, I really am. And don't worry 'bout me 'cause I'll be living in the lap of luxury. Rose talks a lot, but she's nuts about me and who am I to deny her?"

"You gonna have a big wedding?"

Get serious. We're getting married between the third and fourth races at Hialeah."

In my dream, Monica and Joyce were jockeys, and they were riding nude, their jugs bouncing, their bushes right up on the saddle, their hair blowing in the wind, whipping their horses, trying to beat each other to the finish line and win the prize, which was me. Except I really wasn't me. I'd turned into Joe Louis and was beating the shit out of Pepper Katz, I was pulverizing that tall bald bastard, knocking him silly, hurting him bad, when all of a sudden he turned into Winthrop Carrington who, like a nasty schoolboy, was sticking his tongue out at me—he didn't even know how to throw a punch—when, from out of nowhere, he threw a big black typewriter at my face and there wasn't time to duck and . . .

I woke up drenched in sweat.

"No sweat," said Monica. "You don't gotta tell me now. You don't even have to think about marriage. See, I got patience. I got my old job back at Minsky's. I'm buying a car so I can drive back and forth to Newark. No more trains for me. I'm independent now, Danny. I can do for myself. I'd rather be an honest dancer than go down on some two-bit Hollywood producer turning out sleazy movies. 'White Slaves' never even made it to New York. But Minsky's still believes in me, Danny. They got a whole new get-up for me and they're making me the feature dancer on the midnight show. I'd love for you to come watch, I'd feel like I was expressing myself just for you, Danny, I really would."

So on a snowy night in February I went to watch. She was

billed as a cowgirl—"Kitty Colt and Her 45's." Her tits were twirling in opposite directions and under the spotlight her body looked like silk. You should have seen Monica move. Her bumps and grinds were delivered with heart-stopping conviction, her customers yelping like dogs, begging for more. Sitting there, I couldn't help but think that every one of those guys would have died to have her in bed, and there she was, mine for the asking. Afterwards, she came up to Harlem and put on the same show, wearing the same fringy cowgirl outfit, for me and me alone.

Wasn't I one lucky son-of-a-bitch?

I asked myself the same question the next night as I sat in a lecture hall at the New School for Social Research. There must have been a hundred horny college boys watching Joyce's every twist and turn. They were pretending to take notes, but I could see them drooling over my girlfriend standing in front of the lectern in a tight pink sweater and clinging blue skirt. They wanted to yell "take it off, baby, take it off"— I know they did—but they had to act like gentlemen, their elbows on their hard-ons, as they listened to her lecture.

"Sexuality," she told the boys, "is one of the most important components in establishing any individual's psychological makeup. From infancy to adulthood this preoccupation determines patterns of behavior—some normal, some excessive— that are often unalterable."

"What's excessive?" I asked her on the way back to my place.

"That's a good question, Danny, but difficult to answer. I can refer you to a fascinating book."

"I don't like to read, but I liked looking at you up there. I liked listening to you. You were really getting your boys hot."

"That was hardly my aim."

I wasn't sure, but I wasn't about to argue. I was more interested in being excessive.

I ask you: Was having two loves at once excessive? I know it wasn't completely honest, but it'd be suicide to tell one about the other, and I didn't have the heart to cut off either. If I took Monica to a hockey game at the Garden on Wednesday, I might go with Joyce to Carnegie Hall on a Friday. Monica was comfortable and easy, but Joyce was challenging; she was always throwing new shit at me, like a big Beethoven symphony or a movie where everyone talked French with little English words running across the bottom of the screen. That was different. But it could also get boring—I don't read that fast—which was when I'd take Monica to a bowling alley in the Bronx where she'd throw a turkey and beat me silly. Sometimes it's fun to get silly and sometimes it's stimulating to be serious. I was caught in between, and except for the little lies I had to lay on the ladies, I was happy to be trapped in the middle. If it was a mess, I was used to messes, thinking of Mom and Pop and Peg and how hard it was for anyone in our family to avoid messes.

"WOMAN
ſUEſ DOCTOR,
OWN HUſBAND"

"The story's in the Sunday Brooklyn *Eagle*," Peg told me over
the long-distance wire. I was at Lake Louise with Joyce enjoying a lusty March weekend of walks through the woods and
hot toddies by a roaring fireplace in a cozy cabin on the top of
a hill overlooking this gorgeous valley.

"How'd you find me here?" I asked.

"Clifford. I told him it was an emergency. It's all here in
black-and-white. How could this have happened? Did you
know anything about it? Why'd you keep me in the dark?"

"What does it say?"

"That Dr. Shotkin—*our* Dr. Shotkin, the same Dr. Shotkin
who took care of us as kids—is being accused of sexually mo-
lesting his patients. This according to our mother. Do you
believe it?"

"Look, Sis, I should've told you before, but I didn't want to
get you upset, I wanted to keep you out of it. But Mom and
Shotkin have been seeing each other for years now."

"What do you mean 'seeing each other'?"

"Screwing—that's what I mean."

"Jesus."

"So when Mom left Pop she expected Shotkin to leave his wife. Except he didn't. What you're seeing now is Anita's revenge."

"The woman's really crazy, isn't she?"

"What does the *Eagle* say about her and Pop?"

"That she's suing him for the business."

"I'm not surprised."

"Oh, Danny"—she started crying—"I never want to see either of them again. They're freaks. I'm glad they didn't come to my wedding. I don't want to have anything to do with them—ever!"

"When your baby arrives in a couple of months you'll feel differently."

"Aren't you embarrassed, Danny? Can you believe the way our own parents are behaving?"

"I believe it and I'm also embarrassed but all the publicity will probably be good for Pop's business."

"How can you think of such a thing?"

"'Cause that's the way Pop thinks."

"Has he contacted you?"

"He calls from time to time looking for sympathy."

"And you actually talk to him?"

"What am I supposed to do, hang up on my own father?"

"I would. All his horrible womanizing has finally caught up with him."

"I wouldn't exactly call our mom Florence Nightingale."

"I want this all to go away."

"Pop asked about you, Peg. I told him how big you'd gotten, and he wanted to know if he should call. I told him it'd be better to wait 'cause you weren't supposed to get upset. But he cares about you. He loves you. And after all, the baby's his first grandchild. Don't let this newspaper thing upset you, Sis."

"I'm trying not to, Danny, especially now that my gynecologist has heard *two* heartbeats."

"Twins?"

"I'm afraid so."

"What's to be afraid? That's great news! Twins are a blessing. I didn't think Winnie had it in him. How does he feel about all this?"

"He doesn't know yet. He's in Chicago for a music conference."

"Sounds just like him, leaving you alone at the moment of truth. Soon as I get back in the city I'm coming over to see you."

"Joyce has a pretty cabin up there, doesn't she?"

"You've been here?"

"Once—a while back. Anyway, I'm glad you're with her. Tell her hi."

"Take care of your babies."

"Babies?" asked Joyce, who'd been reading a new book with the strange title, *1984.*

"My sister's having twins."

"Wow! How wonderful!" She put down the book and came over to the couch to kiss me.

"I didn't do it," I said.

"You're going to be an uncle twice over, you must be thrilled."

"I'd be a lot more thrilled if Metronome magazine sent Winnie on a five-year furlough to study jazz in northern Nairobi."

"But what's all this other news?"

"You really wanna know?"

"Your family fascinates me," she said. "Yes."

It took a while, but I told Joyce the whole story. When I

was through, she could hardly speak—but, being a professor, she managed.

"So in the family dynamic," she said, "you're the man in the middle, the son who validates everyone. Your mother has relinquished a tremendous amount of her own parental power. She's given it to you. What your parents lack in their own relationship, they look for in you. It's what we call covert incest—"

"Now wait a damn minute..."

"Danny, it's a classic case of role-reversal."

"With all this college book-talk you really remind me of Sis. I know you're bright but you're also talking bullshit, you're not telling me nothing."

"Darling," she said, removing her square glasses and putting her arms around my neck, "one of the reasons I love you is your naivete."

"Does that mean you like the way I rock you?"

She answered by slipping her sweater over her head.

I slipped into the apartment as quietly as I could 'cause I heard Cliff at the piano. He was sounding beautiful and I didn't want to distract him. The poor guy had been killing himself trying to come up with a hit. As I walked down the hallway towards the living room, though, I heard another voice—it wasn't Cliff's—and it only took me a few seconds to realize who it was.

"Woody! What the hell are you doing here?"

"If it ain't Mr. New York himself," he said, getting up and giving me a bear hug.

Cliff was sitting on the piano stool next to him. "Soon as Woody arrived in the city," he said, "first guy he wanted to see was the hat salesman."

"I hear you got yourself a whole hat store now," said the big boogie-woogie piano player, his Adam's apple bobbing up and down, his smile revealing a mouthful of bad teeth.

"Who's taking care of your bar in Birmingham?" I wanted to know.

"One of my women," he said.

"You bring Marvis with you?" I asked hopefully.

"Couldn't get her out of that schoolroom. She sends her love, though."

"This your first time up here, Woody?"

"Got here once in '41. Cut a little record and ran back home. City made me nervous."

"It can get a little frantic around here," I said, "but I'm sure glad to see you. What's the occasion?"

"Cliff sent me a ticket."

Surprised, I looked over at Cliff, who said, "I needed a writing partner so I figured I'd get the best."

"You guys come up with anything yet?"

"I can't write words quick enough," admitted Cliff, "to keep up with Pappy's melodies. The shit just pours out of him."

"Let's hear what you got."

They played some blisterin' rhythm stuff, then some mid-tempo tunes, but it was this ballad that got to me. Woody played the high part, Cliff followed along on the bottom, and it sounded prettier than "That Lucky Old Sun," Frankie Laine's current hit.

"Play the love song again," I said. "I love that love song."

"Who said it was a love song?" Woody asked.

"The women," I answered. "We gotta go for the women this time."

They kept playing this haunting refrain, again and again. Cliff started humming until the hums became words and the words became lyrics. He was singing something about "our secret."

"'Our secret' what?" I egged him on.

"Our secret is safe in my heart," he sang.

The longer Woody played, the more Cliff sang, the story began to come together—boy and girl sharing a secret love, leading a secret life.

> I knew from the start
> They'd keep us apart
> So our love went inside
> Our love had to hide
> But our secret is safe in my heart

"Think you can sell it?" asked Cliff.

I just sat back and smiled.

"I need your advice."

"Please, Mom, I need my peace of mind."

"I'm having a settlement conference and I need you there."

"I'm not coming."

"You have to."

"You have to leave me alone."

"Your father's suing Shotkin."

"I thought you're the one suing Shotkin."

"We both are. Me for malpractice, Myron for alienation of affection."

"How's Shotkin taking all this?"

"He's back in Bermuda with his wife. He'll never practice in Brooklyn again."

"How's your friend Ida taking all this?"

"What's Ida got to do with it?"

"I thought you knew."

"What's there to know? Ida and her Bernie have been very comforting throughout my ordeal. Why do you mention Ida? What are you saying about Ida?"

"I'm saying good-by."

"Was she involved with Shotkin? Was my best friend Ida Gruntstein carrying on with that man, too? Is that what you're implying, Danny?"

"I'm implying that I'm dying to get off the phone."

"If I died," said my dad, "your mother would be happier."

He looked terrible. After weeks of avoiding his calls, I finally agreed to meet him at the baths on Hester Street. We were sitting in the steam room with towels wrapped around us. The average age in the place was seventy, the average weight two hundred fifty. The room was filled with cigar coughs and aching backs. I wasn't happy.

"What about the business?" I asked Pop.

"Let her have the business," he said. "The business has turned to shit. Benny X. Pushman is no Danny Klein, that's for sure."

I was happy to hear it. "What happened with Pushman?" I asked.

"His sales slipped on a banana peel and he's breaking my ass—that's what happened. The guy's been stroking me. So I say, let her sue, let her win, let her have the fuckin' business. I'm through fighting, Danny."

"That doesn't sound like the Myron Klein I know."

"Let her run the business, let her face the aggravations."

"Hasn't she been running it for years?"

"She's been running over me, that's what she's been doing. She's been screwing with my books and she's been screwing my doctor, that's what she's been doing."

Pop's face was so drenched I couldn't tell the sweat from the tears.

"Sorry it turned out like this, Pop."

"You're sorry. You're out already."

"What can I do?"

"Talk to her for me. Tell her I want peace."

"I can't. I won't."

I kept my pledge. For the rest of the week, I dodged calls from Mom and Pop. I worked hard in the store, getting the Easter displays ready. If you're in the hat business, Easter's a big deal on 125th Street. Blue Notes Under a Green Felt Hat was going great guns. In fact, a couple of imitators had already opened—retailers combining records and hats—but no one could duplicate our flair. I was featuring a midnight-blue tapered crown featherweight wool for spring. I had 'em in the window piled up in the shape of a pyramid and surrounded at the bottom by dozens of jars of a new men's hair pomade called "Jazz," high-priced grease in a pretty package. I had Woody Herman's "Four Brothers" blasting from the speakers and all the customers I could handle.

But as I waited on the people, inside my head I kept hearing the string of songs Cliff had recorded since last December. Every last one of them had bombed. I wouldn't call myself discouraged, but I was sure a hell of a lot more cautious. My confidence was slipping; I'd even given up our plan of finding other artists to record. But I hadn't given up on Cliff. I'd been concentrating on studying the marketing side of this business— in short, how to score a national hit without getting fucked in the ass. It wasn't easy, especially if your artist was colored, and especially if you wanted to have something more than a "race record." I never even knew that I'd been raised on race records, never knew race records meant music made by blacks bought by blacks. The way I figured it, blacks made music meant for everyone—and the only reasons they didn't sell to everyone was 'cause the system was set up by and for whites. Sometimes someone like Nat Cole would break through. But that was rare. In my heart and my head I knew that Cliff sang with the best of them—Tony Martin, Johnny Desmond, Perry Como, Vaughn Monroe, even Sinatra. It was just a question of marketing him right. That meant finding the right song.

Now the rhythm song—"Be-Bop Blues"—had been right but I hadn't done my homework. I needed a major distribution deal *before* releasing the record, not afterwards. That was the only protection from bloodsuckers like Katz. Yet the majors had passed on every one of our half-dozen releases since "Be-Bop." Worse still, the majors had been right. The songs didn't sell. So why was I so sure about this new one?

Maybe it was Woody. Maybe I remembered that Woody had been there at the birth of "Be-Bop Blues." And "Be-Bop Blues," in its whitewashed Johnny Jones form, *was* a national hit. Even more, "Our Secret" wasn't a gimmick like "Be-Bop." It was no novelty song. It was a tender ballad; it expressed the sort of sentiment that anyone could feel. I felt it; it gave me chills. And as Woody and Cliff kept refining it, it started sounding even better, deeper, the kind of thing that might have been written by Johnny Mercer or Hoagy Carmichael. I was sure it was a standard. I was confident enough to go all out. I told Cliff to take his time on the arrangement, to let the thing build in his mind. I told him to hire some fiddlers. The hell with the cost. We were going to do this sucker up right.

Now on the night of April 7 I had tickets to the opening of a big new musical called *South Pacific*. This was something of a dilemma 'cause both Joyce and Monica loved these kind of shows. Usually my cultural events were easy to figure—take Joyce to see *Death of a Salesman* where Lee J. Cobb made her cry; take Monica to the Roller Derby where she screamed for the broads to elbow each other in the neck. *South Pacific,* though, would work for both of them. In fact, I didn't know which way to go till Monica reminded me I'd promised to take her to St. Nick's to see Gorgeous George wrestle. So the night before I took Joyce to the Majestic Theatre, where the opening-night crowd of socialites and sports figures, tycoons and tightasses, princes, high-priced whores and even *shmatah* salesmen like me poured into the place.

Mary Martin played Ensign Nellie Forbush and Ezio Pinza played Emile de Becque—they were the two leads—with Juanita Hall as the outrageous Bloody Mary.

The show was tremendous. I never heard so many gorgeous songs—"There Is Nothin' Like a Dame," "I'm Gonna Wash That Man Right Outa My Hair," "Bali Ha'i'," "A Wonderful Guy," "A Cockeyed Optimist" and the unforgettable "Some Enchanted Evening."

Let me tell you something: We walked out of that place humming those tunes along with everyone else in the audience, happy and carefree and thoroughly entertained from our heads to our toes. Yet, in spite of all that—and this is the part that excited me—I still remembered "Our Secret"! I was still singing Cliff's song! Believe me, I wasn't taking nothing away from Mr. Rodgers and his buddy Hammerstein. Those boys knew what they were doing. But so did Cliff and Woody. They'd given me what I wanted, what I needed, a major-league song that everyone was going to love.

"You seem a little distracted tonight," said Joyce as we walked down Broadway to where I'd parked.

"It's this new song," I said. "We've been working on something new. If you don't mind, I'll take you home 'cause I promised the boys I'd be back up at the studio."

"It doesn't sound like I have any choice," she said.

When Joyce left her husband, she moved into an apartment in the Village, only a couple of miles away from Monica. Driving downtown, full of thoughts about the song, I barely heard her ask, "What's happening with your parents?"

I told her about my most recent conversations with them. "It's getting wilder by the week," I said. "I hate it."

"I think you like it. In fact, I think you love it."

"How can you say that?"

"You relish the role."

"What are you talking about? I won't have anything to do with them."

"All you do is deal with them. This triangular pattern is almost an addiction for you."

As we passed by Monica's apartment in Chelsea I kept my mouth shut. I was in a hurry to get Joyce home, and I didn't come in. Maybe I was oversaturated with sex, maybe I was tired of Joyce's psycho-babble, or maybe I was just anxious to tell Cliff and Woody about the score from *South Pacific*.

Anyway, I rushed back up to Harlem, to the studio above the store. It was past midnight, but the lights were on and the music was playing. Ciff and Woody were working on the arrangement to "Our Secret"—the recording session with the fiddlers was planned for the following week—and I started gushing about *South Pacific* and how I thought we measured up to the best.

"Woody had quite a night himself," said Cliff. "You better listen to what happened."

Something in Cliff's voice made me worry.

"Went by to see my old partner Fatha Hines," Woody explained.

"You know Earl Hines?" I asked.

"Been knowing Fatha since he came through 'Bama in the Thirties. Anyway, he's playing in a club not far from here, so I stop by and naturally he sees me and makes a big ol' fuss. Gets up from the piano and makes me sit down and play, saying all this nice shit about me, so I play a little boogie woogie and the folks seem to like it cause they're applauding and wanting me to play some more. So Fatha and I play some shit together and now the place is going wild—maybe 'cause these New Yorkers don't get to hear the real blues every day—and here comes this white boy wanting to talk to me—he looks like a doctor—he says, 'sir, you are an amazing piano player and I'd like to write something about you and record you.'"

"Winthrop Carrington?" I want to know.

Cliff nods his head. "He called here a little while ago wanting to set up a session."

That's all I need to know.

I'm off.

I run downstairs and jump in the Chevy and head towards Gramercy Park. Rain starts to fall, the streets are slick, but I don't care, I'm crazy, I'm zooming, I've taken all I can from this brother-in-law bastard of mine, this wimpy son-of-a-bitch who's stuck his nose in my business one time too many.

I'm skidding, I'm slipping, I'm sliding, but I finally make it over there and I buzz the buzzer and hear my sleepy sister and say, "Peg, sorry, baby, I'm really sorry to disturb you, but please tell Winthrop to come downstairs 'cause it's an emergency."

"You okay?"

"Fine, just fine, just tell Winnie I need him down here."

Five minutes later he appears in his bathrobe and right there in the lobby—I can't contain myself—I grab him by his pajama tops and say, "First you fuck with my sister, then you fuck with my pal, now you're fucking with my pal's pappy. Leave this Woody alone before I bash you so bad your own mother won't recognize you."

He pushed me back. "Woody is a genius . . . he deserves wider recognition . . . if you really cared a fig about him you'd allow me to preserve his music—"

"He ain't no dead museum, he's a man, he's a songwriter and he's writing songs for *me*."

"God help him."

"You asshole."

"Shut the hell up," yelled one of the tenants whose front door practically opened off the lobby. "If you're going to fight, fight outside."

We went outside where it was really raining hard, rain soaking us to the skin. But we had things to say that'd been building up for months. "I'm telling you, keep your dirty paws off Woody," I said.

"And I'm telling you, Klein, your vulgarity cheapens everyone you touch. Your musical ignorance blinds you to what's good and bad. You'd do anything for a buck. You don't distinguish between a song and a straw hat. You appeal to the lowest common denominator. Exploiters like you are the reason jazz is undervalued and underappreciated. For the right price, you'd sell your own sister."

I started to hit him. It was going to be a perfect right hook, clean and straight to his chin. He was supposed to stumble over and fall in the rain and then I'd pick him up and hit him again. But I couldn't do it, I couldn't deliver the punch because a split second before I threw it we heard a bloodcurdling scream above us—Peggy had pushed up her window and was yelling that something was happening, something was wrong, and she had to get to the hospital—*now*.

BLE**SS**ED EVENT

The rain got crazy. It was coming down in buckets. I was driving and Sis was next to me, her gigantic stomach resting on her lap like an oversized beach ball. Her eyes were closed, she was moaning and crying and I was holding her hand while Winnie was in the back—get this: he was reading, or at least was staring at some music book—with me telling Sis to be calm, be cool 'cause we'd be there in a flash.

We arrived at the emergency room of Beth Israel Hospital and soon some doctor was telling me to sit and wait. He said he'd be out as soon as he could, and there I was, sitting next to Winnie who seemed out of it. When the doctor finally reappeared, nearly an hour later, he said things were complicated and it could go either way for the mother and the kids.

"What the fuck does that mean?" I said.

"It's a life-threatening situation . . . all around."

I couldn't stand to look at Winnie anymore and went to the phone and called Mom at my place and Pop in Brooklyn and told them, "Look, you gotta get down here, we all gotta help her pull through this thing."

And sure enough they came down, and we cried and hugged—it was the first time we'd all been together since God knew when—and there was Winnie, book in his lap, and there we were sitting up all night, forgetting about the law suits and the fights when a different doctor came out, telling us Sis was in a long labor, she'd lost lots of blood and was fighting for her life, fighting for her babies' lives, and we tried napping on a couch, sleeping in a chair, but we were too scared, pacing back and forth, and soon it was the next day, it was noon, it was three o'clock in the afternoon. Winnie had already gone home and come back. He looked all clean, he had actually showered and changed. Me and Mom and Pop were haggard, circles under our eyes and fear in our hearts. Mom tried knitting and Pop tried lighting a cigar, but she'd drop her stitch and he'd drop his match—their hands were shaking—and there was nothing to do except sit and wait and wait some more.

At five o'clock Monica showed up—she'd heard what happened from someone at the store—and started kissing and comforting me, right there in the waiting room, right when Joyce walked through the door. Joyce had been told what had happened by a neighbor of Peg's. I was short of choices so I quickly introduced her to Mom and Pop and Monica. I was praying that she'd think that Monica was a cousin, but I could see the fury in her eyes and Monica whispered, "Who's this Joyce?" and Joyce whispered "Who's Monica?" and all I could say was, "Not now, not now," but while we waited my two girlfriends went out in the hall together to talk or size themselves up—I didn't know which—but it didn't look good for me, even though the thing with Peg was a million times bigger; her *life* was on the line.

If my shit was falling apart, at least Mom and Pop were sitting next to each other, at least they were talking, maybe this is what it took—who knew? who knew anything?—except when the doctor walked into the room at seven PM we'd been there for seventeen straight hours, and it didn't look good, seeing his stern face, and already I was crying inside.

"She's just fine," he said. "And so are the twin girls."

Winnie looked up from his book, I screamed "Hallelujah!" jumping up and hugging Mom and Pop who were sighing and crying all at the same time. Joyce and Monica, avoiding my eyes, followed us following the doctor to the nursery.

"They're in incubators, of course," he told us. "They're very very small—each weighs barely five pounds—but their vital signs are strong and the mother is finally out of danger."

There must have been thirty babies behind the glass. The boys had blue labels on their tiny cribs, the girls had pink. There were several incubators so it took us some time to locate the one with a sign that said "Carrington." Mom was the first one to spot it.

"There's some terrible mistake," she said to the doctor who was standing by our side.

"What do you mean?" he asked.

"Those babies are brown, they're colored babies."

"I was a bit surprised myself," he told her, "but those were the babies that I delivered. I can assure you that they are your daughter's twins."

For the first time in her life, Anita Klein fainted.

PO*S*T-PARTUM
DEPRE*SS*ION

What's the definition of a nervous breakdown?

I couldn't ask Joyce, 'cause Joyce wasn't talking to me. I couldn't blame Joyce and I couldn't blame Monica. Monica wasn't talking to me either. I couldn't ask Mom 'cause she wasn't talking to me—or Pop, who swore he'd have nothing to do with me or Peg for the rest of his life. I couldn't ask Cliff 'cause I'd fired him. I threw him out of the store on his ear; I told him never to step in the studio again.

See, the moment I saw those little babies, I saw Cliff's face. It was so clear to me. If Joyce and Monica felt fucked-over by me, I felt a million times more fucked-over by Cliff. I felt betrayed and sick at heart. All this time I thought Winthrop was the motherfucker, or the sisterfucker, but it wasn't Winthrop who'd messed up Peg's life, it was Cliff. When Winnie saw the brown babies, he didn't even scream. He just turned around and left, like he was walking out on a movie he didn't like. He'd obviously been kicked in the nuts, but this guy was too weird to show any feelings. He just hightailed it outta there in a flash.

"How long have you been fucking her?" I asked Cliff before firing him. "I want to know the first time."

"It isn't like that, Danny. It isn't about fucking. It never has been. It's about love."

"Save your sweettalk for my sister, it ain't working on me. When I think of the shit I've done for you, when I think how I worked my ass off—"

"Wait just a goddamn minute," he said. "You were working as much for yourself as for me. You thought we both were going to make money."

"It wasn't just money, I believed in your music."

"And you still do."

"I can't hear your music without throwing up—that's how I feel about you and your fuckin' music."

"All because I fell in love with your sister."

"Don't talk about love. You ain't interested in love, you're interested in pussy—and if it's white pussy, so much the better."

"I never thought I'd hear racist shit coming out of your mouth."

"I never thought you'd fuck my sister behind my back."

"'Fore you throw any more stones, Mr. Danny Klein, you oughta look in the mirror where you'll be staring at one of the biggest fuckin' pussy hounds in the history of fuckin' pussy."

"Least I ain't betraying friends."

"How 'bout Joyce? How 'bout Monica? Are they your friends?"

"They're none of your business."

"Well, neither is the love between me and Peggy."

"What you call love, I call lust."

"I'm sorry this has hurt you, Danny, I really am, but Peggy and I are going to be together. We've decided."

"Why the hell didn't you have the guts to at least tell us what was going to happen before it did?"

"Because the honest-to-God truth is that we didn't know. It wasn't that she never made love to her husband. It was just that it didn't happen too often. She didn't know whose kids the babies were going to be."

"The kids are going to be a mess."

"They don't have to be."

"The world'll never accept them."

"You mean, *you'll* never accept them."

"No one's gonna accept them. No one's gonna accept you and Peg. Can't you see what you've done? Can't you see that you've ruined everyone's life?"

"I can see that you've turned into an asshole," he said, fighting back tears.

"You don't even want to see me?" asked Peg.

"Not if he's around."

"Winthrop's gone. He packed up and was out when I got back from the hospital."

"I don't mean him, I mean Cliff."

"I fell in love with Cliff the first time I saw him play. You felt that, deep down you must have known."

"I don't want to hear about it. If you need money, I'll send money."

"I have money of my own."

"Good, then you don't need shit from me."

"I need your love."

"You got what you want. You got Cliff."

* * *

"You were supposed to be taking care of your sister."

"I don't want to hear about it, Mom."

"How could you have let this happen?"

"*Me?* What kind of example were *you* setting?"

"I thought you loved me," said Monica.

"I did love you. I do. I wasn't lying."

"You were lying and you were cheating."

"You can't cheat if you're not married."

"They could put your dick in a cast, and you'd still find a way to cheat."

"Your family is dysfunctional," said Joyce. "Your whole family is hopelessly neurotic."

"I don't even know what that means."

"I think you know perfectly well. It means you grab whatever you can get."

"If you're talking about cheating, you did a pretty good job on your husband."

"Because I loved you, because I fell in love with you."

"Everyone throws around the word 'love.' Everyone uses 'love' as an excuse to cheat—that's all it is, an excuse to cheat. You, Cliff, Peg, my mother—maybe even me, I don't know, I don't care, I just want everyone to leave me the hell alone."

"It's not cheating, it's control. Your family is in the midst of a battle for control. Your device is the triangle. You're the link. You hook up with two people, like you hooked up with Cliff and Peg—"

"You don't know what you're talking about. I didn't get them together."

"Unconsciously you did. You set them up, you saved them during the shooting, just the way your parents set you up to save them."

"Bullshit."

"Look at the triangles—Cliff, Peg, Danny; Mommy, Daddy, Danny; Monica, Joyce, Danny. Who's the common denominator? Danny. Who's the controller? Danny."

"You're full of shit."

"I'm glad to hear you express anger, because you're an angry man without the courage to express it."

"What are you trying to do, get me really angry?"

"No, I'm writing a paper about you, I'm calling your neurosis 'projective identification'—people who can't express anger so they use others to do it for them. You use your mother to express the anger you feel for your father; you use Monica to express the anger you feel for me; you use me to—"

"I ain't using anyone! What the fuck is going on here? *I'm* the son-of-a-bitch who's being used—and everyone's been doing it, starting with Pop making me go back on the road—"

"See how angry you really are . . ."

"At you, you bitch. Does it make you happy to hear me angry, well, okay, I'm angry, I'm pissed, I'm fuckin' furious!"

"And you're also all alone. The links of your triangles have all rotted and fallen away, ruining your relationships and leaving you utterly alone . . ."

Joyce's words haunted me. I knew she wanted to hurt me, but I also knew she wasn't wrong. But so what? If I was alone, at least it was my own choosing. These people hadn't dropped me, I'd dropped them, avoided them, never called them 'cause I didn't need them anymore. I didn't need anyone. I didn't need to know the definition of a nervous breakdown 'cause I wasn't nervous and I wasn't breaking down.

Okay, maybe I was feeling a little lonely, but I had the store. The store was my baby. The store was still beautiful. I sold my spring hats and records during May, my best month yet. The store was going strong. Sometimes I even slept on a cot in the back rather than be alone at home. When I went to my apartment, I'd start wondering why certain people wouldn't call me and why I wouldn't call them, but then I remembered how they had hurt me, how they'd lied and cheated, and how I wanted nothing to do with them.

I like Scotch, so what's the harm in having a couple of Scotches every night after the store is closed? I worked my ass off; I was entitled. And if I had a hard time sleeping, what was the harm in having a couple more to dull the pain and let me drift off? Saturdays were rough—and maybe I'd keep a little pint behind the counter and start taking nips at noon, just to keep me going, and Sundays didn't matter 'cause the shop was closed and I could stay smashed long as I wanted.

Sundays were the loneliest. Loneliness hung around me like the flu, giving me chills and cramps, making me feverish and sometimes getting me scared. On this particular Sunday early in June, it was seven at night, I was still in my pajamas, I was feeling sick—an entire fifth of Scotch had fogged over my brain—when I decided to call Uncle Nate in Miami.

"You gotta come here," I said.

"What's wrong, kid?"

"Not feeling well."

"Sorry to hear that. Wish I could help, but Rose needs me, Danny, she really does. She wants to open a second laundry. She also found a way to get me off the ponies."

"How?"

"She starting making book. She's my bookie. She lets me have my little fixes, but never lets me go too far. It's a beautiful marriage."

"I'm glad, Uncle Nate, but I'm hurting, I'm hurting pretty bad."

"You can't call your Mom?"

"I'm calling you, Uncle Nate."

"What about Peg?"

"I can't explain now," I said, ready to puke, "but I don't have anybody, I don't . . ."

"Maybe at the end of the summer, kid, maybe in Augu . . ."

I dropped the phone and ran to the bathroom, where I was sick to my stomach. By the time I got back, the line was dead.

I felt dead. I opened a half-pint and drank straight from the bottle. The booze was no longer working. Instead of making me feel good, it was making me feel bad. Everything and everyone was turning on me. I went to bed and tried to sleep, but my stomach wouldn't let me. I felt afraid—afraid that I'd never get better, that no one wanted me, no one loved me, that I didn't even love myself. Then I remembered a small amount of pot hidden in my sock drawer.

Sometimes I smoked before sex. Monica might join me, but not Joyce. Joyce said she didn't trust dope; it made her lose control. Yet she was the one who called me a controller. Now I was losing control, losing my mind. I wondered—*What's the definition of a nervous breakdown?*

The reefer was powerful. I smoked up a whole joint. I got royally potted. Then I got to feeling worse. Worry waves were crashing over my head. Like little monsters throwing darts at my heart, questions kept piercing me—*Why was I alone? Why had everyone deserted me? Why did they all hate me? Why did everyone want to hurt me?*

I needed to talk, needed to talk to someone, anyone.

Joyce, Joyce would understand.

"What's wrong?" Her telephone voice was ice cold.

"I'm hearing knocks at my door," I said. "Mean knocks. I won't answer 'cause I'm scared. There are people out there trying to get me. I know there are."

"Guilt has turned to paranoia. You're a case, but you're no longer my case. Sorry." And the phone went dead.

Monica. Call Monica. Monica would understand.

But the man who answered the phone wouldn't.

I hung up in his ear.

In my own ear, I heard ringing. Loud horrible ringing. It wouldn't stop, then noise on my ceiling, then a smudge or a face at the window, I couldn't tell which. Maybe it was a killer, people wanted to kill me and now these knocks and I ran to the bedroom to call the cops and tell them that the knocking wouldn't stop, to ask them—*what's a nervous breakdown? who can tell me? who's after me?*—ran back to the living room to bar the door, put a chair under the knob, keep out the killers, the killers had me scared shitless, tears pouring down my face, scared of the knocking, the knocking got louder and I started screaming—that's how scared I was—"no, no, don't come in . . . don't hurt me, don't kill me" —when suddenly I heard a voice clear as light say, "No one can hurt you except yourself."

When I opened the door, Marvis Summer stared me straight in the eye. The last thing I remember is collapsing in her arms.

"OUR SECRET"

"You've had so many secrets locked up inside you," said Marvis the next morning, "it's a wonder you didn't go crazy long ago."

After putting me to bed, she'd slept on my couch. When I woke up, my head ached like I was recovering from brain surgery, but the fresh pot of coffee smelled like heaven. In my little kitchen she made me a stack of flapjacks dripping with maple syrup.

"You need nourishment," she said. "And then you need someone to talk to."

"I got nothing to talk about," I said. "I don't even know why you came."

"To see my grandchildren, to see my son, and to see you— that's why."

"Okay, you've seen me."

"What I've seen is a shadow of the Danny I saw in Alabama."

"That Danny is dead."

"Harsh words."

"Harsh world."

"The world is what we make it. And you're making it mighty hard on yourself."

"Look, Marvis, you might mean well, but you're not doing me any good."

"Well, you can do me some good by introducing me to your parents."

"That's impossible."

"That's just good manners. You'll call your mama and tell her that you're taking me by to meet her tomorrow. Is that clear?"

Marvis was wearing a starchy straight beige skirt, a bright yellow blouse and pretty yellow pumps. She looked like the schoolteacher she was. Her hair was clipped short and sprinkled with gray, neat and distinguished. Seated across the big black-lacquer dining room table in my former penthouse was Anita Klein. She was resplendent in a long lounging robe covered with tower-sized tulips. She'd just dyed her hair the shade of a shimmering blue-white diamond. Her long tapered fingernails looked like little red knives.

"You look terrible, Danny," she said, "you look like death warmed over."

"Marvis took care of me when I was sick in Alabama," I told my mother.

"I appreciate that, Mrs. Summer," said Anita, whose only contacts with colored women were the domestics or workers at Pop's place. "That was kind of you," she added, her tone still frosty.

"I asked Dan to bring me here," said Marvis, "only because I thought it was important for the grandmothers to meet. I intend to be part of my grandchildren's lives. I know you have the same intention. I know, because you're a smart woman, Mrs. Klein, you'll agree that in this crazy world our grandkids will have it rough enough without having to endure animosity among their parents' families."

Mom didn't say a word.

Marvis didn't blink an eye. "No doubt, Mrs. Klein, there are differences between us, but that doesn't mean that we can't talk to each other as two women with a common concern. We owe the babies that much."

"I need time," said Anita. "It's still too new."

"And we have time, we have plenty of time. The Lord provides all the time we need. Right now you need time to be with your son and I need to run."

"I'll take you back to your hotel," I said.

"No, Danny, you stay here with your mother."

Marvis left and I stayed. It wasn't easy talking to Mom. She was tough, bitter and headstrong. We didn't resolve anything, but at least we made a start. At least we were talking.

It was Wednesday night and I had just closed the store. The help had gone and I was going over register receipts when I heard a tap at the door. Standing quietly on the street was a strange couple—Marvis Summer and Myron Klein. She towered over him. He was wearing a black silk suit and chewing an unlit cigar.

I opened the door.

"Look who I found," Marvis offered, smiling. "I couldn't believe it when he told me that he'd never seen your beautiful store. 'We need to fix that, Mr. Klein,' I said, 'we need to rush up there right now.' So here we are."

"Come in," I said.

They came in, and without talking to me, without even looking at me, Pop went straight to the hat side of the shop, where he conducted a long and thorough inspection.

"You make a nice hat display," he finally offered. "You bought quality goods. I'm proud."

I'd never heard my father say that before.

"My son's meeting me at a lecture on Isadora Duncan at Hunter College," said Marvis with a small smile. "So I'll leave you two alone."

After a long stretch of horrible silence, my father finally said, "That's an amazing woman, that Mrs. Summer. To come walking in my office like that, unannounced, uninvited. When she shakes your hand, she's as strong as a man. And I'll tell you something else, she's not stupid."

"There's something else I want to tell you, Danny."

"What?"

"Your mother came home to me last night."

"That's nice."

"We had sex for the first time in . . ."

"There you go again, Pop, using me as your audience. I don't need to know this stuff."

"But you do need to know that we're finally through messing around. We're going to try and just concentrate on each other. We've decided to sell the business."

"Is that what you want?"

"Is that what you want, Danny?"

I thought about Pop's place—the smell of dye, the stacks of raw hat bodies, Aunt Bea's ladies in the trimming room—and fought back tears. "I don't care," I said. "Do what you want."

"Who is she, your therapist?" Joyce asked me, pointing to Marvis. We were at Ratner's dairy restaurant down on Second

Avenue. "Are we in therapy here?" the professor wanted to know.

"She's Cliff's mom," I said on Marvis's behalf. "I've been talking about you, she said you sound interesting, and I said, 'Well, come meet her.'"

"If I knew your surrogate mother was coming along, I'm not sure I would have agreed to meet you."

"I don't even know what that means," I told her.

"It means that you're so weak you need your hand held," Joyce said.

"I'm interested in your profession, Joyce," Marvis broke in. "I've read a little about it, but I want to learn more. I want to learn more about this notion of ending a relationship. I'm not sure whether I understand—you know far more about this than I do—but am I right to assume that you psychologists believe that when two people end a relationship it's important for them to express their feelings, to say good-by in an open and honest way? I suppose the theory is that leftover anger doesn't do anyone any good."

"Where did you study, Mrs. Summer?" asked Joyce, suddenly impressed.

"Yuma County Library, Yuma, Alabama."

A few minutes later, Marvis left me and Joyce alone. It took us a while to say what we needed to say. We got angry then we got sorry. We both apologized, but it didn't matter too much. Our thing was over.

"I got the roses and I got the note, but I'm still not sure, Danny, I'm still not sure I can ever see you again."

"I'm just calling to say I know I acted like a louse. I don't expect you to forgive me. I just hope you understand me."

"I love you," she confessed, "I've always loved you."

"I don't feel like I deserve to be loved."

"They're photographing me for a Wash Away soap ad next week, Danny. They're shooting me in a bubble bath—nothing's gonna show 'cause of the bubbles—but I'm in the bath and underneath it says, 'Wash Away your worries with loving care.' Don't you think that's beautiful?"

"I miss you, baby."

"I miss you too, Danny, but I'm scared of you on account of how much I love you."

"So many things are missing from my life."

"Have you seen your sister? Have you seen the twins, Danny?"

"No, and I'm not going to—"

"Why? Why are you mad at the little babies? The babies didn't do nothing to you."

"I don't think babies can get too much attention," said Marvis as I drove us down to Gramercy Park. "But your sister is certainly trying. She never lets them out of her sight. She's a good mother."

"And a lying sister."

"There's no reason to go in if that's your attitude."

"How about your son's attitude about the truth?"

"I am not defending my son. I am merely concentrating on the babies."

I tried to clear my mind, but it wasn't easy. Images of Cliff and Peg kept jumping back into my brain—cheating, lying, screwing behind my back. Besides, who wanted to see a couple of screaming babies?

"The babies are asleep," said Peg as soon as she opened the door. I had to admit that she looked beautiful. Her eyes seemed happy. Her skin was glowing. She was wearing a white babushka over her head. She almost looked like one of those Lower East Side women just off the boat. Her sophisticated college look was gone. She kissed me on the cheek. I didn't kiss her back. She hugged Marvis.

"Let's go in the kitchen for coffee," she said.

"I'm going shopping," said Marvis, "you two have catching up to do."

"I don't want to see Cliff," I told Peg when we were alone.

"You won't have to. He's asleep."

"Good."

She gave me a cup of coffee in a kitchen filled with baby bottles and nipples. We sat across from each other as sunlight splashed through the window.

"I know that Clifford and I have hurt you," she said, "but please try and understand . . ."

"Certain things I can't understand."

"Look, Danny, I made a marriage not for myself, but as a way to make Mom and Pop mad. Winthrop has moved to San Francisco, he's publishing more than ever before—and I haven't heard a word from him. That's how loveless our marriage was. I simply used him to rebel."

"And by carrying on with Cliff—wasn't that the same thing?"

"No."

"Says you."

"I know it wasn't, and you know it too. You know better than anyone because you know Cliff. And I know you, Danny, I know you love him."

I took a bite out of a bagel and closed my eyes. I wasn't sure I wanted to be here.

"I also know," Peg carried on, "that deep down you do want Pop's business. Well, he's finally ready to turn it over to you. Either that, or it'll be sold."

"I've got the store."

"And enough energy for five more stores and three more businesses. Don't let pride ruin your happiness, Danny. Take what's yours. No one can run Myron Klein Hats Limited except you."

I started to argue but was stopped by a baby's cry. Peggy got up to see what was happening. I sat and finished my bagel. Sure, I was curious, but I was determined to stay put. Then the other baby started crying, and I figured, what the hell, maybe Peg needed help, maybe I'd just take a peek.

She was sitting in a rocking chair and had both babies in her arms. They'd gotten a lot bigger. Man, did they look healthy. I couldn't help but be glad for that. They had Cliff's nose and Peg's eyes and hardly any hair. Soon as they looked up at me they stopped crying and started smiling—I swear they did—and I tried to tell them apart, but I couldn't, they were identical, identically gorgeous, 'cause I'm telling you these babies were unbelievably beautiful, the color of coffee and cream. I offered them each one of my fingers, and they grabbed me with their tiny hands, they squeezed me, they even giggled. You could tell they were nuts about me.

"Want to hold them?"

"I don't even know their names."

"Ella and Billie."

"I never held a baby before."

"They're light."

I picked up Billie, who felt like a feather. She smelled so good—baby powder is the best perfume in the world—and I rubbed my nose against her forehead and kissed her chubby little cheek. We sat in the rocking chair and I rocked her back and forth and sure enough, she went right back to sleep.

"Okay, wiseguy," said Sis. "Now try this one."

She gave me Ella, who was a lot squirmier but no match for

Uncle Danny. I cooed her and calmed her and don't you know that in a few minutes I had her snoozing.

Back in their crib, sleeping side-by-side. I just looked at them with wonder. I put my ear close to their mouths so I could hear them breathe.

"They're angels," I said out loud.

Musical notes drifted into the room, notes from a piano.

"Isn't that going to wake them?" I asked Peg.

"Clifford's music is like a lullaby. It helps them sleep," she said as we tiptoed out of the room.

I stayed out of the living room—that's where Cliff was playing—and went back to the kitchen. One more cup and I'd leave. But as I sat there, I couldn't help but hear a melody I hadn't heard in months. I still knew it. I had to admit it. I still loved it. I heard him singing softly, "I knew from the start... they'd keep us apart... so our love went inside... our love had to hide... but our secret is safe in my heart..."

My own heart was hurting so bad, feeling so sad, feeling so happy. In spite of myself I walked into the living room. Cliff looked up from the piano and smiled, just like he had smiled the first night me and Peg had seen him at the Outside Inn. The guy was talented, there was no getting around it.

"Still a good tune," he said.

"Real good tune," I agreed.

P.S.

In case you're interested, "Our Secret," sung by my brother-in-law, was the number-one song of 1950, bigger than anything by the Ames Brothers or Andrew Sisters. If America knew the real meaning behind that tune, we would have been burned at the stake.

That same year, I got Cliff a big-money deal on Decca, and Peg got her master's degree from Columbia.

Mom and Pop retired to Miami. Sometimes I wonder whether they ever run into Woody, who closed his bar in Birmingham and bought a sandwich stand by the beach with his composer's royalties from the song.

I also keep hoping that one day Mom and Pop will have a change of heart and see the twins.

Joyce moved to San Francisco—the shrink business was booming in California—where she started a private practice. Someone said she was dating Winnie the Pooh.

Marvis Summer made semiannual trips to New York to visit

her grandkids. She would have come more often, but was planning a run for the Alabama State Senate.

Doctor Shotkin ran his practice and his family out to Missoula, Montana.

Meantime, Uncle Nate got thrown a curve. His wife Rose died, leaving him both laundries. It took him less than a month to lose the laundries to the nags. Now he's thinking about moving back to New York. Him and Pop still don't talk. Neither do Mom and Ida Gruntstein, who fell in the tub and broke both hips.

Pepper Katz? Got caught for tax fraud and wound up paying me a fat fee to manage his property while he did time.

Benny X. Pushman came by the other day looking for work. I felt sorry for the guy, but what could I do?

Mr. and Mrs. John Hampton White of Richmond, Virginia, got divorced after Annabelle got caught with her daughter's husband.

Me? I kept the store on 125th Street, opened a second one on Lenox Avenue and kept the family business alive. I ran up the highest profits Myron Klein Hats Limited had seen in a decade. Meanwhile, Monica quit Minksy's and went to school to learn bookkeeping. Who would've guessed that she'd turn out to be good with numbers and a great big help to me?

Nowadays, between the hats and records, I never stop ripping and running, though sometimes on a Sunday afternoon in winter, if they sky is gray and there's a chill in the air, I'll drive out to Coney, all by myself, and sit on a bench on the boardwalk and watch the waves come crashing in, and maybe see some weird guy swimming in the ice-cold ocean, and smell the salt from the sea and the garlic from the pizza stands and think of my Aunt Bea, and the summers I spent at Sea Gate with my family, and how things change, and how things never change.